RUST-COLORED RAIN

WRACK AND RUIN

BOOK 1

OTTO SCHAFER

SOUND EYE PRESS

Published in 2023

ISBN 979-8-9860760-7-2 (hardback)
ISBN 979-8-9860760-6-5 (paperback)
ISBN 979-8-9860760-5-8 (ebook)

Cover design and illustrations by Rafido @99Designs
Editing by The Blue Garret

Sound Eye Press
www.ottoschafer.com

For the ones stockpiling, preparing for the day the dead refuse to die. We know what's coming.

CONTENTS

1. A Gut Feeling 1
2. Victoria's Secret 6
3. Supernova 18
4. Call 911 23
5. Princess 34
6. Gooey, Gooey Gumdrops 41
7. Hungry 46
8. The Judge's Chambers 50
9. Dancing in the Rain 64
10. The Restroom 73
11. The Church 82
12. Five-Inch Stiletto 98
13. Spare Set 108
14. Angel 120
15. Girl Power 127
16. The Neighbor 131
17. Well, What Would You Call Them? 142
18. Worst-Case Scenario 152
19. Tiny Monsters 159
20. Nailed It 166
21. Reflections in the Dark 173
22. Coming Clean 177
23. Broken Promises 181
24. Undead or Zombies 188
25. Answers 196
26. Shakespearean Nightmares 205
27. No Soliciting 213
28. The White Worm 221
29. The Horde 226
30. The Plan 230

31. Come and Get Some 238
32. The Bus Stop 245

Acknowledgments 257
About the Author 259
Also by Otto Schafer 261

CHAPTER 1
A GUT FEELING

ZOE REACHED OVER and slapped the snooze button on her iPhone. She didn't want to wake up. She didn't want to go to class. She just wanted to lie here in the warmth of her blanket, close her eyes, and go back to sleep.

"Did the alarm go off?" Oliver asked, stretching and yawning as he rolled towards her.

They had stayed up too late having the same tired argument that always ended in the same tired place. But this time it was really bad – so bad that she'd lain awake for another hour after it ended. She simply couldn't afford not to get sleep, not at this point in the semester. "Yeah, you better get up or you'll be late," she said evenly, the glow from her phone illuminating the outline of Oliver's bewhiskered face as she swiped up and then dragged her finger over the screen, switching off the snooze.

"Still mad?" Oliver asked.

She rolled away from him. "No, Oliver, I'm not mad. I'm just... I'm just tired."

"We stayed up too late." He pressed forward against her as he tried to kiss her neck.

Zoe pulled away, throwing back the blanket only to be assaulted by the cold as she pushed herself up. How is it that a man can always find a way to ask the dumbest question at the worst time? Did he think she would go to sleep at the peak of their fight not speaking to him, and then somehow what little sleep she had would make her wake up happy and horny – like what, like last night never even happened?

They'd been arguing a lot, but this time she'd finally told him she didn't believe he was working late. Why couldn't he just tell her what he was really up to? She found it hard to believe the garbage company had him running so much extra route that it would keep him out late into the evening – several hours later than normal. And just because she was going to nursing school and pulling shifts at the hospital didn't mean she couldn't tell he was up to something. For God's sake, they had cameras on the house! But when she'd pressed him on it, he made excuses. Excuses that just didn't make sense. Plus, he wasn't acting himself, and when she'd said as much, he got all dodgy and defensive.

Behind her she felt the bed shift, and Oliver cleared his throat. "It's only five – you don't have to get up yet. Why don't you lie back down for a bit? Maybe try and get some more sleep before class?"

"No, I really need the time to study." Which was exactly what she should have been doing last night.

"Okay, well, don't forget we have date night tonight. It's supposed to be cool enough for a fire."

"Yeah," she said flatly, adjusting her bra before pulling her shirt over her head.

"Maybe we can project a movie on the side of the woodshed like last time? Oh, and hey, don't forget the contractor for the patio will be here tomorrow, and he said we have to have the permit. I already checked. The courthouse in Bloomridge opens at eight. Do you mind..."

"Yeah, Ollie." Zoe sighed. "I already figured you'd be working late... all that extra route they got you guys running, right?"

"I... well... yeah... It's just that you're going to be in Bloomridge anyway and—"

"I'll grab it before I head to class."

"Thanks, babe. I'll get home as soon as I can."

She knew he was full of shit, but she didn't have it in her to call him out. And besides, he'd just deny it anyway.

Two hours later, Zoe slid into the driver's seat of her Xterra, dropped her coffee mug into the cup holder, and backed out of the driveway.

Zoe's typical morning routine consisted of listening to Shakespeare plays on her thirty-minute commute to school. Sure, Shakespeare was a far cry from her medical studies, but she enjoyed them so much and, weird as it sounded, it really helped her get into the right mind-set for her advanced physiology class. Her favorite and current listen was *Hamlet*.

On this particular morning, she was listening to one of her favorite scenes. It was the skull scene with Hamlet and the gravedigger. "Alas, poor Yorick! I knew him, Horatio." But after last night's fight with Oliver, she just couldn't get into it. "Something is rotten in the state of Denmark," she said to no one as she switched off the audiobook. "Call Alexis," she said into the phone.

On the third ring, a woman's voice answered. "Hey, girl, heeeyyy!"

"Jesus, Alexis, really? Do you have to sound that damn chipper?"

"Fuck you, bitch, what's got your panties all bunched? Wait! Let me guess? It starts with an O and ends with asshole?"

"We had a horrible fight last night. I swear he's cheating on me, Alexis!"

"He isn't cheating on you! Jason was a cheater, and that's why I left the prick. No way Oliver would ever cheat on you."

She wanted so badly to believe that, but something in her heart told her he was having an affair. He was coming home later all the time, and he wasn't talking. She knew in her heart it was another woman. He was probably screwing some whore on the trash route. But no. Sam would tell her if Oliver was screwing around on the route. But then who? One of the women in the dispatch office?

"Did you hear me?" Alexis asked.

"Sorry... what?"

"I said you need to talk to him. Really talk... without blaming and without yelling. You love him, right?"

"Of course, but I think we're past talking it out." The truth was, after eight years of marriage and all the shit that had gone along with it, she didn't know if she loved him, but something inside her wasn't ready to admit it... not out loud.

"Bitch, please! You aren't past that. Jason and I were past talking the third time he put his dick in someone else, but you two still have hope. But *only* if you talk it out. Tell him how you feel, how you really feel, and leave the blame behind. Then ask him how he feels."

Zoe clicked her turn signal, turned onto Route 9, and

pulled a sip from her coffee. Anxiety filled her stomach, and she felt her palms starting to sweat. If he really was cheating, there would be no coming back from it.

"Are you still there?"

"Yeah, sorry. Maybe you're right. We have a date night tonight. After my shift at the hospital, we're supposed to build a fire, roast marshmallows, and watch a movie on the projector."

"That's perfect! And of course I'm right – just talk to him."

CHAPTER 2
VICTORIA'S SECRET

A SOFT GLOW on the horizon illuminated the streets of River City. Oliver peered out through the windshield of the old Mack garbage truck as one by one the streetlights switched off. Grey shadows replaced the artificial glow in the awkward in-between of a spent night and a new day.

Fall in Illinois was his favorite time of year. The cooler temps after a brutal summer were welcome. The early hours were becoming chillier with each passing day, but by late morning he'd be ditching his grey hoodie. Outside, the leaves had turned from green to an array of burnt oranges, ruby reds, and dark chocolate browns. As much as he loved the season, soon the leaves would drop and the after-hours leaf pickup would begin.

River City Disposal paid their employees salary. Whether you took your time and stayed out all day or busted butt to get done as early as possible, the pay was the same. But this wasn't the case for after-hours leaf pickup, which paid by the hour. Finish your route, dump the garbage at the transfer station, then the clock starts. Back out you go to fill the trash truck up with bag after bag of leaves. Leaf pickup didn't pay much though, and frankly Oliver didn't care. Leaf pickup was optional, and he had no plans of signing up anyway. If he played it right, he could simply tell Zoe he was volunteering to work even later than she already thought he was, allowing him to keep up the charade for a bit longer.

He smiled to himself, knowing that he needed a better excuse not to come home and that leaf pickup would be just the alibi he needed. Leaves couldn't fall soon enough.

Gripping the worn wooden knob bolted to the steering wheel, Oliver gave the wheel a spin, swinging his rig into the alley. Braking hard, he slapped the gear shift into neutral and pulled the air brake in the same practiced motion he'd already done a hundred times today. His hand instinctively slipped to the door handle. *Two cans,* he thought, hesitating. After running the route practically by himself yesterday, his shoulder felt stiffer than usual, stubborn about moving at all. Even on the best of days, the old wound never allowed him to forget just how close to death he'd come, how close the bullet had come to taking everything away from him. He shook off the memory. It had only been twenty minutes since he'd taken ibuprofen, and it probably hadn't had time to work its magic just yet.

Well, screw it, he thought, lifting the latch as he shouldered open the door and leapt from the seat to the road, skipping the step altogether. He ran to the back of the red-and-white truck and grabbed the second can off the curb, a blue Rubbermaid. His helper, Sam, had already popped the top on both cans as soon as she'd stepped off the truck. Oliver jerked the can onto his back as he spun toward the rear of the garbage truck, dumping its contents over his shoulder and into the hopper.

"Two cans, Ollie! I didn't need you for this one," Sam scolded.

Oliver dropped the now empty can off his shoulder and back onto the curb. "I know, but I really want to tell you about yesterday."

"Fine, but you're going to put us off pace, and I already feel bad enough for bailing on you yesterday," she said, tossing the lids back onto the cans.

"First off, you didn't bail, you were sick. I get it. Second, it's our lightest day, and if we get done any quicker, we'll have to hide until at least ten o'clock. You saw what happened to Dusty and Ray Ray."

"Yeah, and I told that dumbass Dusty not to be going back into the shop at eight in the morning. He didn't listen, and sure enough HQ added three more hours to his route. Now they have to make an extra trip to the transfer station because they can't get the whole route in one load," Sam said, shaking her head. "Well, that's what they get."

"That's what they got alright, but that isn't going to happen to us, so no need to set a record today. Oh, and third, I'm not mad you missed, but don't think for one second you're getting out of hearing how bad I had it just because you feel like crap for not showing up." Oliver bent, snatched a discarded paper plate from the ground, and flicked it like a Frisbee into the hopper. "Besides, this was the most epic thing I have ever seen, and if you *had* shown up for work yesterday, I would have missed the story of a lifetime," Oliver said, popping his knuckles.

Sam narrowed her eyes. "You realize you're setting yourself up for a story that couldn't possibly live up to this kind of hype?"

Oliver grinned. "Oh, my dear Sam, that's where you are sorely mistaken."

"Well, wipe that shit-eating grin off your face and get on with it, bro!"

Oliver drew in a dramatic breath. "You know that house on Melody Court? One green can always full, but the owner tends to—"

"Tends to forget to bring out a bag of trash until the last possible second," she said, finishing his sentence. Smiling mischievously, she added, "Well, she pretends to forget."

"Wait, what do you mean she pretends to?" Oliver asked.

"Ollie, come on. Typical fucking guy, you. How did you even end up married? Wait, let me guess, you were in a bar... no, a club – not dancing though, just hanging out. Probably with some pals, right? Zoe is dancing with friends. She exits the dance floor, gives you a smile, and you offer to buy her a drink. She slaps you in the face, grabs you by the collar, and throws you in a lip lock. Then she proposes." Sam smiled and shrugged. "Well? Tell me I'm wrong."

Oliver pulled a face. "What is wrong with you? Yeah, totally wrong. For your information, we met at karaoke night. I'm also the one who asked her to marry me! And why would she slap..." Oliver shook his head, waving off the thought. "Never mind. What's this got to do with the lady on Melody Court?"

Sam stepped around the side of the truck and pushed both hydraulic handles inward. The hopper blade swung open, and the packer panel descended. "This is sad, really sad," she said, yelling now to be heard over the whine of the power take-off and the rev of the garbage truck's engine. "Okay, let me explain it so your man brain can understand. She likes to come running out in her robe. The robe that's way too short and tied way too loose." Blinking her green eyes repeatedly, she formed her lips into an O and gave

Oliver a seductive look. In a sultry rasp, she said, "Oh, I'm so sorry, I almost missed you. Thank you for waiting for me." Smiling shyly, she fluttered her eyelashes again.

Oliver's eyebrows bunched.

Sighing, Sam dropped the fake smile and changed back into... well, back into Sam. "It's obvious this chick is flirting!"

Oliver frowned. "I don't remember her ever saying any of those things to me."

The blade reached the seal of the hopper and shut down. This time, Sam gave both handles a pull. The blade curled under to the sound of glass bottles popping, metal twisting, and garbage crunching. Steadily, the hydraulics drew the packing panel up, compacting the contents of the hopper into the belly of the truck. Unknown juices, rancid and brown, spilled down the shiny metal to pool in the now empty hopper. "Silly Ollie, not flirting with you – she's been flirting with me."

Raising his eyebrows, Oliver shouted over the roaring engine. "What? Really?"

"Don't look so surprised. How can you blame her! Having all this show up in front of your house once a week." Sam rolled her hips as she motioned to her body with a wave of her gloved hand.

Oliver laughed. Sam was beautiful though, there was no denying it, even in her uniform shirt that she'd modified by cutting off the sleeves and tying a knot at the waist. It also didn't hurt that she wore jeans tight enough they appeared painted on. And why not with a figure like hers? After all, she was a local CrossFit champion. She was also the only woman to ever work as a helper at River City Disposal. Hell, maybe the only woman to work at any of the garbage companies, locally anyway.

The power take-off kicked off again and the truck quieted to a low purr.

"Oh shit, um, Sam, tell me you weren't interested in her?" Oliver asked.

"Are you kidding me? I've been working her for months. Shit, maybe I'm kidding myself. Maybe she's been working me in that scanty robe of hers. Either way, yeah, Ollie, I'm interested. Next week, she'll be giving me her digits – guaranteed." Sam slapped Oliver on the shoulder.

Oliver snorted. "Hold that thought. Turns out you aren't going to like this story nearly as much as I'd hoped you would."

Sam put one hand on her hip and frowned. "Oliver McCallister! What did you do?"

"Wow! You sound just like my wife when she's pissed. Look, it isn't what I did, Sam. It's what my temp did."

"Insta-Labor?" she asked, pulling a face like she'd bit into a lemon.

"Yeah, and I don't give a rat's ass what HQ says, that was the last time I'm using one of those guys. The next time you don't show up for work, I'm going it alone." It was bad enough two drivers had been robbed by their temps, and while Oliver hadn't had that experience, he'd dealt with his fair share of unusual behavior from these guys.

Insta-Labor was a service provided to companies who needed low-skill manual labor in a pinch. Oliver and the other forty-plus drivers, who from time to time had to use the service, could expect to pull into a parking lot and be faced with a lineup of folks who often appeared to be homeless individuals down on their luck or even drug addicts looking to make enough to cover their next fix. As the driver, you had the barbaric task of selecting a helper for the day based on appearance alone. The questions that ran through

Oliver's head when trying to select a helper for the day went like this: Who looks least likely to rob me? Who looks most sober? Who appears to have showered in the last week? Then with safety and hygiene covered, he moved on to the key question: Who looks most physically capable of making it through the route?

With the hopper emptied, Oliver motioned to the truck. "Okay, let me pull up to the next stop and we'll continue this," he said, running for the cab.

"Hey, what happened to not wanting to get done too early?"

"Nothing," he shouted over his shoulder. "But I don't want to rush this story." He laughed, climbing the two steps back into the cab.

"Fine, but you're only making the likeliness of this being epic even more remote, you know!"

"It's going to be so worth it!" he shouted back, slamming the cab door as he slapped a palm against the air brake knob and shoved the truck into gear. Glancing into his driver's-side mirror, he ensured Sam was on the helper step and holding on to the handrail, then punched the gas pedal.

At the next stop, Sam had already dismounted the step and was waiting for him with hands on hips and an unhappy expression on her face. She pulled off her gloves and ball cap, adjusting her auburn ponytail. "Why do you do this, Ollie?" Sam asked, looking up the long concrete drive of the single-story ranch.

Oliver climbed up the helper step and onto the lip of the hopper. He reached above his head where two carry-out barrels rested on a wide ledge. Grabbing the handle of one, he pulled it down, letting the big black barrel fall onto his back. "You don't have to come, Sam. But if you do, you get to hear my story sooner."

"Ugh! Fine. But the old hag could pay for carry-out service just like everyone else who doesn't want to drag their trash out to the road. Look at this place! She can obviously afford it."

"She doesn't pay for carry-out service because she doesn't want us to carry out her garbage for her. She wants to do it herself."

"Yet here we are, walking up her long-ass driveway."

"Ms. Richmond is getting old, and sometimes she struggles to get her trash out. But if she paid for the service, then she would never have a reason to make this walk. Look at it as us helping her stay motivated," Oliver said.

"You know, Ollie, you are an annoyingly good guy. How do you even remember her name?" Sam asked.

"I try to remember all our customers' names. Especially the ones that leave us a tip at Christmas," Oliver said, smiling.

"Oh, shit! This is the lady that makes that pound cake every year. That nasty dry pound cake?" Sam laughed. "Not sure I would consider that a tip. I prefer good old-fashioned cash money. With the exception of that one guy on Rosewood who makes his own wine and always leaves us a couple bottles. Now that guy is alright."

"Yeah, J. Crumley, good guy. Owns a BBQ joint on Sixth Street." Oliver punched a code into the garage door keypad.

"Like I said, you're a good dude."

The garage door lifted to reveal a tan-colored Cadillac and two brown garbage cans. Oliver flipped the lid off the first one to reveal white bags covered in maggots that were likely the product of a warm garage and spoiled food.

Oliver turned his head, drew in a breath, and held it. Maggots were the worst – squirming opaque creatures that had their own special smell. Nothing that he'd ever encountered compared to the vile smell of maggots. He popped the lid on the other can. No maggots. Quickly he dumped the maggot-free can into his carry-out barrel. "Yeah, good dude, huh? Well, maybe you should hold that thought until I finish my story."

Sam crossed her arms and frowned.

"Alright, so back to yesterday and the lady on Melody Court. By the time I got to Insta-Labor, pickings were slim, but unfortunately the guy I was forced to choose wasn't. He was... let's just say, a robust and jolly fella that reminded me of a young Santa Claus – if Santa were homeless... and possibly on meth."

"Meth? Jesus, Ollie, that's odd," Sam said.

"Really, meth-heads at Insta-Labor are odd? Since when?" Oliver asked, climbing into the carry-out barrel and jumping up and down. The garbage compressed under his weight, allowing enough room for him to get the contents of the maggot-filled can into the barrel.

"No, but you said he was a big guy. Usually meth-heads are skinny."

Oliver knelt, lifting the barrel onto his knee and then rolling it onto his back. "Oh, I don't know, maybe he was just getting started. Anyway, we're on Melody Court, and I pull up to 'tiny robe' lady's house. And before you ask, no, I actually don't know her name. Anyway, she only had one can, only ever has one can, so I don't plan on getting out. I'm watching in the mirror as Shorty jumps off the step, grabs the can, and disappears behind the truck—"

"Wait," Sam said, placing the lids back on the cans and slapping the button to close the garage. "His name was Shorty? Was he really short or really tall? Just want to picture this right."

Oliver snorted. "Neither. He was about my height, with a long brown mullet and a full-blown brown beard to match. Introduced himself as Shorty, and I didn't ask any questions."

"Got it. Please continue."

"So I'm looking in the mirror, and I don't see Shorty. A minute goes by, then two, and still, I don't see the guy. I'd shown him like three times how to run the hopper, but the hopper wasn't running. This leads me to think he must have found something in the trash that interested him. After another minute goes by, I'm like what the hell? I hit the air brake and jump out, praying I don't find Shorty eating old pizza out of the trash like the last guy."

Sam's face screwed up in disgust.

"It can't be more than a day old!" they both said in unison and laughed.

"So I round the corner of the truck and find the can sitting upside down in the hopper. And there's Shorty, dancing," Oliver said, pausing for effect.

"Dancing? Like dancing to the music from the hopper?"

Their garbage truck was rigged with a speaker mounted above the hopper and wired to the radio. Sam and Oliver listened to *The Morning X* talk show every morning and, on the days when the route stretched into the afternoon, they cranked up the tunes and rocked out as they threw trash.

"No. I didn't even have the hopper speaker on. He was literally just dancing to whatever music was playing in his own head, but that's not the best part. It seemed Shorty had found something in the trash. A pair of white panties trimmed with pink lace," Oliver said, as the two reached the back of the garbage truck. He tipped the carry-out barrel over his shoulder, emptying its contents, then tossed it back above the hopper. The barrel landed with a small bounce before settling into place.

"Eww! He found the panties and started dancing?"

Oliver nodded. "Oh, that's not the half of it! Hang on, I'll pull up."

"What?! Bullshit you'll pull up! Oliver McCallister, you will not leave me hanging after that! Not even for one more stop!" Sam argued, crossing her arms.

Oliver laughed, throwing his hands up defensively. "Alright! Alright! So, I round the back of the truck, and there's Shorty dancing... with the used panties on his head! The pink lace waistband sat perfectly across his hairy mustached lip, with the dark stained crotch covering the bridge of his nose," Oliver said, making a stank face. "Shorty has the elastic waistband stretched over his ears! And there he is, hopping from one foot to the other, jazz hands, jazz hands!" Oliver mimicked the dance as he hopped from one foot to the other, his arms extended as he twisted his hands back and forth.

"No fucking way!" Sam laughed.

"Yes fucking way! But it gets better!"

"How? How could that get better?"

"Because as he's dancing, and I'm laughing so hard I can't breathe, guess who appears from around the corner of the truck with her forgotten bag of trash?"

"Oh, no!" Sam breathed, throwing a hand over her mouth.

"Oh, yes! And she's mortified to find her discarded panties on the head of a homeless-looking Santa Claus meth-head, who now stands frozen in mid-dance, balanced precariously on one foot, holding the other about a foot off the ground. He looks at her from around the crotch of her stained underwear and smiles. Tiny robe lady's face is shaking as her face flushes red. She drops the bag of trash, runs back to her house, and slams the door."

"Oh my god! You were right! That is the most epic story I have ever heard."

"Well, HQ didn't think so."

"Oh shit!"

"Yeah, I barely made it to the cab before I heard the call over the radio: 'We have a customer on Melody Court claiming your helper is wearing her discarded underwear on his head.'" Oliver grinned mischievously. "I respond, 'That's ridiculous – Sam wouldn't wear another woman's underwear on her head. Not if they had been discarded anyway.'"

Sam punched him in the shoulder. "Dick!"

Laughing, Oliver said, "So then HQ says, 'Sam doesn't have a beard either. Well, way to go – we have one less customer on Melody Court.'"

"Wait. What?" Sam asked, her smile slipping.

"Yeah, remember when I said you weren't going to like this story after all? Well, we don't pick up 217 Melody Court anymore."

"Shit, Oliver! I was about to shoot my shot! And she was digging on me hard too!" Sam slapped her hands against her hips.

The hidden speaker above the hopper chirped with the *beep, beep, beep, beeeeeeeeep!* of the emergency alert system.

"Don't 'shit, Oliver' me! This is on you. You're the one who didn't come to..." Oliver trailed off, looking toward the hopper speaker. "What's that about? It isn't the first Tuesday of the month."

"Please stand by for a special announcement from the president of the United States."

"C'mon, let's jump in the cab and see what's up," Oliver said, nodding towards the cab.

CHAPTER 3
SUPERNOVA

OLIVER AND SAM climbed into the cab just as President Ona Freeman began her announcement.

"A large asteroid – estimated to be ten kilometers wide – has been discovered and could enter our atmosphere in the next fifteen minutes. The US military has joined forces with our allies to execute a plan that will intercept the asteroid's path, shifting it onto a safe course. The world has been preparing for an event like this for a long time, and we are ready. Over the Americas, expect to see multiple bright flashes, followed by colors similar to the aurora borealis. You may experience power outages and a short disruption in communication. This is all to be expected. Do not be alarmed."

Oliver and Sam, both of them stunned, stared at one another.

"An asteroid? Holy shit, Ollie! An asteroid! What should we do?" Sam asked, but before Oliver could answer, his radio lit up with other drivers.

"Base, mobile seven is coming in. I... I need to be with my family. Over."

"Base, mobile ten is coming in too. Over."

"Mobile twenty-eight to base. I'm staying out. I don't want to have to make all this up tomorrow. Over."

"Mobile sixteen to twenty-eight, you're assuming there's going to be a tomorrow, Doug. Over."

From there the floodgates opened, everyone talking over one another. Oliver reached across and shut off the radio. "Son of a bitch, they're going to nuke it!"

"What? They... they didn't say anything about nuking it." Sam shook her head, deep creases forming on her brow.

"They didn't have to. Bright flashes, power outages, and lights similar to the Northern Lights. That has to be nukes, right? Sam, I got to try to get to Zoe, but I can run you in to base first and drop you off."

Sam looked at him and frowned. "Ollie, I got no family close and no one waiting for me at home. Rather than driving across town, let's just go! Head to your house right now! You'll save at least thirty minutes."

Oliver swallowed dryly as he tried to process what they'd just heard. Was this really happening?

"Ollie?"

Sam was right. But even so, Zoe was at school in Bloomridge, and he worked in River City. The two cities were thirty minutes in the opposite direction from their home in the tiny town of Mackinaw. "They said they'll intercept the asteroid in fifteen minutes. It'll take thirty to get to my place."

"Yeah, but they also said we have nothing to worry about. Look, even if whatever their plan is doesn't work, we'll have more time, right? We'll still have a chance to get Zoe before... before the end."

Oliver pressed his lips into a tight line and nodded. It would be enough. It had to be. Of course, that was assuming

Zoe heard the alert and would come straight home. But she would, right? Of course she would. A ten-kilometer asteroid was about to enter their atmosphere. "Thanks, Sam," he said, slapping the shifter into gear. Sam was an incredible friend, his best friend, and no matter how this turned out, what she was doing for him now wouldn't be something he'd ever forget. "Okay, Mack, you old beastly bastard, let's see what you got!"

They raced down the alley and turned onto Sixth Street. Sam kept her eyes glued to the sky as if she expected the meteor to show itself at any second.

"Here, dial Zoe for me." Oliver tossed her his cell phone as he dropped the stick shift into the next gear. "I want to make sure she heard the emergency alert and is on her way home."

"The phone isn't ringing through!" Sam said.

"What? Shit, everybody's probably trying to call someone! I bet the network's overloaded or something. Keep trying!"

Sam nodded, redialing.

As Sam continued to try Zoe, Oliver guided the garbage truck east down Route 74 and onto the Murray Baker Bridge. Below, the Illinois River flowed silently southward towards the mighty Mississippi.

"What could change the course of a ten-kilometer asteroid? It'd have to be a nuke, wouldn't it?"

Oliver nodded. "Nothing else has that kind of power." He slammed his hands against the steering wheel as traffic slowed to a crawl. "C'mon! I got to get home," Oliver said.

"It's okay. We'll make it."

"You don't understand. I screwed up, Sam. Zoe and I got into a huge fight last night."

"Does that have something to do with why I got a text from her saying that she needs to talk?"

He glanced over. "What? Zoe texted you? And you didn't tell me?"

"I was going to but then... Well, this happened."

"What did she want?"

"She said she had to ask me something. She said you haven't been coming home after the route. That you told her we've been working late covering extra routes."

Oliver felt his face flush as Sam's accusing eyes bored into him. "Dammit," he breathed. "So, what did you say?" he asked, not taking his eyes off the road as they neared the end of the bridge.

Sam crossed her arms. "Well, I didn't rat you out, if that's what you're asking, but I'm not lying to Zoe either."

"So... how did you answer?" Oliver asked nervously.

"I didn't respond yet. But I'm going to have to, Oliver! So what the hell is going on?"

"It's complicated."

"Uncomplicate it!" she said, raising her voice.

As they exited the bridge, a flash lit up the morning sky.

Oliver slammed on the air brakes, throwing Sam forward into the dashboard. "Ugh," she grunted.

"Shit! Sorry, Sam! Do you see it?" he asked, pointing toward the sky.

"Yeah, let me just... just peel myself off the windshield."

Oliver glanced over. "Sorry! Hey, buckle up, okay?"

Ahead, three lanes of traffic lit up in red brake lights. Tires shrieked, metal crunched, and horns blew. The light in the sky grew brighter, as if the sun were going supernova right before their eyes. But this was no supernova.

"The nukes!" Sam breathed.

Oliver looked away from the sky as a red SUV shot past

them, rear-ending a small white sedan. The driver of the SUV must have jerked his wheel at the last second because it cut to the side and flipped into the air. Oliver's eyes went wide as the SUV rolled airborne across the tops of several other cars before finally colliding with a panel van.

"Jesus! What the shit! No way the driver lived through that!" Sam said.

"Don't say that. There's still a chance that—"

From beneath the SUV, a pool of fuel ignited with a *whoomph,* followed by an explosion.

CHAPTER 4
CALL 911

ZOE ASCENDED the last steps to the second floor of the Bloomridge courthouse. They were doing some remodeling and had the main stairwell closed, along with the elevator. But after following the signs, she had finally made her way up a narrower set of stairs and onto the white marble floor. Now she just needed to find the county clerk's office.

What a crap morning. She'd had just about enough of the special kind of stupid she'd already had to deal with today. Some jerk had nearly sideswiped her as she pulled into the parking lot, and then another idiot had almost backed into her as she tried to find a place to park. Oliver was going to owe her big for this.

After making her way across the atrium, she looked back, thinking she must have missed the clerk's office, when someone slammed into her, knocking her onto the marble floor. Zoe landed hard on her hip, banging her elbow as her phone and purse slid away from her. "What the F!" she shouted.

"I'm sorry! Jesus!" a tall, heavy-set man said, pushing himself up from the floor.

Zoe scrambled for her phone and purse, expecting the guy to at least offer to help her up, but when she turned, the prick had already climbed to his feet, completely ignoring her as he bolted away.

"Jerk!" she shouted as the man rushed for the stairs. Across the atrium, a courthouse door burst open, and a flood of people began moving quickly toward the stairs too. *What the hell is going on?* It was only just after eight. Shouldn't court just now be starting – not recessing?

A woman in a business suit and glasses with her hair in a bun walked briskly towards her. Zoe hurriedly shoved the spilled contents of her purse back inside and pushed herself up, rubbing her elbow. "Ma'am. Ma'am. Excuse me. What's happening?" Zoe asked, half expecting to hear gunshots or screaming from the direction of the courtroom.

The woman stopped and glanced over. Her face was grave, but Zoe could see she wasn't really looking at Zoe at all. The woman's eyes were distant, like she had just witnessed something awful. "You didn't hear? They announced it ten minutes ago! Thank god someone ignored the no cell phone policy, or we would have spent our final minutes arguing fucking traffic violations."

"Final what? Announced what?" Zoe asked, pleading for understanding.

"A massive asteroid is about to hit the Earth. They're going to bomb it or something to try to change its path!"

"What? But... Wait, what?"

The woman's eyebrows knitted together. "I... I'm sorry. I... I have to go," she said, brushing past her.

An asteroid? That doesn't make any sense. What was she talking about? Across the huge atrium, a sign mounted above a large wooden door read COUNTY CLERK. Zoe made her way through the throng of people, all of them holding phones to their ears. Somehow she managed to stay on her feet as they shouldered their way past her, all with panicked voices and wide eyes. Finally, she pushed open the door to the county clerk's office. On the opposite side of the long counter, several employees stood with their backs to her, staring out several massive floor-to-ceiling windows. All their eyes were on the sky.

"Excuse me," Zoe said.

A mousey, balding man with a primly trimmed rim of hair just above his ears, a collared shirt, and grey sweater-vest called over his shoulder. "I'm sorry. Given the situation... we, well, we're closed."

"Okay. But can you tell me what's happening?" Zoe asked, her own eyes drawn to the windows and the sky beyond. She didn't know what she was looking for, but all she saw was an early morning blue sky.

"Tom. I... I think we should go to the basement – to the take cover area," a grey-haired woman said.

"Yes... yes, of course, Ginger," Tom said. "Everyone away from the windows." Then, as if in agreement with Ginger, an alarm sounded.

Zoe startled, wincing at the too-loud bell clanging above her head. It rang for what felt like forever, stopped, then rang again for at least another ten seconds, stopped again, and repeated.

"If it's short, leave the fort! If it's slow, go below! That's the sound to go below! Come on, everyone! Let's get to the basement!" Tom shouted.

As the staff moved from the windows towards the counter, the sky lit up with a blinding white light.

Everyone spun back around.

Zoe's eyes squinted against the ever-growing light, forcing her to turn away as she fumbled for the door handle and shoved. Behind her, the sky changed from bright white to crimson red. She pushed, stumbling out into the atrium of the courthouse ahead of the others.

Zoe stole a glance back over her shoulder and saw that Tom was climbing over the counter while others crowded through a narrow opening between the counter where a hinged wooden gate read PERSONNEL ONLY.

Hurrying across the atrium, Zoe made for the stairs, but with the main stairs closed, the crowd was thick, everyone shoving and shouting. Her instincts told her to stay clear. She moved to the side and pressed herself against the wall between a protruding column and a water fountain. With the alarm sounding, all the office staff plus the occupants of two other courtrooms were piling out, filling the atrium.

"How long before impact if the missiles didn't work?" a man shouted.

"I don't know! Seconds... We need to get to the basement!"

The crowd panicked, surging forward. Someone screamed as the group on the stairs fell like dominos.

"Dear god!" Zoe breathed, throwing her hand over her mouth. In the middle of the atrium there was a railing that surrounded a large opening – open to the first floor below. Directly in front of her, a man climbed over the rail and lowered himself, hanging from the rail by his fingertips.

"No!" Zoe shouted, pushing forward toward the man. She could see the panic in his eyes as he realized he'd made a horrible mistake. The drop was too far.

"Help me! Please!" the man begged, trying to pull himself back up.

As she struggled past people, Zoe could see that the man – heavy, with thin arms – wasn't in good enough physical shape to pull himself up. She slung her purse over her shoulder and grabbed the man by the wrists. "Help! Help me!" she begged the surrounding crowd, but the ringing bell swallowed her words. Didn't they see him? Maybe some did, but they were in full-on panic. Like a stampede of frightened cattle, they continued to push their way towards the stairs, ignoring everything and everyone else. "I can't hold you if you let go! Don't let go! Help! Please!" she tried again.

The bell stopped again. "Lady! Please don't... let go... of me!" The man's eyes were wild.

The bell started again. "I can't! I can't hold on! Help, please! I'm sorry!" Zoe shouted as the man slipped.

The bell stopped.

In the silence between rings, the man struck the floor with a slap and the all-too-wrong pop of a snapping bone.

Several in the crowd gasped.

"Oh god! Jesus Christ! I broke my leg!" the man screamed.

Zoe stared over the rail as blood pooled beneath the man, a jagged bone protruding from his thigh.

Outside, the crimson sky darkened and a low rumble grew louder.

The bell rang again.

The crowd surged with renewed force. On the stairs, people were climbing over the fallen while others slid down the rails. Some made it, while others fell or jumped to the floor below as they neared the bottom. The man with the compound fracture wailed and bled.

Zoe knew she should be trying to figure out how to get

to cover, but all she could think about was the man with the broken leg and how to get to him to try and stop the bleeding. Already a registered nurse, Zoe was in her last year of nurse practitioner school, and she knew the man was likely bleeding out. If she didn't get to him now, he was going to die.

Down on the first floor, a man appeared from the exit, pushing his way through the fleeing crowd and into the atrium. He raised a handgun towards the ceiling and fired.

The report was deafening.

All at once the crowd dropped low, ducking their heads, everyone going silent except for a few people sobbing on the stairs and the man with the broken leg still wailing for help.

The bell stopped ringing – for good this time as the lights flickered and went out. Red-tinted light spilled through windows and skylights, casting the atrium in an eerie hue.

"Everyone shut up!" the man with the gun shouted. He was covered in red liquid, like someone had just poured iodine over him. "Everyone just stop! They did it! They blew the damn thing up! Look at me! It's raining red out there! The asteroid is destroyed!" He laughed. "It's just rain! Red rain!"

The crowd seemed to exhale all at once. And all at once, they seemed to realize what they had done, looking around at each other.

"Hey, this guy needs a doctor!" the man covered in red shouted, tucking his pistol into his waistband. "Do we have a doctor?"

Zoe looked around, thinking there must be a doctor in the crowd, but when no one answered, she heard herself say, "Here! I'm here. Let me through please!"

"Let that lady in the blue uniform through!" the man shouted.

This time, the crowd parted, allowing Zoe to make her way to the stairs. She stepped past a pregnant woman who sat sobbing and holding her head but didn't appear to be in life-threatening distress.

"Help me, please!" the pregnant woman begged.

"Are you okay?" Zoe asked.

"I hit my head and banged my knees up pretty good, but I don't think anything is broken," she said.

"Okay, good," Zoe said, feeling the urgency to get to the man with the broken leg. She was acutely aware that the femoral artery runs down the leg; if the man's bone had severed that artery, she had to hurry before he bled out. "I'll come right back to check on you," she said, hurrying past the woman.

Zoe passed more injured on the stairs. A few had been shoved and or had fallen, like the pregnant woman, but a couple others had been trampled by the mob descending the stairs. Panic crept in as she realized she was going to need a lot more help. "Does anyone else have medical training? We need more help! And can someone dial 911, please?"

A smartly dressed man in a suit and tie knelt next to her. "I've been trying, but I can't get through. I'll keep trying."

A few people from the crowd stepped forward to help others as Zoe knelt next to the man with the broken leg.

"It's going to be okay, sir. We're going to get you help." Zoe turned to the well-dressed man. "Thank you. He's bleeding bad. We need to stop it. What's your name?"

"Ben," the man said, dialing 911 again.

"Ben, can I have your tie, please?"

"Of course." He pulled his tie loose and handed it to Zoe.

"Hey, he don't look so good!" the man covered in red said, pawing at his eyes.

Zoe glanced down at the man with the broken leg just as his eyes rolled back and he passed out.

"He's passed out from blood loss." Zoe looked back up at the wet man, who was still pawing at his eyes. "Hey, are you okay?"

"Yeah, my eyes just sting a little. What are asteroids made of... iron or something? I probably got some metal dust in my eyes. It's pouring like hell out there. Got it in my mouth too. The stuff tastes kind of like rusty water." The dripping man blinked as a puddle of burnt-orange liquid pooled beneath him.

Zoe looped the tie around Broken Leg Guy's upper thigh and cinched it as tight as she could pull. Bright red blood smeared the back of her hand, standing out against her ebony skin. Normally, she would never treat a person without gloves. What she wouldn't give for a pair right now. "Put your hand here," Zoe said, motioning to the rain-soaked man.

The man did as directed, and she was able to secure the tie with a double knot. The blood gushing from the man's bone-punctured flesh slowed to a trickle.

Ben remained next to Broken Leg Guy as he kept trying to get through to 911, while she went back and checked on the pregnant woman.

Placing a hand on the woman's stomach, she asked, "Did you hit your stomach?"

"No. I twisted when I fell to protect my baby. That's why I think I took the worst of it on my knees and head," the young mother-to-be said, rubbing the side of her head.

"No pain in your abdomen?" Zoe asked.

"No. Just my head... and my knees." She looked up at Zoe, eyes filled with fear and worry. "Do you think the baby is okay?"

Zoe smiled at her. "I think you did great, Mama. I see you have a good-sized goose egg, but your head isn't bleeding. Your knees are skinned pretty good, but you won't need stitches. Now, I need to check on the others, but as soon as we can get through to the hospital, I want you to get checked out by a doctor, okay? Just to be safe."

The woman forced a smile and nodded, wiping her eyes with a tissue from her purse.

Through the glass doors, it looked as though blood rained from the sky.

Umbrellas swooshed open, clicking into place. The crowd was thinning now, many having already left, while more filed out into the rain, one after the other. Zoe tried Oliver, but like the power in the building, the phone service seemed to be out as well.

Making her way back to Ben and the man with the broken leg, Zoe knelt once more, taking his pulse. It was weak, but it was there. "Ben, can you find something we can cover his leg with? If he wakes and sees the bone again, it could throw him into shock."

"Of course," Ben said, taking off his suit jacket. Zoe laid the jacket over the protruding bone.

The wet guy with the pistol began rubbing his head and pacing back and forth. "It hurts so much. What? No. No... I don't know."

"What's that?" Zoe asked, looking up. The man's complexion looked ashen. She realized it was probably all the blood from the broken leg making the man ill. Blood didn't bother her at all, but some people didn't do well with it. "You don't look so good – maybe you should sit down."

The man froze and blinked, looking suddenly confused. "Sit down? Oh, you'd like that. That'd be rich, wouldn't it. Rich like this suit over here?" The man turned and glared at Ben. "What are you, some kind of lawyer?"

"Hey, what's your name?" Zoe asked, sensing something was off. The man had been so helpful when she had needed him to help secure the knot around the injured guy's thigh, and if he hadn't come in and calmed the crowd, who knew how many might have died.

"Chuck. And I ain't no suit, I'll tell you that. You see these hands," he said, holding them out palms up. "They didn't get this way talking fancy and pushing a pen."

"It's okay, Chuck. There's no reason to be upset. Are you sure you feel okay?" Zoe asked.

Chuck bent, his hands going to his stomach. "It hurts... you know? The hunger... it's too much." He lowered his voice, whispering as if talking to himself. "I know but I can't just..."

Ben glanced up from rolling up the sleeves of his dress shirt. "Pal, you don't look so good."

Suddenly, Chuck's eyes snapped back from wherever they had been, stretching cartoonishly wide as his lips twisted into a grotesque sneer.

Ben froze, glancing at Zoe and then back to the man towering over him. "Chuck. Listen, we're just trying to help—"

"Oh, you damn right!" He yanked the pistol from his waistband and thrust the barrel down toward Ben's face.

Ben gasped, his voice shaking as he found words. "Now just stay calm. Let's not do anything—"

Chuck pulled the trigger.

Blood and brain matter sprayed Zoe as a now faceless Ben fell across her lap.

Her eyes went wide as all sound was replaced with the deafening ring of the report. Zoe turned her spattered face toward Chuck as he pressed the warm barrel against her forehead.

CHAPTER 5
PRINCESS

THE RED SUV ignited in a ball of fire as the explosion lifted the vehicle and tossed it back towards Oliver's garbage truck.

Oliver grabbed Sam by the wrist and pulled her down into the seat.

"Ollie!" Sam screamed, as outside metal crunched and twisted and something struck the windshield of their garbage truck with a pop, fracturing the glass.

Oliver peeked over the dash to find flaming carnage. It wasn't the SUV that had struck them but something thrown from the vehicle when it landed. The windshield was cracked in a few places, but it had held. The SUV now sat perched precariously upside down atop two other vehicles engulfed in flame.

Oliver's attention was pulled back to the sky as it changed from bright white to a red hue. "Sam, are you seeing this?"

The sky above darkened as it filled with dense red clouds that seemed to materialize out of nowhere.

Sam leaned forward to peer up through the windshield. "What the hell is that?"

"I don't know, but I think... I think it must be what's left of the asteroid! Maybe the nukes worked!" Oliver said. "Look, we need to find a way off this highway or we're going to be stuck here for hours."

A low rumble sounded from the sky.

Sam's eyebrows bunched together. "You hear that?"

"Thunder?" Oliver guessed.

"No! Not that! That! Listen, don't you hear it?"

Oliver shook his head. "Hear what?"

Sam held up her hand for quiet. "There! Someone's screaming!" Her eyes sprang wide. "It's a kid! Look!"

Beneath the burning SUV, a tiny hand stuck out the window of a grey car.

Sam jerked the door handle up and was out of the truck before Oliver could protest.

Oliver looked to the sky as the red clouds roiled. "Jesus, Sam," he breathed, lifting the door handle and jumping down onto the pavement.

With traffic at a standstill, people were climbing out of their cars, eyes fixed on the sky. Some were cheering, others applauded. A man shouted, "USA! USA!"

Oliver made his way around two cars to get to the back of the grey sedan. The heat coming off the burning SUV was almost unbearable. The SUV had smashed the front windshield and crushed the driver. The hood was crushed too, and liquid fire was dripping onto the front of the car. It was only a matter of time before the sedan burst into flames.

The rear window was only a quarter of the way down. "The door is stuck!" Sam said, yanking on the handle. "Little girl, will the window roll down?"

The girl, who couldn't have been older than six, looked scared shitless.

"Get back, Sam! We got no time!" Oliver picked up a chunk of heavy steel debris from the road. "Little girl! Little girl, get back!" Oliver shouted, motioning with his hand and then pointing at the window.

Above them, the thunder grew louder and the first drop of rain fell, splatting fat against the pavement near Oliver's feet. He smashed the window in one swing. "It's okay! Come here!"

The girl climbed across the seat and reached out her hands.

Oliver jerked her through the window and made for the cab of his truck. "Come on, Sam!"

Splat, splat, splat – a few more drops fell from the sky. Oliver pushed the girl into the cab and climbed in.

"My Princess!" the little girl shouted.

Sam stopped and turned back. "I got it!"

"Sam, don't! That car could go up any second!"

"I got it, Ollie! Back in a sec!" Sam shouted over her shoulder.

Dammit, Sam, Oliver thought, slamming the door.

Outside, the sky let loose a torrent of rain. But it wasn't like any rain Oliver had ever seen before. The rain was so thick and dark... and red. He couldn't even see Sam two car lengths up. "Dammit! Listen, kiddo. Stay here and I'll be right back, okay?" Oliver said, reaching for the door handle.

The little girl threw herself onto his lap, wrapping her arms around his neck. "Please don't go!"

Oliver patted the girl's back. "Whoa, easy. It's okay."

A shadow appeared from the rain, the door opened, and Sam climbed up into the cab.

"You look like someone dumped a bucket of red Gatorade over your head," Oliver said.

Sam reached beneath her seat and produced a towel. "Yeah, that's like some biblical shit out there!" She dried her hands and face, tossing the towel onto the dash before reaching beneath her shirt and producing a small Black doll with a gold dress and a silver tiara. "I kept it dry for you!"

The little girl smiled, grabbed the doll, and hugged it. "Princess!"

"Are you hurt?"

The girl shook her head. "Where's Mommy?"

Sam pressed her lips into a tight line and looked at Oliver. "Shit, Oliver, what do we do?"

Oliver unclipped his route list off the visor and wrote down the plate number of the sedan. "I got the license plate number. Once we get to Zoe, we'll call the authorities."

Sam nodded. "What do you make of this rain?"

"That's got to be asteroid dust." Oliver felt his heart begin to race with panic. "I'm not sure I can drive in this, Sam."

"Well, maybe it will slow soon and we can get moving. Hey, at least the Earth is still here, so that's good news." Sam grabbed the towel off the dash and wiped her face again.

"Yeah," Oliver answered absently as he started the truck up again and tried to maneuver around the traffic. He managed to get past the burning SUV as the last of the flames were doused by the strange rain – a rain that poured in an ever-thickening sheet from the dark red blanket of clouds above. *Please be safe, Zoe.* Hopefully she wasn't stuck in traffic or worse.

Twenty long minutes passed as Oliver slowly picked his

way forward, making little progress. The little girl played with her doll as Sam kept trying but failing to reach Zoe.

Frustrated, Oliver wiped a sleeve across the sweat beading on his forehead and slapped a palm down on the wheel. "Look at it, Sam! It's getting worse! I can't see past the hood!"

In between attempts to reach Zoe, Sam messed with the radio. She glanced over at him, rubbing at her eyes. "Man, I got to get some food! I feel like I haven't eaten anything in days!"

Oliver frowned, noticing Sam's apparent discomfort for the first time. "Hey, what's wrong?"

"Got that shit in my eyes and mouth. It tastes like I got a mouth full of pennies." Sam blinked as she ground her palms into her eye sockets.

Oliver shifted the Mack truck into neutral and pulled the air brake. "Lean over here and let me look."

"I don't know what you think you are going to see, Ollie."

"Hey, who knows what kind of chemicals could be in that shit. That's nuclear asteroid rain, Sam! You should have got back in the cab with me."

"Way to make a girl feel better, dick. I was trying to get the kid her doll."

Oliver sighed. "I'm sorry. Just let me look."

Sam leaned over the little girl sitting between them as Oliver grabbed his trusty penlight from the cubby on the dash. Sometimes he needed the light when looking at HQ paperwork for new starts or discontinued stops early in the morning. He clicked the light on and shined it into Sam's eyes.

She drew back, slamming her eyelids closed.

"C'mon, Sam, I can't look if you don't let me."

"Sorry, Ollie, but damn if that light didn't sting."

He motioned for her to try again, and Sam leaned over and opened her eyes as wide as she could. When the light hit, she flinched a little, but she forced herself to hold still.

Oliver stared into Sam's eyes, noticing right away something looked wrong. The whites of her eyes were completely bloodshot. No, not just bloodshot – they were bleeding.

"What the..." Oliver trailed off, his forehead wrinkling.

"What do you see?" Sam asked, blinking. A blood-red tear spilled from each of her eyes.

He reached down to his drink holder, lifting a half-empty bottle of water. "I want you to rinse your eyes out, Sam."

"Why? What do you see?" Concern filled her voice as she continued to blink... and bleed.

"I think you got some of that crap in your eyes is all. If it's irritating them, we should flush them."

"Why are your eyes bleeding? Do you have an owie?" the little girl asked.

Sam pulled down the visor and stared into a mirror she'd attached to the back. "What the fuck?"

"Ummmm," the little girl said, covering her mouth.

"Easy, Sam. It's probably just the rain in your eyes. Tip your head back and let me rinse them." Behind them, horns blew angrily, indicating he could pull up. He ignored them, motioning with the water bottle.

Sam snatched the bottle from Oliver's hand and poured the liquid into her eyes, forcing them to stay open as the water washed through. "Check again!"

Oliver checked again. This time, his heart raced as he noticed small perforations in the whites of Sam's eyes. They were probably in her corneas and pupils too, but he couldn't tell. Slowly, as Oliver watched, Sam's eyes filled with blood and began to leak.

Sam didn't wait for Oliver to say anything this time as she began pawing at her eyes. "Shit! Oliver, am I going to go blind? What the fu—"

"Stay calm, Sam. We'll get you to a doctor. It'll be okay—"

"Okay? My fucking eyes are bleeding!" Sam was as near to a full-on panic as Oliver had ever seen.

"Can you see now?" Oliver asked.

"Yeah, I can see, but my eyes are bleeding, Ollie! And... and they sting too." She pressed her fingers into them and rubbed.

"Stop rubbing them – you might just make them worse. Earlier, you said the rain tasted like pennies."

Sam took a mouthful of water, rinsed, and spit crimson onto the floorboard, her face twisted into pure terror.

Oliver frowned. "What is it?"

"My mouth! It still tastes like metal, Oliver! Metal and blood!"

CHAPTER 6
GOOEY, GOOEY GUMDROPS

CHUCK'S EYES flashed wildly as those remaining in the atrium screamed, everyone throwing themselves down onto the cold tile floor. "Arrrgggh! Shut up! Everyone shut up!" Chuck shouted, pressing his empty hand against his stomach.

Zoe sat frozen with Ben's blood pooling over her nurse's uniform and soaking her right leg. She blinked up at the crazed man, the barrel of his gun pushing against her head – pushing and trembling.

The ringing in her ears faded as, outside, rain fell and water spilled from a downspout, slapping against concrete in a gush. Zoe could hear it all. The held breaths, splashing gutters, and a crazed Chuck, arguing with himself. But her wide eyes stayed fixed on the man's trigger finger, stained red like his face, as he slowly squeezed. She was going to die. She was going to die just like Ben!

Zoe sucked in her final breath, her eyes spilling like the gutters outside as a silent sob squeaked from her throat.

Beside her lay Broken Leg Guy, unconscious until that

very moment. His eyes popped open as he let out a wretched moan, filling the atrium with the sound of agony.

Chuck's bloody eyes flashed to the man with the broken leg, and he swung the gun down and away from Zoe's face, firing once, twice, and then again.

The screams of those in the atrium were blotted out by another round of ringing in Zoe's ears.

The man looked down at her and raised the gun again, but this time he didn't put it to her head – he put it to his own. "Oh, come on! I don't know! Do you smell it? Jesus, can you smell that?"

If she hadn't been looking right at his face, she wouldn't have been able to make out the words, and even now they weren't making sense. Zoe wanted to tell him to stop – to just please, stop – but she was afraid to so much as blink. All she could do was watch helplessly as blood leaked from the man's eyes, trailing down his cheeks and into his salt-and-pepper mustache.

Chuck kept mumbling, looking at the crowd now as he started tapping the gun against his head. "Starving... starved... hung—" Suddenly he stopped, lowering the gun as he began sniffing at the air like a dog on a scent. Glancing down, he locked his pleading eyes with Zoe's. Crimson tears leaked from them. "You smell it? Please... you can smell it, right? It isn't just me? It shouldn't be, but... it's good, right? Oh... noooo," the man whimpered, squatting down next to her. He placed his face close to hers now. "It's on your face. All the little grey bits. God, they shouldn't be! I shouldn't!" He reached forward with his empty hand.

Zoe flinched back, recoiling from the bloody-eyed man, but she couldn't get away. Ben was still there, lying across her lap, anchoring her to this nightmare.

As Chuck's fingers touched her face, Zoe turned her head away, her breath hitching with terror.

Chuck picked something off her cheek and looked at it as if he were staring into a crystal ball. He brought the grey matter to his nose and drew in a deep breath. "Oh, yes!" he breathed. "It smells like... like a flower... like the sweetest flower!"

Horror gripped Zoe as she watched Chuck pop the grey matter into his mouth like a gumdrop.

Chuck closed his bloody eyes and fell back onto his ass as he lowered the gun to the floor, his tongue working slowly across his teeth. He laughed, swallowed, and licked his lips.

Oh hell, no! With the gun on the floor, Zoe seized her chance. She put her hands on Ben's shoulder and side and pushed. Ben rolled off her, his limp hand slapping the blood-drenched marble with the sound of raw meat being dropped onto a cutting board.

Chuck's eyes popped open.

Zoe gasped and kicked the gun.

The gun slid towards a group of people lying facedown at the bottom of the stairs. Zoe planted her feet against Ben's body and kicked, scrambling back in the slippery mess.

Chuck lunged forward, but he didn't grab for Zoe or the gun. He grabbed for Ben.

By the time Zoe had climbed to her feet, Chuck had his index finger buried all the way to the bottom knuckle in Ben's head wound. He glanced back at her, pulling his hooked finger from Ben's head as if he were lifting it from a mixing bowl. But it wasn't cookie dough coating his finger. Hurriedly he shoved it into his mouth. His eyes rolled back as if he'd taken a mouthful of his favorite ice cream, and then he pulled his finger from his mouth and began chewing. His bleeding eyes swooped back to Ben as he shoved the appendage back into the head wound.

People were screaming now, and those who were able were on their feet and running for the door.

A uniformed man stepped forward from the fleeing crowd and raised a gun... Chuck's gun. "Stop that! Stop right now!" he shouted, but Chuck paid no attention.

The man fired twice into Chuck's chest. This time, Zoe had managed to get her hands over her ears before the shots were fired.

Chuck fell onto his back, his whole body seizing. Then all at once, the crazed man relaxed into death.

"You all saw what he did! I had no choice! He wouldn't stop... stop eating that man! Jesus Christ, you all saw, right?" the uniformed man said, running a hand over his face. "Ma'am, you saw, right? I had no choice."

Zoe didn't answer, as all around her more people screamed and ran out into the rain. *The rain!* she thought, regaining her senses. Finally, finding her voice, she said, "I don't think we should go out there!"

No one heard, or if they did, they didn't care. This time, she shouted. "Everyone! Listen! Don't go out in the rain!"

Only the security guard or whatever the uniformed man was seemed to hear her. He released the magazine in the gun, checked it, and then shoved it back in with a click, tucking it into his waistband. "Why? Why shouldn't they go in the rain?"

Zoe swallowed, pointing at Chuck's lifeless body. "There was something wrong with him, and he'd been in the rain. He was acting weird, and his eyes were bleeding."

The guard looked toward the door. "Shit."

Outside there were screams and the sound of more

gunshots. Headlights shone through the glass doors, lighting up the atrium in a red glow.

"Run!" the man shouted, grabbing Zoe by the hand as they made for the stairs.

She was on the fifth step when the pickup truck slammed into the double glass doors, exploding them inward in a shower of twisted metal and glass shards. The truck managed to make it halfway inside the building before jolting to a stop, its horn blaring.

Zoe and the guard stopped and spun back around. Through the busted windshield she could see that the driver was slumped over the wheel and wasn't moving.

"Hey, do you work here?" she shouted to the guard over the blare of the horn.

"Yeah, for three months now."

"What's your name?"

"Deandre," the guard said.

The horn stopped.

Zoe glanced back at the truck, but she no longer saw the driver slumped over the wheel. *Maybe he'd come to*, she thought. "Deandre, we need a safe place we can go to wait out this rain. It isn't safe to go out there." Zoe took a deep breath. Her heart was racing in her chest, and she needed to calm down before she had a panic attack.

"Okay. We can find a place upstairs. Maybe the judges' chambers." Deandre looked back down at the scene below. "Hey, Je... sus... what the... ?!"

"What's wrong?"

"The guy!" the guard said, pointing.

Zoe followed his finger to where Chuck had been lying on the floor only a moment ago, but Chuck was gone.

CHAPTER 7
HUNGRY

RED RAIN CONTINUED to pour from the sky as Oliver steered the red-and-white garbage truck slowly toward the exit ramp.

"Sam, how are you doing?" he asked, looking over at the tiny girl who sat between them, huddled in a lavender North Face jacket with her doll, Princess, sitting on her lap.

Sam was leaning against the door, her forehead pressed against the glass of the passenger-side window. "Hungry," she said quietly.

"Well, that's good. You have an appetite. Hey, I've got a granola bar in the glove box." He motioned toward the glove box but didn't take his eyes off what little he could see of the road ahead.

"No. You know I don't eat carbs. Besides... I'm craving something else. Something..."

Not only did Sam not eat carbs, but Oliver knew she didn't eat on the route... ever. She fasted until at least noon and then didn't eat again after six – or maybe seven? In fact, he didn't remember ever hearing her complain about being hungry. He squinted through the windshield. The clouds above were like red velvet, so thick they blotted out most of the sun's light. It was dark. Not pitch dark, but more like dusk during a storm – *if the storm were bleeding*, he thought. As he eased the truck onto the off-ramp, shapes came into view, forcing Oliver to slow to a stop. "Shit, it's blocked, Sam. Traffic must be backed up all the way down onto Route 29."

"Try and pass them on the shoulder," Sam said, lifting her head from the glass.

"I don't know. I think we may have no choice but to wait. But I think the rain is slowing a little."

"Ollie, I can't wait. We need to go. I need—"

"I know, and I'm trying to get you to the hospital, Sam."

"No. First, I need to eat. I have to eat," she said, drawing in a deep breath through her nose. "I can smell it, Ollie. Can't you smell it?"

Oliver frowned. "Sam, I don't smell anything. Food can wait. We need to get you checked—"

On the dash, Oliver's phone buzzed. "Zoe!" He snatched the phone and pressed his thumb to unlock it. There was a text message from Zoe: "Did you go in the rain?"

Oliver quickly typed back, "No. But Sam did. Are you okay? Did you go in the rain?"

Zoe's reply came through immediately. "Is she with you? Is she with you now?"

Oliver started to type a response when a horn blasted. The garbage truck jolted forward. Oliver threw his arm out in front of the little girl, his cell phone flying from his hand and onto the passenger-side floorboard. "Dammit. Someone rear-ended us!" Somewhere behind them, Oliver heard the distinct sound of a gunshot. "What the hell?"

Outside, silhouettes of people ran past his truck.

"Tell me you smell that, Oliver? How could you not smell that?" Sam asked, shaking her head. It was like she was oblivious to what had just happened. She leaned down, placing her nose in one of the little girl's Afro puffs, and drew in a deep breath. "Oh... Oh, that's where it's coming from, isn't it?" She moved her nose toward the girl's ear.

Another shot sounded outside, and someone screamed.

Oliver's eyes widened as he stared into the side mirror, trying to see what the hell was happening out there. Through the rain he saw the flash of more gunfire. Jesus, it was right behind the truck!

"Hey! Stop that! It tickles," the little girl said, moving away from Sam toward Oliver.

Oliver glanced over and frowned. "Sam, what are you doing? Hey, can you grab my phone? It's down there by your feet somewhere. That was Zoe texting me!"

Sam looked down at the floorboard, but she didn't reach for the phone. "Why is she scooting toward you? Why? Why do that? Why won't you just let me? Don't you want me to feel better? Oh, it hurts so much, Oliver." She breathed out and winced, her eyes still fixed on the floor.

"Sam, I don't know what's wrong with you, but I need my phone and we need to get you help," Oliver urged, pulling the little girl closer as he pointed to the floorboard.

Sam screamed, "You can't smell it? Or you want it all for yourself? Well, I smelled it first, Oliver! And I'm the one starving!" She stomped her right foot down onto Oliver's phone. "I... smelled... it... first!"

Oliver's full attention was now on Sam and her contorted face. "Sam, what the fuck?!"

Sam's bloody eyes flashed to Oliver and then to the girl, widening insanely as she lunged forward.

The little girl screamed, pushing herself into Oliver's side as she pulled her doll to her chest.

Sam's lips drew back, tongue showing as she prepared to bite.

Reflexively, Oliver thrust out his hand as if to shove, his palm colliding with Sam's forehead. "Jesus...! Sam!"

Sam's head bent back as her mouth snapped shut hard enough to crack teeth.

Oliver pulled on the little girl's arm, dragging her onto his lap, as the force of Sam's momentum pushed Oliver back into the door.

Sam was fully on the seat now, stomach down with her own feet pressed against the passenger door, knees bent to give her leverage. Her sneakers squeaked against the metal door as they found purchase. Sam pushed. "Mine! Mine! Mine!" she growled, teeth gnashing as she grabbed one of the girl's legs and pulled.

The little girl screamed and kicked.

Oliver's arm began to fold in. Sam could leg-press five hundred pounds. With one arm holding the little girl, there was no way he could hold her back. "Stop, Sam! What the hell is wrong with you?"

Outside, the red rain spilled from the sky as if it were an open wound.

CHAPTER 8
THE JUDGE'S CHAMBERS

ZOE STOLE a few quick glances around the atrium as Deandre shouldered open a large wooden door that read Courtroom B.

Screaming continued to filter up to them from the lower level.

"C'mon, there's a judge's chambers in the back." The security officer motioned as he cautiously stepped into the darkened courtroom.

As Zoe started through the door, she heard feet shuffling behind her intermixed with the clacking of high heels on tile. Pausing, she glanced back to find a tall blonde with a mascara-streaked face, short skirt, and large breasts that strained the buttons of her white blouse. She was running behind a familiar man, slight in build and balding. *Tom?* Zoe recognized the mousey man from the county clerk's office.

"Tom! Over here!" Zoe motioned for the two to follow.

The four of them ran across the courtroom. The place was eerie, with the backup light putting out a dim reddish glow.

Quickly the four crowded into the reception area for what, according to a nameplate on the door, was the chambers of Judge Pastel.

"I heard screams and... and gunshots! What the... what the fuck is happening down there?" the blonde gasped, trying to catch her breath.

Tom ran a hand over his face and pushed his thumb and index fingers beneath his glasses and into his eyes. "Some crazy bastard drove his truck through the building! Nearly killed me!"

Deandre crossed over to the judge's chamber door and flung it open.

"Can I help you?" called a frightened voice.

"Judge Pastel?"

"Yes. What's this about?"

Deandre leaned into the reception area. "Sorry, Judge, I didn't mean to startle you, but I didn't think you'd still be here. Listen, something's happened."

"Deandre? Please come inside."

Deandre entered the reception area fully now as Zoe and the others followed. "We need a place to hide... to hole up until things calm down."

"All of you, come – please come inside." The judge beckoned them forward into his office as he crossed over to his desk.

Zoe had never been in a judge's chambers before, but it basically looked like any other office she had been in. A giant desk, wood-paneled walls, and bookshelves, presumably full of law books. It also had two big floor-to-ceiling windows with blinds drawn closed. "Excuse me, Judge Pastel?"

Judge Pastel pulled up short of sitting down, his eyes bunching up. "My god, you're covered in blood! Come over here, sit down, and let me get a look at you. What the hell has happened?"

Zoe glanced down at her bloodstained scrubs, realizing she must have been a gruesome sight. "I'm okay. The blood isn't mine."

"But I don't understand." The grey-haired man turned back to Deandre. "Deandre, do we have an active shooter? Was that what I heard?"

"You don't know?" Zoe asked, approaching the judge.

"Know? I... Well, I wasn't scheduled for court until nine. I typically arrive early to prepare. A little while ago, I heard the screams and gunshots. The whole building shook. I only just unlocked my door and ventured out into the reception area. I was trying to peek out to see what was happening when you burst in."

The blonde shook her head in disbelief as she crossed over to the two large windows. "You don't know about the giant fucking asteroid, the nukes, or the sky raining blood!"

"Sky raining blood? My dear girl, what drugs are you on?"

The blonde pulled the chain on one of the curtains to reveal glass splashed in red water partially obscuring the dark sky beyond – an alien sky. "I'm not on shit, and I'm not your girl."

Judge Pastel approached the window, his eyes wide. "Oh, dear lord! It's all true."

The blonde crossed her arms and raised an I-told-you-so eyebrow. "Uh-huh."

As they all gazed out the window, Deandre quickly brought Judge Pastel up to speed. Zoe tried texting Oliver again: "Oliver, please answer me!" The blue bar slowly stretched out and then froze. Below the text, the message changed to red, and a notification appeared: "Message failed to send."

"Shit!" she breathed, trying again: "Did you go in the rain?" Again, the blue bar stretched out, but this time it didn't stop. This time, the message that appeared below the text turned blue and read "Delivered."

Zoe gasped, leaning back on the edge of Judge Pastel's desk as she stared at the screen. *Please, please, please!* Her phone chimed with Oliver's reply. Her relief at his "no" was quickly replaced with alarm that Sam had gone in the rain.

Oh, no! Quickly she typed back, "Is she with you? Is she with you now?"

Zoe waited for ten seconds, then twenty... nothing. Oliver didn't answer. Frantically, she thumbed the screen on her phone. "Come on, Oliver! Text me back! Don't do this to me right now!"

She stared down at her phone, hoping with all she had. *Please, Oliver! Answer me!*

"Your phone worked? He answered?" Tom squeaked. Zoe hadn't even noticed him standing next to her. Something in his tone made her glance up. She looked at him... really looked, as if assessing a patient. His once neatly kept hair was now disheveled, like she imagined a clown might look on his day off. Tom started blinking repeatedly, like he had a nervous twitch or maybe from the stress of the situation. Zoe realized only now that the scrawny clerk looked like he was losing it. "It's Tom, right?"

Tom nodded, frowning down at his own phone. "Mine won't work at all. Is yours actually working?"

"Hey, did you say your phone is working?" the blonde asked.

The others turned from the window and gathered around Zoe. Tom's panicked eyes darted between them.

Zoe shook her head. "Yes. I mean it was. I did get through with a text and he answered, but now he's not responding. I'll keep trying." Maybe if texting was working, then ringing through would work too. She punched Oliver's name with her index finger, and it actually began to ring!

"Can I use your phone to try my Laura? Please?" Tom asked, reaching for her phone.

Instinctively, Zoe pulled back. "Wait. It's ringing!"

Deandre frowned and held up a hand. "Take it easy, Tom. Let's see if she gets through." He looked back at Zoe expectantly.

She shook her head. "Voicemail."

"Damn. But, hey, at least you got through," Deandre said.

Tom lunged forward, grabbing her phone.

"Hey!" Zoe protested, backpedaling into the desk. A container holding pens, a pair of scissors, and a long letter opener tipped, scattering its contents across the desk.

"I... I have to try and reach my Laura. She'll be worried sick, what with all this going on!" Tom opened the dial screen and frowned.

"Well, that was quite rude! You don't go around snatching something that doesn't belong to you, son. For god's sake, its borderline assault," said Judge Pastel.

Deandre sneered, giving Tom a look like he might twist him into a knot.

Zoe composed herself. "It's okay."

The blonde pulled a face at Tom. "No, it's not okay, you little pip-squeak!"

"Shut up, you filthy whore," Tom said, still frowning at the phone screen.

"Hey, asshole! How dare you—"

"Stop!" Zoe said, waving off the woman but keeping her eyes fixed on Tom. "It's okay, Tom. Call your wife."

"I... I can't remember her number," Tom said.

"Can't remember your own wife's number?" Judge Pastel asked skeptically.

Tom used his empty hand to try and straighten his wire-framed glasses, but they appeared to be hopelessly twisted. "It's just that in my phone, her number is programmed in... I don't ever dial it."

The twisted glasses drew Zoe's eyes to Tom's, confirming her suspicion. Tom's clothes were spotted in what might have been blood spatter, but now she realized it wasn't blood at all. "Tom, your clothes. Did you go out in the rain?"

"I tried to get... get home to my..." he stuttered, squeezing his eyes up tight as if trying to remember.

Zoe swallowed dryly as a bloody tear leaked from the corner of Tom's left eye.

"To... to my Laura!" His eyes popped back open to reveal one blood-red sclera.

Zoe's medical training told her what she was seeing was beyond bloodshot eyes. The man's eye looked severely damaged, and his other eye looked only slightly better. Without a closer examination, she couldn't tell what was causing the bleeding, but she wasn't sure it mattered. The bloody eye was only a symptom of something else. Something affecting the man's mind.

Tom shook his head. "But see, that's when all hell broke loose! There was a truck smashing through the parking lot. I ran back inside just before it smashed through the darn building."

Zoe glanced at the rain-slicked window and then back

to Tom's red-stained clothes. "How long were you out there, Tom?"

"Who gives a shit!" the blonde said. "Look, if you can't remember your own wife's fucking phone number, please, pass it over. I need to make sure my ride is still outside!"

"No," Tom said flatly.

"What do you mean, no?" the blond asked.

"I think I'll keep it till I remember. It's on the tip... tip of my... tip of my taste. It will come to me," Tom said quietly. Then he began to sing softly, "My baby... my bay... beeee."

The blonde barked out a laugh. "This guy's losing his shit!" She turned away, walking to the other side of the office. The woman threw herself down in a dark chocolate leather chair and began thumbing her own phone. "You guys can keep crazy over there. I'll figure this shit out myself."

"Give her back her phone, Tom, or I am going to make you give it back," Deandre said.

Tom's lips twisted into a sneer. "You think so?"

Zoe placed a gentle hand on Deandre's shoulder. "Let him try his wife. The rest of you come back into the reception area and help me block the door."

"Block the door? We can just lock my office door. Do you really think blocking the door to the outer office is necessary?" Judge Pastel asked.

Zoe nodded. "I do. And I need all your help. Except Tom. Tom needs to stay here and call Laura. She'll be worried."

Tom's brow furrowed at the screen as he busied himself punching in wrong numbers.

Deandre shook his head. "Lady, we all got people we're worried about out there, but this guy took your—"

"Forget it," Zoe cut in, motioning with her eyes to the clerk and then pointing to her own eye.

The big security guard's brows tightened as he looked at Tom anew.

The clerk's left eye was leaking blood in a steady trickle now, and the other was beyond bloodshot.

"Am I missing something?" Judge Pastel asked.

"Yes. People are acting strange out there. Please, Judge, come help us with the door." Zoe turned to the blonde in the leather chair. "You too."

The blonde looked up with a frown and started to protest.

Zoe shook her head and nodded toward Tom. Deandre pointed at the door.

The blonde's eyes darted between them, an eyebrow raised in curious confusion, but she stood and followed them out of the office. Once in the reception area, they made their way across to a large wooden door.

From the office, Tom's singsong voice became a chant. "My baby... I know you must be hungry... my baby... hungry... don't you smell it... smell it... smell... smell... smell..."

"Everybody," Zoe whispered, "we need to leave now."

"Shoot, I need to grab my jacket," Judge Pastel said, turning back to the office.

Zoe reached for the door handle that separated them from the courtroom. "Forget it."

Judge Pastel shook his head. "I can't, my car keys are in the pocket. I'll be quick." Before Zoe could protest again, he vanished back into the office.

"Shit!" she said, her hand on the door handle.

From the other side of the door came a gut-wrenching scream followed by a great *boom*!

The door shook. Zoe yanked her hand back as if she'd just touched a hot stove, and Deandre threw himself against the massive wooden door.

Boom!

"Grab a chair!" Deandre shouted, motioning behind him.

Another scream. Another boom. The wooden door cracked.

Then nothing. Through the open door of the chambers, Tom chanted softly to himself.

Zoe and the blonde grabbed one of the plush leather chairs and carried it over to the door.

From the other side of the door, a quiet voice spoke. "I can smell you."

"What the hell is happening?" the blonde asked, her voice breaking as she helped Zoe wedge the back of the chair under the door handle.

Zoe shook her head. "I... I don't know."

Deandre backed away from the door and looked at Zoe, fear filling his eyes. "That dude downstairs was dead, and then he... he disappeared. What if the dude on the other side of this door is that same dude... that brother that was... was eating the other guy?"

"The guy you shot in the chest twice? He was dead. That much I'm sure of. My guess is someone else dragged him away," Zoe said, keeping her eye on the door.

Boom! The door shook again.

"No," Deandre said, shaking his head. "He was lying in a pool of blood. If he was dragged off, it would have left a red streak across that white marble. He wasn't dragged."

Zoe gave that a half second of thought before the door shook again. *Boom!* "Let me the fuck in!"

"This chair isn't going to hold the door for long!" Deandre warned.

Another voice came from beyond the door. This one was deeper. "I'm starving to death!"

Boom!

"I need to get out of here!" the blonde said.

Zoe grabbed the now sobbing woman by the shoulders. "What's your name?"

"Angel," the woman said between sobs.

"Angel, we're going to get out of here together. Deandre, is there another way out?"

Boom!

"Judge," Deandre called over his shoulder. "I saw a door at the back corner of your office – please tell me it isn't a closet?"

Judge Pastel didn't answer. Suddenly, Zoe noticed she no longer heard Tom's creepy-ass chant. "He went to get his jacket," she said, sharing a worried look with Deandre.

Boom!

"Come on!" Deandre shouted, running for the office door.

Once inside, Zoe and the others pulled up short, frozen by the horror of Judge Pastel's prone body sprawled twitching across his desk. Tom straddled the man, a blood-slicked letter opener in his hand. Beneath the judge's robes, a pool of viscous dark liquid spilled off the desk.

Pastel's head was turned away from them. Tom, paying them no mind, was stabbing the older man over and over in the temple. "So hard to... to get into!" Tom shouted to no one. Then, forgoing the letter opener, he plunged his thumbs into the man's skull. Tom's tongue stuck out of the corner of his bloodstained mouth as he concentrated and strained, trying to pull the opening in the man's temple apart as if he were trying to split open a watermelon with his bare hands.

Angel screamed.

Tom's head snapped around as he noticed them for the first time. The balding man's face contorted as his lips drew up into an awful sneer.

"Run!" Zoe said, pointing to a door at the back of the office beyond the gruesome scene atop the desk.

From the reception area came the sound of splintering wood.

Deandre slammed Judge Pastel's office door closed. "They've broken through! Go! Go! Go!"

They ran, darting around the desk. First Zoe, then Angel.

Zoe grabbed the door, turned the latch, and pushed, stumbling out onto the landing of a stairwell. The staircase fell away into the darkness below. Angel, close on her heels, slammed into her back.

Zoe stumbled forward, grabbing the handrail to keep from falling down the stairs.

"Sorry!" Angel grunted.

Zoe spun and grabbed the woman, pulling her to the side to clear a path for Deandre so he wouldn't knock them both down the stairs.

"Hey!" Angel cried, her stiletto heels sliding across the tile as she fell into Zoe's arms.

But Zoe paid no attention as she stared back through the door, her eyes snapping wide. Tom had thrown himself from the desk and onto Deandre.

On the opposite of the office, the door shook and cracked.

"Get off me, motherfucker!" Deandre shoved Tom back. A gun fired. *Crack! Crack! Crack!*

All three shots hit Tom in the center of the chest, staggering him backward into one of the giant windows in a crash of breaking glass. The man's bleeding eyes opened wide as he fell back.

Zoe was sure Tom would fall out the window, but the small man's flailing hands grasped the jagged window frame at the last second. Despite the glass shards digging into Tom's hands and the fatal gunshots to his chest, he somehow held fast, pulling himself forward only to collapse onto his knees and finally tip onto his face.

Tom's body began to spasm then, twitching and jerking before going still.

Outside, the rain poured.

Across the office there was a final snap of wood as the door swung inward.

"Hurry!" Zoe shouted, motioning for Deandre to run.

A short, portly man with a beard and bleeding eyes burst into the office, followed by a tall man with a blood-smeared face.

Deandre staggered through the door, pulling it shut with one hand as he unbuckled his belt and yanked it free of his waist with the other. "Help me!"

"How?" Zoe begged.

From the other side, bodies slammed into the door.

Deandre grabbed the handle and leaned back with all his weight. "Quick! Wrap my belt around the handle, loop it through, then wrap the other end around the handrail!"

Zoe wrapped the belt around the handle and looped it through.

The door jerked open a few inches. The short, bearded man's face appeared in the crack, teeth bared and snapping open and closed as he sniffed at the air.

Deandre braced his foot against the doorframe, tugging the door closed with a grunt. "Hurry!"

"How do I fasten it to the rail?" she asked.

"Just tie it the best you can!"

She looped it through and knotted it best she could, but it was leather, and leather doesn't make a good knot. "I'm not sure how long this will hold," she said, looking over at the guard and noticing for the first time his arm was bleeding—bleeding bad. "Deandre, your arm!"

Deandre let go of the door and gave Zoe's knot a firm jerk. "Yeah, that little freak Tom bit me!"

CHAPTER 9
DANCING IN THE RAIN

SAM'S TEETH clacked as red tears spilled from her eyes and onto Oliver's windbreaker. "I'm so hungry, Oliver. It hurts. It hurts! Please!" the woman begged, and then screamed, "Ahhhhh! Give it!"

"Sam! Dam... mit... Don't!" Oliver pleaded.

The little girl kicked her foot free and climbed over the steering wheel and onto the oversized dashboard, wedging herself against the windshield of the garbage truck. But Sam paid no attention to the girl now as her face pressed in closer to Oliver's.

Now, with Sam fully focused on him, he couldn't hold her off... couldn't stop the CrossFit champion from collapsing his arms and biting his face.

Oliver closed his eyes, turning his face away from his best friend and the horrible visage of desperation she'd become.

Suddenly the passenger door popped open, and Sam collapsed onto her belly.

Oliver peeked one eye open, his head snapping around to see what had happened, half expecting to see someone there in the doorway. But there was no one. Quickly he realized Sam's foot must have lifted the truck's door latch. She'd lost her footing and with it her leverage.

Sam drew back and scrambled onto her hands and knees. New hope surged as Oliver saw his fleeting chance slipping away.

The little girl screamed.

Oliver twisted, lifting his right leg and pressing his back against the driver's-side door.

Sam snarled like a wild animal, like a goddamned wild animal. She lunged forward again.

Oliver clenched his jaw and planted his foot atop Sam's shoulder. Now it was Oliver who had all the leverage. "Ahhh!" he shouted, kicking with all he had. "I'm sorry, Sam!"

Sam's bloody eyes went wide as the force of the kick flung her off her hands and knees and onto her bottom near the edge of the bench seat. The crazed woman's hands stretched out as she fell backward out of the truck. "Please!" she shouted, vanishing into the rain.

Oliver's heart sank; he knew a headfirst fall from the height of the truck could be serious, if not fatal. But Oliver didn't wait to see. He shoved the truck into gear and stomped on the gas pedal. The truck lurched forward, the sudden force slamming the passenger door shut just before it would have crunched into the vehicle in front of him.

The little girl grunted, falling back off the dashboard and into the oversized steering wheel.

Grabbing a glove off the seat, Oliver used it to quickly depress the lock on the rain-slicked passenger door. "Climb down," he said, breathing hard. The little girl was crying, but she seemed to be uninjured.

"Are you okay?" he asked desperately. "Did you hit your head?"

The girl shook her head, wiping tears from her eyes. She gripped her doll like it was a lifeline. "I want my mom," she said, her lips trembling as her eyes glistened with fresh tears.

Oliver's heart broke as he fought back tears of his own. "I know. I know. Listen," he said, hesitating. His own thoughts scrambled as he tried to rationalize what just happened. He realized in the twenty or thirty minutes since he'd picked up the little girl, he hadn't even asked her name. "What's your name?"

"Jurnee," the girl said between sobs. "But not like... like when you're going on a trip but like this." One by one, the girl spelled out the letters. "J U R N E E."

Oliver blinked. "Jurnee," he whispered back. Here they were, two strangers, and that name – that word – Jurnee. He wanted to believe that meant something. But he'd stopped believing in signs and greater cosmic reasons when... He frowned, trying to shake the thought away, but he couldn't. Jurnee was the name he and Zoe were leaning toward before... He closed his eyes and swallowed. It felt like he was trying to swallow a cat... Before they'd lost the baby.

Even the spelling was the same. Sure, they'd spotted it on a list of trending girls' names, but still, what were the odds he would meet her here and now, in this moment of uncertainty? And where was this journey about to take them? He didn't know, but a feeling inside him he couldn't explain was urging him, *You have to keep this little girl safe*.

Oliver opened his eyes and looked at the little girl. "Well, Jurnee, I'm Oliver, and I'm going to keep you safe until we find your family, okay?"

Tears spilled down Jurnee's small round cheeks, but she managed a slight nod.

"Okay, now I need you to do me a favor and stay good and far away from that door. Don't touch anything wet, okay?"

Jurnee nodded, scooting closer to Oliver.

"Good. Now let's figure out—"

There was a thump on the passenger-side window as a fist smashed into the glass.

Oliver jumped and the girl shrieked. Outside the window, Sam jerked on the locked latch and punched the window again. "Muuuuuaaaa!" she moaned. Her head was twisted funny and a viscous stream of blood covered one side of her face, visible even through the streaks of red rain.

Oh, Jesus, Sam. Oliver yanked back on the shifter and stomped on the gas pedal. The truck reversed as the backup lights and beeper burst into action. *Beep! Beep! Beep!* A moment later, the hopper smashed into a vehicle behind them, and Sam fell from the step.

"Hold on, Jurnee!" Oliver shifted into first gear. The heavy rain was slowing enough that he could see the shape of the other vehicles filling the off-ramp. Steering onto the shoulder, Oliver shifted into second and then third, speeding past the jammed-up motorists. He grimaced as he sideswiped a blue SUV. Horns sounded but he kept going, navigating the truck down the curving ramp.

A large brown king-cab pickup truck eased out onto the shoulder in an effort to block him from passing. *Not the time to be a dick, pal!* Oliver thought. He put his arm across Jurnee's chest, as if he and he alone could stop gravitational force from throwing the girl into the dashboard.

Fortunately, the pickup offered little resistance when

the half-full garbage truck hit the front passenger-side quarter panel. The truck spun away, back into the waiting traffic. "That's what you get!" Oliver shouted, glancing into the side mirror.

Staying on the shoulder, Oliver turned right onto Route 29. To his right, there was a Kohl's department store, and just past that there was an explosion of movie-set proportions as a gas station went up in a fantastic ball of fire. Oliver realized in that moment that something was clearly wrong with the world around him, and he remembered the text from Zoe. *Did you go in the rain?* Of all the things she could have texted, that's what she'd asked him. Not *Are you okay?* Not *Are you home?* But *Did you go in the rain?*

His thoughts flashed to the tiny bleeding holes in Sam's eyes. It was more than metal particles in the eyes, more than asteroid particles. Something had infected her, changed her – something in the rain. Something that made her want to eat him. What the hell was going on? The gunshots, the explosions. It wasn't just Sam; the rain was changing people. He had to get home. He had to get to Zoe. Screw traffic laws. He was done playing by the rules, and god help anyone who got in the way – he was going home.

Up ahead was an intersection. If he tried to turn left, there would be no shoulder. He could go straight past the CVS and take Springfield Road out of town, but there would be sections with no shoulder that way too. He had to be smart and stay on the roads with a shoulder as much as possible.

Mackinaw was thirty minutes east on a normal day, but this was anything but normal. *Well, damn.* He supposed his best bet was the path of least resistance. He'd take his chances with Springfield Road. If he could just get out of East River City, he should be home free. Oliver glanced at his phone lying on the floorboard. He didn't need to retrieve it to see that Sam had stomped the shit out of it. Zoe was probably freaking out. But something she'd said had given him comfort. She had asked him if he'd gone into the rain, which could only mean she knew not to. Thank god she knew not to. *I'm coming, Zoe.*

Oliver swung the truck around the front of the line of cars and into the intersection. "What the shit?" he said, noticing there was a crowd of a dozen or so people standing in the rain. No, not standing... dancing.

"Oh, you dumb sons of bitches!" Oliver said, shaking his head in disbelief. *Look at them,* he thought. *Happy to be alive and not knowing they're killing themselves.* His thoughts flashed back to Sam, a lump forming in his throat.

"You sure say lots of bad words, Oliver," Jurnee said disapprovingly.

"Oh, um, sorry, Jurnee," Oliver said, feeling strangely embarrassed.

Jurnee sniffed, wiped her nose on her coat sleeve, and giggled.

The giggle felt right somehow. Sam would have laughed at this, at him being scolded by a little kid for his potty mouth. Oliver cleared his throat, pushing down the lump and forcing a smile. "Everything is going to be okay, kid," he said, more to himself than to the girl. "Old Mack will get us where we need to go."

"Who's Mack?"

"Oh, didn't I introduce you? Mack is my truck – says so right on the front grille." Oliver patted the dashboard. "Mack, this is Jurnee! Say hello." He revved the truck's engine a couple times.

Clutching Princess close, Jurnee giggled again. "Hi,

Mack! This is Princess," she said, holding her doll out as if to show the truck. "Maybe you two can be friends."

"Well, alright! Now that we're all acquainted you hold on, okay?"

Jurnee clutched Princess tight to her chest and nodded.

He stared past the group of dancers and towards a row of cars stretching bumper-to-bumper across the intersection from the other direction. *Sorry for this*, he thought as the people shuffled out of the way. He aimed the truck between the front end of a grey Toyota Corolla and the trunk of a black Cadillac. Both vehicles desperately honked their horns as Oliver eased the front bumper into the two vehicles, his headlights filling their cabs. The two cars were pushed aside like a set of squeaky French doors.

Once through the intersection, Oliver turned off Route 29 and onto Springfield Road. Ten miles per hour – at this rate it would take him two and a half hours to get home. He pushed his way through another intersection and dropped his rig into low gear. Slowly he maneuvered the heavy beast up the steep hill adjacent to a small park.

As Oliver crested the hill, he saw a woman running down the street in nothing but a bra and underwear. A man chased after her with a garden shovel raised high above his head and cocked for a swing. *Good lord!* His instincts tugged at him to help the woman, but what could he do? If the rain was poisonous, she was dead anyway. Still, he had to do something. "Close your eyes, Jurnee, and don't open them till I say, okay?"

Jurnee nodded and shut her eyes up tight.

Oliver pressed down on the gas pedal and aimed the corner of his rig toward the man with the shovel, clipping him as he passed. The shovel flew from the man's hands, clanging into the grill of the truck as the man spun down onto the pavement, sliding away from Oliver's sight.

The woman continued to run.

Slowly they crept forward as the rain tapered off to a steady shower of doom. Gunshots fired from somewhere in the neighborhood, first on his left and then from somewhere even closer on his right. Oliver tried to see beyond the street and the front yards, but it was still no use. The few cars on Springfield Road were moving now, and high above, the rust-colored sky seemed to brighten just a little. It was only midmorning, but the sky glowed as if poured full of molten iron. Oliver hoped this was a good sign. Perhaps he was seeing the last of this alien rain as the clouds were wrung like a washrag to splatter blood red over the world.

"Can I open my eyes?" Jurnee asked.

"Shit! I mean yes. Look at the sky, Jurnee. I think it's brightening." Some small relief filled him. He wanted to drive faster – to get home to Zoe.

They crossed through their last intersection, and a few miles later they drove into the small town of Groveland. But despite the hope of sunshine to come, the rain continued to stubbornly fall.

As he passed through the tiny town, he noticed carnage. A car crashed through the front of a home, a gas station ransacked and burning. Another home billowing smoke. Through his driver-side window, Oliver saw three people crouched on the sidewalk. They were bent over a fourth. Oliver squinted, trying to understand what he was seeing. *What the... They were. No... no, that can't be right.* But there they were – kneeling in the rain, doing the unthinkable. They were eating a woman's face.

Oliver sped up, shifting through the gears. He looked

down at the little girl and dragged a hand down his whiskery face. *What the hell was happening out there?*

On his dashboard a light flashed, catching his attention. Oliver frowned, not sure he'd really seen it, but then it flashed again. The third time, the service engine light didn't flash – it stayed on, bright and red and damning.

CHAPTER 10
THE RESTROOM

ZOE BOUNDED down the tile stairs leading away from the judge's chambers and onto the first floor. Straight ahead, a metal door exited into the midmorning rain. To their left was a dark corridor, presumably leading back into the courthouse atrium.

"Smell you! We smell you! Smell... youuuuuuu!" a disturbed voice trailed after them. High above, the belt-strapped door banged over and over.

Somewhere beyond the hallway, a woman screamed. It wasn't a scream for help or a scream of someone running in fear; this was the scream of someone being murdered.

Zoe pulled up short.

"Don't stop," Deandre said with a grimace, his right hand pressed tight over an oozing wound just above his elbow. "We have to go this way. We can't go back up, and we can't go outside!"

"The backup generator kicked on earlier, so if the power isn't out, who the hell turned out the lights?" Angel asked uneasily. "Look, I think I'll take my chances with the rain."

Zoe stepped in front of the taller woman, blocking her

path. "No! He's right! You can't go into that rain! Don't you see? It's the rain, Angel! The rain is causing them to go crazy!"

From the darkness, something banged. They all jumped as another scream gargled and faded.

"Well, I'm not going down there," Angel said, her eyes wide and full of panic.

Deandre pointed down the hall. "Listen, there's a bathroom on the left. Maybe we can hide in there until the rain stops." The tall man looked at Zoe hopefully. "Upstairs, I got a look through the window. I think the rain is slowing."

Zoe had noticed it too when Tom broke the window. It did look like the rain was slowing, but Zoe would be damned if she stepped one foot out that door until she was sure she could make it to her car without getting a drop on her. She nodded. "Yeah, it's slowing. The bathroom is a good plan, and we can get that bite wound washed up."

Angel crossed her arms. "Okay, fine. But for the record, I don't like being trapped in a room with only one way in and one way out."

Behind them laughter spilled down the stairs, accompanied by shuffling feet.

"Shit, it didn't hold! Hurry, this way!" Deandre said, running for the bathroom.

Pushing their way inside the men's room, they scrambled past six puke-green stalls and into the seventh and final one. There they stood, trying to control their breathing as their eyes darted back forth, listening for the door to pop open. Deandre lifted the pistol and looked at it as if surprised he still held the weapon. "Get behind me," he whispered. "If they come in, I'll shoot..." He swallowed dryly, trailing off.

Seconds passed, then minutes. Jesus, it felt like hours.

Zoe's mind raced. Oliver, the rain, the crazy man, Chuck eating Ben's brains right off her face. Instinctively, she reached over and wiped her face across her shoulder. Then her thoughts flashed to Judge Pastel, Tom, and the letter opener. What the hell was in the rain that made people want to kill each other and... and eat each other?

"Well?" Deandre asked, frowning.

Zoe blinked. "Huh? Oh, sorry, what?"

"I said they must have passed by now. It's been fifteen minutes," Deandre said, nodding towards the door. "You think it's safe to go out?"

"I think we should wait another fifteen minutes," Angel said, texting something on her phone. She'd been trying the whole time, but her texts weren't sending.

"Okay," Zoe whispered. "We can stay and wait, but let's get you over to the sink. Your arm is still bleeding."

They agreed and eased open the stall door, making their way to one of the sinks where they stood frozen, listening.

"There's no lock on that door. Someone could burst in here any second," Angel said.

"If you'll look at my arm, I'll stay focused on the door," Deandre said, placing the gun next to the sink. "I'll have plenty of time to shoot. I just need to make sure I aim for the head."

"Angel, as quietly as possible, get me a bunch of paper towels." Zoe gestured towards the paper towel dispenser.

Angel nodded and began depressing the lever on the dispenser ever so slowly.

Zoe turned on the cold faucet and washed her hands. "Bend down here and let me wash it out. But just know, it's going to hurt like hell and the soap might burn too."

"Just do it," Deandre said, fixing his jaw.

Hoping to take his mind off the pain to come. Zoe said, "Tell me what you meant by aim for the head?"

Deandre looked at her hard and pressed his lips into a tight line. "I mean there's only one way to kill a zombie – aim for the head."

"A zombie?" she asked in disbelief as she dispensed a palm full of soap. This guy couldn't be serious. "Don't be ridiculous, Deandre. There's a logical explanation for this. Now take your hand away and let me see."

Deandre pulled his hand back and cringed. "Ridiculous? People are changing, craving brains, and that guy I shot in the chest multiple times got up and walked away. What the hell would you call it?"

"I don't... I don't know, but I have some theories. And you don't know that Chuck got up and walked. You didn't see him move after you shot him," she argued, assessing the damage to his arm. The bite was bad, but at least Tom hadn't bit out the whole chunk. He'd sunk his teeth in good though, deep into the tissue of Deandre's lower triceps muscle. At a minimum, the man needed a hospital and stitches. It was also likely he'd suffered tendon damage, which could require surgery. She wet her hand and rubbed soap over the wound.

"Like... what... theory?" Deandre grunted.

"Hey, sorry, but we have to clean it."

Deandre nodded, squeezing his eyes shut. "I know, I know. Do what you have to do. I can handle it. So? What... theories?"

Zoe winced, wishing she could numb the wound area. "Well, I think there is something in the rain."

"No shit, honey. You said that already," Angel said, her eyes locked on the door.

"Yeah, I did. Well, my best theory is some kind of

bacteria or maybe a parasite. Something small. Since it has to be in that strange rain, who knows… something we've never seen – but something that moves fast."

"A parasite that makes you want to eat brains. Lady, what the hell for?" Deandre asked.

Deandre's arm was a mix of soap lather and blood. "Bend down, let me rinse it."

Deandre bent, sticking his elbow into the sink.

"You might be amazed at what parasites can make the host do, and I'm not even talking about alien ones."

"Like what?" Angel asked.

Five came to mind. Zoe remembered them from a semester on parasites in nursing school, but she didn't want to talk about any of them or the horror of what they could do. "Doesn't matter. It's just a theory." She folded the paper towels into a bandage.

Deandre nodded. "I have a theory of my own, and I like mine better than yours. You see, they had to have fired nukes at that asteroid. And doesn't 'nuke' mean radioactive?"

"Yeah, I guess so," Zoe said, patting the wound dry before wrapping the folded band of paper towels around Deandre's arm.

"Of course, sure it does," Angel said, nodding along.

"Right… well, maybe there is… is some kind of radioactive shit in the rain. Jesus, that hurts."

"I know, sorry, but the next part is going to be worse. I need to tie something around this tight or it's just going to keep bleeding," Zoe said.

Deandre removed his uniform overshirt and handed Angel a small folding knife from his front pocket. "You mind cutting this into strips for me?"

"Sure."

"You said you like your theory better than mine?" Zoe asked.

"Yeah... If you're right I... I probably caught that parasite shit when that little prick bit me. And that would jibe with my zombie theory."

She hadn't even thought about that. Not the zombie part but the spreading of a parasite through a bite. Zoe's heart sank. If she were right – and god, she hoped she wasn't – Deandre could be infected. "I don't think it would work that way," she lied. "Besides you feel okay, right? It's been what, thirty minutes since he bit you?"

"I feel fine considering I killed at least one person today and my arm burns like hell."

Angel handed the strip of grey shirt to Zoe. She wrapped it around Deandre's arm twice, made a knot, and cinched it down tight.

Deandre winced.

"I know this sucks, but one more should do it. What I'm applying is a pressure dressing. It should help to keep pressure on the wound and stanch the bleeding."

Deandre nodded. Then, as if an afterthought, he said, "Man, I'm starving. I mean I feel like I could eat a full-sized horse right now."

Starving? Zoe's breath caught. At a time like this, hunger shouldn't even be a thought. Somehow, her heart, already in the pit of her stomach, found a way to burrow in deeper and deeper as Chuck's words echoed in her mind. *Starving... starved... hung—* Then Tom's strange singing: *I know you must be hungry... my baby... hungry... I can almost smell it... smell it... smell... smell... smell...*

Zoe's body shivered at the memories, knowing those words would haunt her nightmares for years to come – if she lived that long. But with the dreadful memory came a realization. Whatever was happening, starvation was a symptom. And not just starvation but smell too.

"Deandre? Do you smell anything?" Zoe asked carefully.

Angel froze, glancing up from the grey fabric strip.

"Smell?" Deandre blinked and took in a deep breath. "Smells like a bathroom." He shrugged.

Zoe sighed, exchanging a relieved look with Angel. The woman's own relief told her she was tracking along. Maybe the guy really was just hungry.

"But now that you mention it," Deandre said, a smile stretching across his face. He closed his eyes tight, squeezing them, mashing them down as he scrunched his nose up and drew in deep breath. "Aaaah yeah!" he exhaled, stretching out the words. "There is a kind of, I don't know... a sweetness to the air. Do you smell it?" He licked his lips. "It's kind of like when you put your nose really close to a cherry cheesecake and suck in a deep breath. You know when... when it smells so good you can almost taste it."

Tears stung at Zoe's eyes as she tried not to let them fall. She glanced at the gun lying next to the sink.

Deandre opened his eyes. "Well? Do you?"

"Huh? I'm sorry, what?" she asked quietly.

"Smell it? That wonderful fragrance. You think it's something they use to clean the bathroom?" Deandre leaned forward and sniffed. "No... No, wait. It isn't the bathroom at all. I think it must be your perfume!" He smiled again. "Hey, what are you wearing? Maybe I can get some for my girl."

Zoe stared into Deandre's eyes with the focus of an ophthalmologist. But she didn't need to be an eye doctor to see what she feared more than anything. Deandre's corneas had turned light pink. *Oh no.* She leaned in closer. It almost looked like there were small perforations in the whites of his eyes. That would explain the bleeding.

"Why are you looking at me like that?" Deandre asked.

"Chanel Number Five," she answered quickly.

"Chanel Number Five? Well... I got to get some of that for my girl, Teyana. Did I tell you we just got married? Got a little one on the way too. We just found out last week it's going to be a boy," he said, beaming. "We're gonna name him Howard, after my father." Deandre frowned before his eyebrows lifted thoughtfully, his gaze shifting to Angel. He pulled in another long breath. "I'll be damned. You two are wearing the same thing?" The man laughed in disbelief. "Now what are the odds you would both be wearing the sweetest perfume I have ever smelled on the same day?"

Zoe slid her hand across the counter, turning the gun as she lifted it carefully.

Deandre's eyes caught the movement, languidly following Zoe's hand over to the gun. "Now why would you do that? Haven't I done a good job protecting you girls?"

"You have, Deandre, and now I want to protect you for a while."

"'Cause you think I'm changing... changing into a zombie?"

"No," Zoe said evenly, and she meant it. There was no such thing as a zombie. "I just think you're hurt, and you've already done so much."

Rapid footsteps resonated from beyond the door, growing closer. But the sound was wrong. It wasn't the clack of dress shoes or even tennis shoes – it was a slap of bare feet smacking tile.

"What the fuck?" Angel mouthed.

Deandre didn't look at the door, didn't take his eyes off Zoe. "Give me the gun," he said, his voice too loud.

Zoe shook her head. "I... I'm sorry. I can't do that."

Deandre lunged forward, grabbing the gun.

Behind him, Zoe caught a glimpse of a naked woman with bared teeth and blood-filled eyes bursting into the bathroom – and she wasn't alone.

CHAPTER 11
THE CHURCH

OLIVER CHECKED HIS GAUGES. Plenty of fuel. Oil pressure looked good. Battery charge was fine. Temp gauge was... oh come on! The temp gauge was pegged in the red. The old Mack truck was overheating. There was nothing he could do about it now but press on and get as close to home as he could before—

Suddenly the engine sputtered and a loud hiss announced a billow of steam, rolling from beneath the hood of the big diesel.

"Fuck my life!" Oliver shouted.

Jurnee gasped, slapping her hand over her mouth.

Oliver frowned. "Ah, sorry, kid – don't... don't learn that... okay?"

Frowning back, the little girl shook her head. "That's the worst one, Oliver," she whispered as if god himself might overhear.

Steam rose from every seam like a dormant volcano awakened and about to erupt. Oliver squinted against the thick fog of evaporating radiator fluid. Stomping his foot down on the accelerator, he said, "I'm not going to baby you,

Mack! I'm going to push you until you give up on me! Don't you give up on me!" he begged.

The cab bucked as the engine sputtered and cut out again. Twelve miles to Mackinaw, maybe fifteen. "Oh, c'mon!"

"Uh-oh, Oliver. Mack sounds sick," the little girl said.

"Yep, Mack's sick alright!" Oliver said, willing the big beast forward. "Don't you die on me, Mack!" he growled.

They were in the country, a few miles outside Groveland. On his right was a huge brick farmhouse with a four-car garage and five chimneys. The massive home looked more like a mansion than a farmhouse. A wooded creek ran across the front of the property, requiring a short bridge to cross. On the other side stood a wrought iron gate, but the gate was open. Beyond the gate, a gravel driveway led toward the house, where it made a large circle.

Oliver, considering pulling in, took his foot off the gas pedal. As he slowed, he could see a car with the door ajar and headlights on. Maybe the car was abandoned. Maybe he could borrow it. Wait. What the hell? He couldn't be sure through the thick rain, but it looked like the front door to the house was standing wide open. Slowing to a near stop, he squinted to peer up the driveway. The car was completely off the circle drive and sitting in a flower bed. The hood looked crinkled. Judging from a crooked porch pillar, Oliver realized the car must have slammed into the massive porch. Something was wrong. *Damn,* Oliver thought, pressing down on the accelerator as Mack sputtered in protest.

Another mile. Mack began to buck, and this time it didn't stop. He needed a solution and fast. Ahead on his left was a large, modern church with a lot of property attached. Soccer fields, a small pond, and a baseball diamond were all part of the church's complex. Oliver navigated into the parking lot and headed straight for the front entrance to the church.

Attached to the entrance was a large porte cochere, no doubt to allow churchgoers to be dropped off or picked up without the inconvenience of getting wet. It was the most beautiful thing he could hope to find in the middle of a deadly rainstorm. Unfortunately, his truck was way too big to fit underneath, but not his cab – the cab *would* fit. It had to fit.

He coasted forward, the big red-and-white truck choking out its final gasps. Oliver stared up through the red drops as they splattered fat and thick against the window. He smiled with relief as the cab slipped underneath the oversized carport. He let Mack creep as far as it could go before the bed hit the roof with a jolting crunch.

Jurnee gasped.

"It's okay. I meant to do that," he reassured her.

The tiny girl gave him a dubious look.

Mack trembled and wheezed a final time and then stalled. Everything went silent except for the hiss of radiator fluid and the *pit pat* of falling rain.

Staring at the glass doors of the church, Oliver made a decision. He was going to have to go in that church – break in if he had to. He needed to find a phone and call Zoe. Turning on the radio, he heard the familiar test that played every first Tuesday of the month at 10 a.m., but this wasn't the first Tuesday and it wasn't a test. The first channel he checked was 105.7 the X. The station was running the emergency alert system on repeat. As he clicked through the digital display of his and Sam's other presets, he found more of the same. All he could think was, *This is bad, very bad.*

"I need to go inside this building, Jurnee. I won't be long," Oliver said, reaching for the door handle. The rain fell with a constant but calm steadiness. There was no angry thunder, no blowing gusts, leaving him with the hope he could get from the cab to the door without the rain touching him. Then another thought occurred. What if what was happening out there wasn't the rain at all – what if it was in the air itself? Some kind of radiation or something? Suddenly he felt dumb. That couldn't be right. He was breathing the air from out there right here in his own cab. Therefore, it had to be in the rain, right? Sam's eyes had small perforations. Sam had been in the rain and got that shit in her eyes.

Again, he reassured himself, it had to be the rain.

"I don't want to stay here by myself, Oliver. I want to go with you!" Jurnee said, moving toward him.

"I don't... I don't think it's a good idea," Oliver started.

"Don't you know anything about little kids? I'm only six. I can't stay here alone!" the girl pleaded, her eyes welling with fresh tears.

"Alright! Okay," he said, reaching over the girl and pulling Sam's rolled-up rain gear from beneath the seat. Shaking out the jacket, he handed it to Jurnee. "You need to put this on."

Jurnee wiped her nose on her sleeve, laid Princess on the seat next to her, and pulled on the oversized blue rain jacket.

"And Princess stays here. We don't want her getting wet."

The little girl frowned and looked as though she might protest.

Oliver raised his eyebrows.

Conceding, she sat the doll upright in the seat next to

her. "We'll be right back, Princess. What? You want to come? I know, but you don't have a raincoat. Oliver promises we will come right back, don't you, Oliver?"

Oliver frowned at the doll.

Jurnee leaned in close and whispered, "Promise so she won't be scared."

Oliver sighed. "I promise," he said, zipping his own windbreaker.

The truck door creaked open. Moist air, warmer than he expected, met his face. He turned back to the girl. "Hold your breath and close your eyes, like you're going underwater," he said, pulling up her hood.

"Are we going underwater?" Jurnee asked, her voice shaking.

Oliver faced her as he climbed out of the truck. "No, but just pretend, okay?"

Jurnee nodded and took a deep breath, her little cheeks pushing out as she slammed her eyes shut.

Reaching up, he pulled the girl from the truck and turned to the church, quickly carrying her over to the double glass doors. *Please be unlocked.* Grabbing one of the doors, he gave the handle a tug – locked. He tried the other – locked. *Dammit!*

The doors were recessed into a small alcove, protected on both sides. Where they stood it was completely dry. "I got to set you down. Open your eyes and breathe."

Jurnee blew out all her air and sucked in a dramatic breath. "Can we go inside?"

"We will," Oliver said, pounding his fist on the door.

After three tries and still nothing, he turned back to the truck. "Stay right here. I have to get something out of the truck."

"Hurry. I need to go potty," Jurnee said, jumping up and down.

Shit. "Okay. Just hang on." Oliver grabbed a three-foot piece of steel pipe he kept under the seat. Sometimes the meth-heads could be persistent, and you never knew who you might run into on downtown alley day. He drew the pipe from under the seat like a sword from a sheath and ran back to the glass door. "Jurnee, I'm going to have to break this door. Get behind me."

The girl's eyes widened. "Mmmmm, you might get in big trouble, Oliver."

"Don't worry. We can leave a note. They'll understand." With an underhand swing, the steel bar smashed the glass. The entire door shattered, raining down all around his feet. "Don't move," he said, reaching for the girl and picking her up.

Jurnee wrapped her tiny arms around his neck. Holding the girl in one arm and the steel pipe in the other, Oliver carefully stepped through the broken door into a large foyer. To the left along one side was an open-faced oak coat closet with several coats hanging from hangers. Beyond the coat racks were two sets of double doors with a brass-plated sign reading AUDITORIUM. Across the foyer were two more sets of double doors with the same brass signage that read FELLOWSHIP HALL. Scanning to his right, Oliver found still more signs – CLASSROOM A, MOTHERS ROOM, NURSERY, KITCHEN, MAIN OFFICE, and finally, RESTROOMS.

From somewhere beyond the shadows a door slammed, echoing through the foyer.

"Hello!" Oliver shouted. When no one answered, something niggled in his guts, settling uneasily in the pit of his stomach. He decided it was best not to yell again.

"The bathroom is this way. I'm going to put you down," he said, kneeling.

Jurnee let go of Oliver's neck. Her little hand stretched out from the too-long raincoat sleeve. Oliver took her tiny hand in his and led her to the bathroom, making sure it was safe and clear. "Okay, I'll be right outside this door. Do your best to hurry."

Jurnee ran inside, reappearing a few moments later.

"You all good?"

"Yep," she replied.

"Okay, let's try to find a phone," Oliver said, walking deeper into the shadowed hallway. He passed by a group of interior windows, but with the lights off he couldn't see into the room. Letting go of Jurnee's hand, he hooded his eyes, leaned against the glass, and looked inside.

Even with the power off, the dimly lit room beyond revealed desks cluttered with paper, files, computers, and – more importantly – telephones. The church offices! "This way, Jurnee," Oliver said, leading her to the first door on the right. "Um, stay behind me, okay? Let me make sure it's safe."

Jurnee frowned, looking scared. "Because it's kind of dark?"

No, because people seem to be losing their shit and attacking each other... eating each other. Like... like some undead zo... No, he didn't want to put words to what he was thinking. And obviously he couldn't say any of that. "Yeah, because it's dark," he answered instead, reaching for the light switch. "But let's see if we can fix that, okay?"

Jurnee nodded approvingly.

Oliver flipped the light switch, and to his surprise the hallway light came on. The corridor before him offered two doors on the right, which appeared to be offices. To the left was a door that read Conference Room. Moving towards the first office door, Oliver adjusted the pipe in his hand as a sense of uneasiness passed through him like a cold chill.

Surveying the large office space, he quickly spotted the phone and lifted it from the receiver. Nothing. No dial tone... nothing. He screamed internally. *Fuck!* Rummaging around the desk, he found nothing useful. Across the room, someone's brown jacket hung on a coat rack. Oliver searched the pockets, hoping to find car keys. What he found instead was a set of several keys, all of which appeared to be for the building itself except for one. It wasn't a key to a door, but it wasn't a key to a car either; attached to it was a tag that read Spare Set.

Outside the office a door slammed again.

Oliver jerked his head up to see a man, who was missing most of the left side of his face, rear back and slam his forehead into the office window.

Jurnee screamed.

Instinctively, Oliver dropped the keys and raised the pipe to swing, but the glass didn't shatter.

The man, forty-something with an average build and wearing a bloodstained Eddie Bauer quarter zip, slammed his face into the glass window again.

"Jesus Christ!"

The guy only had one eye; the other must have been wherever he left the rest of his face. The single eye stared frantically through the window, searching with desperation. One Eye reared back again, slamming his face into the glass, this time splitting the flesh on his remaining cheek all the way to the bone. *Why? Why was he doing that! Why was he using his own face? Not his forehead, his face! And how in the hell was he still alive with half his face missing?* As the man's single eye stretched wide and darted back and forth,

Oliver noticed it didn't look right. The eye looked gooey and fixed open, unblinking. The guy's remaining cheek had just ripped open to the bone, and yet it didn't bleed a drop. What the hell was going on?

Oliver had plenty of questions, but the guy didn't look like much for conversation. The next strike of One Eye's forehead fractured the office window with a pop, and a spider web of cracks spread across the glass.

Jurnee screamed again and buried her face into Oliver's pant leg.

Gently he pushed her back. "Stay behind me, Jurnee, and get ready to run! And don't look!"

The window exploded inward.

Oliver hurried forward, cocking the pipe. He could hear the man now, but not words – the guy wasn't saying anything. The sounds spilling from the man were all wrong, like a combination of hissing and groaning. Like he was trying to speak without a tongue. But he had a tongue. Oliver could see it between the teeth of his slackened jaw, exposed by a missing cheek and absent lower lip.

The guy threw himself over the sill of the broken office window.

"Buddy, you better stop!" Oliver shouted.

The jagged glass protruding from all around the windowsill did nothing to slow the guy. Nor did he seem to care that he was cutting the shit out of himself.

One Eye flopped onto the floor and began to scramble to his feet. *Am I really doing this? Am I really about to hit a guy in the head with a pipe?* He had already thrown his best friend from the garbage truck and hit a random guy running down the street. But smashing in a man's skull with a steel pipe – that was on a whole different level.

Through the broken window he heard footsteps and

more groaning. If they ran out of the office, this guy was coming after them, and if they got caught in between... "Close your eyes, Jurnee!" Oliver shouted, setting his jaw. As One Eye attempted to push himself to his feet, Oliver swung the pipe, connecting with the left side of the man's skull.

It was a solid hit.

Through the pipe Oliver felt the man's bones crunch. Adrenaline fueled him through the moment, but it didn't stay the wave of nausea sending bile up his throat, threatening to upturn what little his stomach held.

One Eye, never having achieved a fully upright stance, fell down onto his side. The side of his head looked deformed from the blow.

Oliver blinked. The pipe hung slack in his hand. He'd just killed a man. For god's sake, he'd just killed a man in a church. Not that he was religious, but still, in church! Exhaling, he started to turn back to Jurnee when the man he'd just killed twitched and began to move. The one eye, still there, still holding to its ruined face, stared up at him. The man groaned, his teeth clicking as he snapped his jaw open and shut.

What the fuck? No way he could be alive, let alone conscious. Oliver swung again and again, fracturing and destroying the man's skull and with it his brain.

One Eye lay prone on the floor, a huge puddle of blood pooling beneath his smashed skull. He didn't twitch or move again. Outside the office, the moaning grew closer.

Grabbing Jurnee's hand, Oliver made for the door. "Did you keep your eyes shut?"

Jurnee nodded.

Oliver looked down. The poor kid still had them shut.

"Look, you can open them, but be ready to shut them again?"

"Are they monsters?" she whispered.

"They're sick, that's all," he answered, leading her down the short hall that led to the main corridor by the bathroom. But he knew for a fact that was not all. It was insane for him to think it or say it, but maybe this little girl saw it truer than anyone, truer than he had. Kids don't need to rationalize. They call it as they see it. And as he thought of Jurnee's words, he realized that was the closest thing to a monster he'd ever seen.

Back the direction they had come, beyond the reach of hallway light, three shapes stood groaning, hissing, and sniffing at the air like a pack of curious lions on a scent. He couldn't tell in the darkened hallway, but he thought the silhouette of one must have been a child. Monsters or no, he didn't want to kill a kid. "Come on!"

All at once, the three stopped sniffing and ran towards them.

Oliver led Jurnee the other way. They rounded a corner and ran through a door labeled KITCHEN. The large kitchen had a walk-in freezer. Oliver looked inside to find it was full of frozen goods, but they could still fit inside. On second thought, if those things saw them in there, they might not leave and they could freeze to death. Oliver had no interest in becoming trapped in a walk-in freezer. He found a fully stocked walk-in pantry, but it didn't look like a safe place to hide either.

The door they'd come through opened to a chorus of hisses and moans.

On the opposite side of the room was another door. "This way!"

This door opened out into what seemed to be the

Fellowship Hall, a massive space full of dozens of round tables. The dining hall could probably seat two hundred. No wonder they needed such a big kitchen. Oliver grabbed a chair from one of the tables and wedged it under the door handle to the kitchen.

When they'd first entered the church, he had seen the sign for the Fellowship Hall. All they needed to do was cross the room and exit back into the foyer, cross it, and they could get out the way they'd come in. Oliver hesitated. But then what? Mack was overheated. As hard as he'd pushed the big rig, it would be a miracle if the engine block hadn't cracked. Oliver stopped short – something occurring to him. If there were people here, then there had to be other cars here.

Behind him, something or someone crashed into the door. A long, muffled moan rattled thickly from the other side. It sounded like a pained cry from a broken throat shoved full of gravel. The moan was followed by a *boom! boom! boom!* rattling the door in its frame.

Oliver grabbed Jurnee's hand, but he didn't cross to the front of the Fellowship Hall; instead, he ran to the back – towards the exit.

If there were cars parked in the back, and Oliver was sure there had to be, he would need to figure out how to get himself and Jurnee through the rain without getting wet. *Boom! Boom! Boom!* Guess he'd cross that bridge when he got to it. The chair he'd wedged under the handle shifted and squeaked in protest. It wasn't going to hold long.

Circling around one of the large round tables, Oliver felt his foot slip in something. Then he saw her, a grey-haired woman lying prone on the floor. "Jurnee, eyes closed!" he shouted. The old woman lay on her ample belly, her mangled face turned to the side. An oversized handbag lay next to her, its contents dumped and intermixed with her insides... *Jesus Christ!* He lifted Jurnee, carrying her past the dead woman, all the while wishing he'd taken his own advice and not looked. He would never unsee the image of the elderly woman's intestines coiled in a gelatinous goo and spilled onto the floor. Her skull sat broken open and emptied of its contents, but those weren't spilled out like her intestines; they were... gone. Oliver feared he knew where they had gone, and the thought sickened him. Someone had eaten them. If not for the tuft of grey hair still attached in a tangle of the matted mess, he wouldn't have been sure she was old.

Across the hall, the door handle snapped off; the wedged chair fell forward.

Shoving open the exit at the back of the dining hall, Oliver peered out into the rear parking lot. There were three cars. A black Buick Enclave, a red Ford F-150 and a white Toyota 4Runner. At the far end was a short black-and-green church bus. Thank god! There were vehicles, but that wasn't even the best part.

The red rain had stopped.

Oliver tipped his head back to consider the sky. Still cloudy. Still red and otherworldly, but free of rain.

Behind him, a final *boom!* sent the door flinging inward. A boy of maybe thirteen was the first one through. The little shit hissed and jumped onto one of the round tables. More silhouettes piled through – more than the three he'd seen earlier. A final glance back told him several were kids.

Please, if there's a god up there, for fuck's sake don't let it rain! Hugging Jurnee close to his chest, he ran out the back door and straight for the closest parked car. He needed some luck. He needed a car to be unlocked with the keys in the ignition. Just one – he wouldn't be picky.

The first car was locked. He ran for the truck – also locked. *Give me a break!* The Toyota had to be the one. It would be unlocked with the keys in the ignition – it had to be because he willed it so.

The church door burst open, and that little bloody-eyed blond kid sniffed at the air. *Fuck me!* Oliver thought, leaning the pipe against the car as he groped for the door handle. Locked. Fucking locked!

The blond kid's head snapped in the direction of Oliver, and he broke into a run.

Oliver fought the urge to run for the open field. There was no way he could outrun that kid or the ones piling out the door behind him. Not carrying Jurnee. Then he had a last glimmer of hope. *The bus!*

Oliver ran. He rounded the front end of the bus just ahead of the blond kid, who was a good distance ahead of the others. Even if the bus was open, he couldn't board before the kid caught up to him. "Jurnee! Eyes closed!"

"I still have them shut from last time, Oliver!" the girl answered, her voice on the brink of tears.

"Okay! Good. Keep 'em closed, kiddo," he said, setting her down on the asphalt behind him. Oliver quickly turned to find the blond boy was right on his heels, his mouth open for a bite. Cocking the pipe short, Oliver gave a half swing just in time to catch the little shit across the bridge of the nose. The blond fell back onto his ass, his nose a ruin of what it had been, but he didn't seem to notice, and the fountain of blood Oliver expected to see didn't come. Weird.

Letting out a shrill, guttural moan, the kid sprang to his feet, but the fall and recovery had been just what Oliver needed to get a proper swing readied – a home run swing.

The boy's head cracked, the sound reverberating across the parking lot.

Oliver quickly turned away. Maybe it wasn't the smartest thing to do – to turn your back before you're sure you've done the job. But he didn't want to see what he'd done. Would he be forgiven for this? How would he explain it to the authorities? Hissing moans grew close from the opposite side of the bus, and Oliver knew it didn't matter. What mattered right now was not dying – not failing this little innocent girl. He shoved the folding door to the bus, and it opened.

Grabbing Jurnee, he lifted her onto the bus stairs. "Open your eyes and climb up, Jurnee. You're on a bus!"

Jurnee climbed up as Oliver pulled himself onboard, quickly shutting the bifold doors and locking them as the first of the other kids rounded the bus.

Okay! This is it. There have to be keys! Please. Please, let there be keys!

Fists and heads smashed into the glass of the bus door.

Jurnee screamed.

"It's okay! Just don't look at them!" Oliver shouted as he frantically searched for keys. Nothing in the ignition. Next, he searched the visor, dashboard cubby, drink holder, and finally beneath the floor mat. Nothing!

Three adults and five kids stood outside the bus, their jaws snapping and heads twitching as fists, feet, and sometimes whole bodies repeatedly threw themselves against the bifold door of the bus.

What the hell was wrong with these people? They didn't talk and they didn't bleed – not anymore. All they seemed to want was to eat the living. Then what did that make them? That word came to him again. A word so unfathomable he couldn't believe he was considering it. But what else could this be? What else could they be if not... if not zombies?

A large man, clean-shaven with long grey hair pulled back in a ponytail, charged at the bus. He looked fairly normal aside from bloody eyes and a huge chunk of meat missing from his inner thigh. He snarled and ran forward, throwing a fist into the windowpane of the bus door.

The glass cracked.

A renewed energy seemed to fill the mob. A frenzy of excitement. Like they knew they were close to getting what they wanted.

CHAPTER 12
FIVE-INCH STILETTO

THE GUN RIPPED free of Zoe's hand as she fell back, smacking the back of her head into a towel dispenser. She slid down the wall onto her butt as Deandre spun away and lifted the gun.

Zoe barely had time to get her hands over her ears before Deandre fired two rounds into the face of the charging naked woman.

She dropped, the remains of her ruined head slapping wetly against the tile floor.

Two more men were through the door now. A large potbellied man with a greying beard and Tom. *Jesus Christ!* She'd seen the clerk get shot in the chest three times! *How could he still be alive, let alone running?*

Beside her, Angel was pulling at Zoe's collar, yelling something but she couldn't hear – couldn't rationalize what the fuck was happening!

"Give me a taste!" the potbellied man shouted.

Deandre fired again and again. The fat man took a bullet just below the eye, his knees buckled, and he dropped. Bright blood spilled from the man's head wound.

Like a gallon of milk being slowly poured out, it spread and spread, coating the tiles.

The next round hit Tom, but he didn't drop. The bullet went low, ripping through the side of the smaller man's neck. Instantly, Zoe recognized that Tom's blood looked all wrong. It didn't spray bright red or pulse like a jugular injury should. Instead, it oozed out from Tom's neck, like sap from a tree, thick and black as soiled motor oil.

"Glahaglaaaaa!" Tom managed a gargled moan as he rushed forward, colliding into Deandre.

Angel tugged at Zoe, dragging her toward the last stall.

Deandre and Tom fell back, colliding into the wall and landing hard where Zoe had just been sitting.

The gun slid from Deandre's hand across the tile and into the merging pools of the fat man and the naked woman's blood.

Somewhere beyond the bathroom, someone shouted.

"Get in the stall – we can hide until this is over!" Angel urged.

Deandre flipped Tom over onto his back and punched him in the face once, twice, and again.

"Glahaglaaaaa! Glahaglaaaaa!" Tom continued to moan despite the rain of punches ruining his face.

Zoe shook her head. "No. We have to get out of here – they'll smell us!" She scrambled forward, hesitating before crawling into the pool of blood. Would she be infected if she touched the blood? If that were the case, she had already touched Deandre's bloody wound. *Dammit!* She stretched over the pool and pinched the gun between her thumb and forefinger. Climbing to her feet, she ran to the sink and turned on the faucet, depressed a palm full of soap, and rinsed the gun.

"Zoe!" Angel shouted.

Zoe spun to find Deandre standing behind her. She looked to her right. Tom lay on the floor unmoving. He had to be dead... really dead.

"Give me the gun," Deandre said, blood oozing like angry tears down his cheeks.

Zoe knew what came next, and she wouldn't make the same mistake. "I'm sorry," she said and pulled the trigger.

But there was no report. Only a soft *click*. Zoe frowned – the gun was out of bullets, or maybe she shouldn't have washed the damn thing off.

Deandre smiled. "You lied to me, lady."

"I didn't lie to you," she managed.

Deandre thrust his hand out and grabbed her by the throat. "Yes! Yes, you did! It isn't Chanel Number Five. It's so... so much better... sweeter. You tried to hide it! But you can't... No! No! No!" he said, closing his eyes as he squeezed her neck. "I *will* get it out!"

Zoe's eyes bulged, her throat constricting. She pounded her fists on the man's forearms, but it was no use, like beating on thick oak branches.

Fireworks lit Zoe's peripheral vision. It happened so fast, the strength slipping from her arms, the burning in her chest. She couldn't gasp... couldn't breathe. Still, she had to fight, but he was just too big – too strong. Her vision narrowed. Jesus, this was it. She was going to die.

Deandre froze, his hungry eyes shifting to confusion. He let go of her throat, turning slowly.

Zoe gasped and choked, her hands groping her own neck as she tried to catch her breath. As she blinked frantically, her vision returned enough to see a knife handle protruding from the base of Deandre's neck, just off center. Behind him, Angel stood frozen in the horror of what she'd done, her long fake lashes hooding eyes wide as saucers.

Deandre reached back over his shoulder, groping for the knife.

With new breath came a surge of adrenaline. Zoe pushed Deandre sideways. The big man's feet tangled and slipped on the blood-slicked tile. He fell hard, unable to turn his head in time to see the floor coming – unable to get his hands out. The sound of the big man's skull cracking against the floor echoed off the stalls.

As Deandre's body twitched spastically, falling into death, movement from the corner of Zoe's still-clearing vision caught her attention.

Tom was flailing. Only the smaller dead man wasn't twitching like Deandre. This wasn't some aftereffect of death – Tom was trying to get up. Thankfully the slippery tile wouldn't let him find his footing.

"We got to go!" Zoe said, grabbing Angel's hand.

Abandoning his attempt to stand, Tom growled like a wild animal and kicked off the wall, sliding across the bathroom floor through the greasy oil slick of blood and coming to a stop between the two women and the door. He sat up and hissed.

Zoe pulled up short as Tom finally scrambled to his feet, emitting strange guttural grunts and sniffs. The smaller man wasted not a second lunging toward them, his red eyes unnaturally wide and unblinking.

The women backpedaled, scrambling into a stall. "Lock it!" Zoe shouted, climbing onto the toilet.

Tom hit the stall, slamming into the door with his full weight. Angel screamed, a panicked sob escaping her throat. "No – oh! Pleeeease!"

"Climb!" Zoe shouted, pulling herself from the toilet up onto the middle partition. She had to climb over, get out, and make a break for the door.

Hands shot under the stall door, reaching – groping.

"No, please!" Angel cried again, pressing herself between the toilet and the partition.

"Angel, dammit – climb!"

Teeth clacking, throat croaking and hissing, Tom dragged himself under the stall door. Belly down, he reached, grabbing the toilet, and pulled.

Angel stepped up onto the toilet seat as Zoe swung her own leg over the partition. She'd no idea how the woman was going to climb in those stilettos and that miniskirt. Angel couldn't simply kick off the heels; they were strapped around her ankles. "Please! Take my hand!"

"I can't climb over! I can't do it!" Angel's pleading face begged as she looked down at Tom's head.

The undead man's left cheek was pressed to the tile floor as he reached up, grasping the rim of the toilet. One unblinking eye glowered up, fixed on the treat to come.

"You can, Angel! Take my hand!"

"Ohhhh pleeeease! Don't make me!" she moaned, looking down at Tom's thrashing body.

"Angel! What are you doing?"

Angel looked back apologetically. "I don't... I can't... I have to go!"

Zoe shook her head. "No! Wait, Angel, don't..."

Angel closed her eyes... and jumped.

What followed was a sickening crunch as Angel's right five-inch stiletto punched through the fleshy temple of Tom's head, sinking in all the way down to the heel.

The crazed man went instantly still.

Zoe starred down from atop the partition. "Jesus, Angel. Are you okay?"

Angel stood frozen, her heel still buried in the man's

head. "Uh... is he... is he... dead?" she asked, her voice hitching into a sob.

"I think so," Zoe said, climbing back down onto the toilet.

"I mean, is he really dead?"

Zoe nodded. "Whatever this sickness is, I think you have to destroy the brain."

Angel sniffed and wiped her eyes on her blouse. "Just like in those zombie movies."

Zoe's medical mind ignored that. This was an illness, some kind of disease with a logical explanation, not *Night of the Living Dead*. "Come on. It's time to get the fuck out of here."

Steadying herself, Angel sucked in a deep breath and lifted her leg, drawing the stiletto heel from Tom's skull like a dagger from a wound.

Zoe stepped off the toilet and unlatched the stall. After giving a final glance to Tom's lifeless face, she noticed Angel's leg was bleeding. She gasped. "Angel?"

"Yeah?"

"You're bleeding. Did Tom bite you?"

Angel's eyes flashed to her lower leg. "No, it's just a scratch."

There was no way to know if a scratch would infect Angel the same as a bite had infected Deandre. For all she knew, this disease – or whatever it was – could be airborne. *Only time will tell*, she thought. Anyway, it didn't matter because right now. Angel's eyes were clear, not like Deandre's – not yet anyway. *Shit... Deandre!* Zoe eased open the bathroom stall and peeked out, scanning the area for the security officer. Despite the skull-cracking header Deandre had taken into the tile floor, he no longer lay in the bloody mess. The naked woman and the fat guy were both still there and appeared to be dead-dead.

Zoe eased the stall closed.

"What?" Angel asked.

"Deandre isn't there," she answered.

"Shit! I should have shoved the knife into his freaking brain!" Angel's face twisted, and she looked like she might scream or puke. "I can't stay in here with that," she said, motioning down at Tom's corpse. "I'm like five seconds away from losing my shit!"

"Shhh. Stay calm. Maybe he left the bathroom. Look, we can make a run for it," she said, placing a hand on the stall door and peeking out again.

"Wait! Where? Where in the hell are we going to go?" the woman whispered desperately.

"I don't know," Zoe said, holding her hands palm out. "The only way we haven't gone."

"You mean deeper into the courthouse?" Angel asked.

"Well, I don't want to go back upstairs, and we can't go out in the rain," Zoe said.

Angel pulled the hem of her skirt down. "Okay, let's just get to the next room. Maybe one with a lock on the door."

Zoe readied herself, pushed open the stall, and bolted for the bathroom door.

Movement filled her peripheral vision as Deandre lurched towards them from some hidden corner.

Zoe kept her eyes fixed on the slippery floor, an involuntary scream escaping her as she jumped over the fat guy and shoved the bathroom door open.

Behind her, Angel screamed.

Stealing a quick glance back, she gasped as Deandre snagged a fistful of Angel's long blond hair.

Zoe turned back to face him as he lunged in to bite. The man's face twisted. His broken head appeared deformed and cocked unnaturally to the side. But it was his eyes that hitched her breath. They looked all wrong... blood red, yes. But there was something different. She'd seen her share of dead eyes, both in school and in her work. And Deandre's eyes looked just like that – like a dead man's eyes.

Angel's eyes opened wide as her head snapped back, exposing her neck to Deandre's teeth. She reached for Zoe in a desperate grab. "Pleeeeease!"

Seizing Angel's hand, Zoe yanked. The woman's blond hair ripped free of her head, revealing shorter brunette hair pinned down flat with bobby pins. Zoe hadn't even realized Angel had been wearing a wig. The sudden jerk and release of Angel's hair sent her skidding forward. How the woman didn't slip on the blood-soaked floor in those heels was beyond Zoe, but somehow she managed to stay standing as she crashed into Zoe.

This wasn't the case for Deandre. The sudden shift in momentum sent him slipping backward. He tripped over the dead woman on the floor and fell hard.

The two women tangled and stumbled through the door and into the hall.

As the door swung closed, Zoe saw Deandre scrambling over the naked woman's body, reaching toward them, teeth snapping at the air. He hissed and groaned, his eyes fixed and bulging wrongly, as if he were demon possessed. *Jesus, what's happening?*

The bathroom door shut with an echoing clack. That's when she heard them – people running and groaning from the darkness of the courthouse interior. She and Angel exchanged terrified looks as they clambered to their feet. "Run for the stairs!" she shouted.

They ran back down the hall toward the stairs they'd descended less than an hour ago.

Behind them, the bathroom door opened as Deandre joined in with the moans and hisses pursuing them from the shadows. The nightmarish sounds created some sick chorus of undead melody only Satan himself would enjoy. Ahead, near the end of the corridor, a single door stood with a glowing red sign that read Exit, but it might as well have read Certain Death. To the right were the stairs.

"Come on! Run!" Zoe shouted. Angel was running, and pretty damn good too for a woman in five-inch stilettos and a tight skirt. But as they approached the stairwell, more footfalls came – more hisses and moans – but these were coming from above, like a herd of cattle running down the stairs.

"No! Shit!" Zoe shouted.

"What now?"

They couldn't go back or up, and if they went out the metal door, the rain would... would infect them.

Zoe glanced up the darkened stairwell. Shadows shifted as descending shapes came into view. Zoe didn't need to look back to know Deandre and the others were closing in behind them. She could feel them. What now? No other doors; nowhere left to hide.

The Exit sign glowed like a beacon of hope, false as it was. Be eaten alive or press into the rain and become the hungry. It wasn't really a choice at all. Zoe's fight-or-flight was full on flight as she ran forward, reaching for the door; her only chance to live a little longer was in the rain beyond. *I'm sorry, Oliver. I tried, I really tried.*

"We have to get out!" Zoe shouted as she collided with the metal bar, depressing it with a forceful *thwack* and shoving with all she had.

The door swung open, neither woman hesitating a moment as they stumbled across the threshold.

CHAPTER 13
SPARE SET

OLIVER PULLED Jurnee farther away from the door of the bus. Outside, hissing children were scaling the vehicle. One of the kids, fifteen or sixteen, crawled onto the hood. As the kid reared back to kick, Oliver noticed an object sticking out of her chest. *What in the unholy fuck?* Oliver thought, realizing the object was the handle of a butcher knife. It was right where her heart would be. She couldn't be alive!

The kid kicked the windshield, and when it didn't break, she dropped to all fours and started hammering both fists on the glass like a child in the throes of a temper tantrum.

Outside the bus door, the big man's fist broke through the glass.

Shit – he needed a plan and fast.

"Jurnee, go to the back!"

Jurnee let out a short, high-pitched scream as she ran down the aisle toward the back of the bus.

The man's hand reached in, groping for the handle of the door.

Oliver drew the pipe back and swung, smashing the man's hand. The guy didn't let out a cry of pain, nor did he jerk his broken hand back. He just reached in farther, all the way to his shoulder, fingers twisted wrongly, groping for the handle to the bus door. "Jesus Christ," Oliver breathed, swinging again and again, breaking the man's wrist, then his forearm near the elbow. The man withdrew only to turn sideways and reach back in with his good arm. Oliver smashed that one too; all the while, a single insane thought screamed through his mind. *Zombies! They're freaking zombies!* On the hood, the girl with the butcher knife buried in her chest hit the glass again, splintering the windshield in a spider web of cracks.

Without keys, they were sitting ducks in here. Then something clicked. SPARE Set. That's what the strange key on the set of keys Oliver had dropped in the office had said. He knew it now – that strange key wasn't to an office door or a car... it was to a bus.

Oliver spun and ran down the aisle. "Jurnee, listen to me," he said, kneeling in front of the girl. "I need you to lock the back door when I go out and then wait for me here. Can you do that?"

"No! You can't leave me! I'm only six! There are monsters!" she yelled, beginning to cry.

"You have to wait here, but I promise the monsters are going with me. I have to get the key, Jurnee, and then we can leave. I need you to be brave. You have to trust me, and you have to stay here."

The little girl's lower lip trembled as tears spilled trails down her face, but she nodded along despite her fear. If not for being scared shitless himself, Oliver's heart would have broken for the little girl.

On the hood, the teen kicked the windshield again, her

foot punching a small hole in the passenger-side corner of the glass.

"Listen to me," Oliver said, pointing at the back door. "I'm going to lift this lever, open the door, and jump out. Then I'm going to close the door. You have to pull this bar down." He lifted the lever. At the other end of the bus, more glass broke. It must have been the door because the windshield was still mostly intact, but the teen had managed to yank her foot free. *Shit!*

Oliver jumped out the back door, landing hard on the asphalt. "Back in three minutes, Jurnee – I promise. Can you count to sixty?" he asked, looking up at the girl.

Jurnee nodded. "Even... even higher than that," she said, doing her best to hold back the tears that wouldn't be restrained.

"Okay, well count to sixty three times or count to one hundred eighty if you can and either way, I'll be back before you finish. Now as soon as this door closes, pull the lever down!" Despite her tears, he pushed the door shut.

Oliver heard the latch click and turned away. He rounded the corner of the bus to the side with the front door. One of the adults, a woman in bloodstained jeans, had half her body wedged through the bifold door of the bus. A young boy with a mouth crusted in blood – he was maybe ten or twelve, Oliver wasn't sure – was climbing onto the hood where the girl was kicking frantically at the windshield she'd freed her foot from. Oliver couldn't see her, but he could hear her. The rest of the zombies were clawing and pushing at the door.

"Hey, motherfuckers!" Oliver shouted.

Wild eyes whipped sharp in his direction.

"MMMMM!" the zombie with the broken hands called

out. The others answered in a chorus of throaty moans and serpentine hisses.

"That's right, assholes. No one's in the bus! We're back here! So come on! Come get some!"

Not only was Oliver a fan of zombie movies, he'd also listened to several audiobooks in the zombie genre. He was a trail runner, and audiobooks were kind of his thing. It wasn't that he didn't like to read; he just never seemed to find time to sit down and do it, and when he tried, he'd only get through a couple paragraphs before dozing off, no matter how good the book. But with an audiobook, he could go on a long run and listen for hours. His favorite was a series called *Mountain Man.* It followed a drunk named Gus as he tried to survive the zombie apocalypse. This was not the time to be thinking about zombie books, but as he watched the zombies turn and bolt toward him, he realized there was a reason his mind went to old Gus and his samurai bat. In the *Mountain Man* series, just like in most movies and books he'd read on zombies, the bastards didn't run. They shambled slowly or shuffled quickly, but rarely did they flat-out run – or for that matter, climb on top of buses. Well, these things were flat-out running!

Oliver bolted across the parking lot, sprinting as fast as he could push his body to go. As he rounded the side of the building, he stole a glance back at the mob. *One, two, three, four, five, six, seven.* He frowned. There should have been eight. He glanced back again. *One, two, three, four, five, six, seven.* Four kids. Three adults. *Damn!* It was the girl with the knife in her chest. She wasn't there.

Juking left, Oliver ran toward an outbuilding and then cut left again back towards the bus. It had only been seconds, but what if that girl had gotten inside the bus? Jesus, what if...

He could see the driver's side of the bus, but he didn't see the teen on top of the hood. She'd gotten in the bus! Oh god! What had he done? *Oh Jurnee, please no!* Oliver clenched the pipe in his right hand, pumping his arms as he ran back to the front of the bus. When he got to the front end, he slowed, craning his head back, frantically searching the hood.

Behind him, the zombies' hisses filled his ears.

The windshield was crushed inward, and it had a small hole in the lower corner from the teen's foot, but it was otherwise intact. The teen hadn't busted through. So where—

From around the corner, the girl with the knife in her chest appeared, announcing herself with a guttural moan as she lunged to bite. Oliver twisted like a running back trying to shake a tackle.

The pursuing mob was within reach, groping for him. One managed to get a fistful of his windbreaker, but he didn't slow – he couldn't slow. The jacket tore free as Oliver leaned in, pushing forward with heavy breaths. Behind him there was no panting, no breathing that he could hear, only hungry groans. Groans begging for a taste of flesh.

Oliver had the whole mob on him now – all eight of them. Relief that Jurnee was okay would have been welcome, but there was no time for celebration. If he didn't get the keys and make it back, that little girl was as good as dead.

When he reached the front of the church, he practically dove through the broken glass doors, stumbling forward but somehow staying on his feet. *Jesus, they're fast.*

Oliver knew he couldn't lead them directly to the office or he would quickly become trapped. Instead, he shoved open the door to the Fellowship Hall, but with no time to block the door, the zombies piled through hot on his heels.

Stealing a quick glance back, Oliver found a familiar zombie leading the way. With broken hands and dangling arms flopping wildly, the portly grey-haired man ran recklessly into a tangle of folding chairs. Thanks to Oliver's steel pipe work, the overweight man was unable to catch himself and face-planted, tripping up two more and slowing the others. Capitalizing on the opportunity, Oliver spun and grabbed one of the large tables, dropping his pipe atop it. He ran forward, shoving the table into the zombie as it tried to stand.

The table struck the thing under the nose, crushing it and driving the cartilage into the guy's brain with a sick crunch.

The zombie fell back and went still.

A middle-aged woman in a ruffled blouse and beige slacks, besmeared with blood and soiled with urine and god only knew what else, leapt onto the table, shrieked, and jumped for him.

Oliver swung the pipe, cracking the woman in the head before she hit the ground.

The other six pressed forward, shoving the tables out of the way.

Oliver crossed the hall back to the now-familiar kitchen door. Once inside, he didn't mess with trying to find a way to close and secure it – no time. Instead, he knocked over racks of trays and pans as he passed, then shoved a rolling island into the aisle.

Behind him, the kitchen erupted in a crash of banging metal. Oliver stole a glance over his shoulder. The young boy with the blood-crusted mouth was just ahead of the others, scrambling on all fours through a pile of cookie sheets. A few feet behind him was the woman in the blood-stained jeans. A bite-sized chunk of flesh was missing from her neck where her jugular should have been. Behind her, others were filing through the door.

Oliver set his jaw and charged back in, chopping from overhead with the pipe as if he were splitting a log. The boy fell onto his belly and went still. He reared back again, this time over his shoulder, determined to take a swing at the woman stomping her way across the mess of cookware. But the swing went low, missing the woman's head and striking her in her already wounded neck. There was a strange pop as the woman's head fell onto her shoulder.

Oliver's eyes went wide at the horror of it. The woman couldn't lift her head up, yet it did nothing to slow her forward movement. On she came, reaching out with desperation as her sideways mouth snapped at the air. Thankfully, she stepped on a cookie sheet, her foot sliding out from under her as if she were dropping into the splits. Tipping sideways, she fell onto the dead boy, her mouth working like a fish out of water as she scrambled forward.

"F me!" he shouted, his voice echoing through the church kitchen. No time to swing again. The other four zombies, all kids, were there now, clanging through the pots and pans and falling onto the woman in a tangle of moaning undead adolescence and snapping jaws.

Running through the doorway, Oliver escaped into the hallway. Sprinting down the hall, he turned back into the office area and into the first office on his right. He scanned the floor, finding the keys and scooping them up.

Shoes squeaked and scuffed outside the office as the zombies closed in.

Climbing out the broken office window and back into the hallway, Oliver turned left and ran. He climbed back through the broken glass door of the main entrance and sprinted back around the building, across the parking lot, back to the bus. Three zombies gave chase, all of them kids. Maybe Broken Neck Lady was down for the count and had taken another one with her.

"Jurnee! Jurnee! Open the door!" Oliver shouted, banging on the emergency exit of the bus. He hadn't thought about how he'd get back onto the bus.

Fortunately, Jurnee's little face appeared through the glass, her eyes wide with fear. But they weren't looking at Oliver, they were locked on the zombies stampeding across the parking lot. Still, somehow little Jurnee found the courage to lift the handle. Oliver climbed aboard and slammed the door just as the teen with the butcher-knife in her chest slammed into the door, her small fingers bent like claws, raking at the glass with desperation. *Where had she come from?*

"How far... did you get?" Oliver asked, breathing hard as he hurried towards the front of the bus.

"I counted to one hundred and seventy-five," Jurnee said, crossing her arms.

"Wow! You really counted that high?" Oliver threw himself into the driver's seat of the bus. Glancing into the sideview mirror, he spotted Butcher Knife Girl and another kid, somehow still wearing glasses, running towards the front of the bus.

"I can count a lot higher than that, Oliver! I can even do multiplication. Weeeeeell, kind of," Jurnee said, 'fessing up. "I know two times two is four, but so is two plus two. But three times three isn't six. You might think so, but it isn't."

Oliver found the key marked SPARE. *Please let me be right!* He slid the key into the ignition and twisted. The bus roared to life. "Jurnee, get in a seat and hold on!"

Knife Girl was pulling herself onto the hood as Oliver threw the bus into gear and stomped down on the gas. Knife Girl had no hold; she slipped and rolled, landing hard on the asphalt. Oliver glanced over to check the mirror. The kid with the glasses was hanging from the side mirror.

Oliver cranked the wheel left.

"Whoa, Oliver!" Jurnee shouted.

The kid couldn't hold and fell backward. He hit the ground and rolled but then was right back on his feet, running at full speed.

Squinting into the mirror, Oliver said, "I'll be damned. The little shit still didn't lose his glasses."

"You're really driving fast, Oliver. Princess is sure going to be glad you hurried up."

Shit, Jurnee's doll! He drove around the building toward the front. Checking the mirror again, he watched as the two kids rounded the building, running fast. *Where in the hell did the third one go?*

On top of the bus he heard a hollow thudding – mystery solved. "Jurnee, buckle up! And tell me when you're clicked in!"

"Okay!"

"You're clicked in?" he asked, looking up into the rearview mirror.

"Yep!"

They rounded the front of the building, and the garbage truck came into view. Oliver approached fast. "Hold on! We're going to test the brakes!" He pulled alongside the passenger side of the garbage truck, outside of the porte cochere, and slammed on the brakes.

"Whoa!" Jurnee shouted.

The zombie on top of the bus slammed down onto the hood, bounced, and vanished over the front end.

"Stay here! I'll get Princess!" Oliver said, pulling the door lever. The doors folded open as bits of glass fell onto the steps. Oliver jumped up from the seat, grabbed his pipe, and descended the steps only to come face-to-face with the zombie that had fallen from the hood. Part of its face hung in a loose flap, attached only at the jaw. One of its bloodshot eyes dangled from its socket by a string of nerves. *Je-sus Christ!* Exposed gums and teeth gnashed down over and over like a pair of chattering wind-up teeth. The thing didn't even seem to notice its own detached face.

With no room to swing, Oliver kicked the thing in the face. The zombie fell back. Oliver stumbled down the steps, giving chase and drawing back for a swing, hoping to get to it before it could regain its feet. This one looked like an older boy – *had been* an older boy. Now it was something else. Dead but somehow not dead... undead. Judging from the bloody perforations in the teen's Nirvana T-shirt, he'd been stabbed in the side repeatedly.

Over the last three hours, something horrible had happened to these people. Just like it had happened to Sam. As Oliver swung the heavy pipe down across the back of the teen's head, he couldn't help but wonder how the whole thing had gone down.

The red sky rumbled deep and long. No doubt a warning of more rain to come. *Wonder later, dumbass – right now, move!*

Hurrying around the front of the bus to the passenger side of the garbage truck, he yanked open the door. From behind the bus came the sound of shuffling feet, hissing, and moaning. In a single leap, Oliver jumped up onto the top step, reached into the cab, and snatched Princess off the seat.

As he went to climb down, he felt hands grope his legs

and ass, pulling at his waistline. "What the fuck!" He spun. The lady whose neck he'd broken earlier was clawing at him, her crooked head bent to the side, right cheek resting on her shoulder, mouth snapping like a Doberman.

Frantically, he kicked and crawled back into the truck, across the seat, and out the driver's side. Oliver slammed the door behind him and crossed in front of both the garbage truck and bus, sliding on the wet pavement as he rounded the corner.

Inside the bus, Jurnee was screaming.

Oliver flew up the stairs, his heart racking his chest as his eyes flew wide. The girl with the butcher knife in her chest was climbing over a seat, reaching for the little girl. Tossing Princess and his pipe into an empty seat, Oliver grabbed Butcher Knife Girl by the back of her hair, dragging her backwards down the stairs and off the bus.

The teen hit the ground and rolled onto her hands and knees. Oliver kicked her in the head, turned, and climbed back up the bus stairs. "Did she bite you?"

Jurnee, still screaming, didn't answer.

Oliver scanned the girl, looking for any sign of injury, but she was balled up in the seat, her face buried in her arms.

Outside, more moans. They were out of time. Oliver turned away from the girl and jumped into the driver's seat, threw it in gear, and stomped on the gas. "Jurnee!" Oliver yelled over his shoulder. "Are you hurt? Did she bite you?" He pulled out onto the country road that had brought them to this nightmare and stared up into the rearview mirror. "Jurnee, please! Did she bite you?"

Jurnee looked up, her inhales broken as she hyperventilated. She tried to speak but couldn't. Instead, she nodded.

"What? You're hurt?"

Jurnee continued to nod.

Oliver's own breath caught. He glanced forward and then into the mirror again. "Did she bite you?"

The girl's breathing worsened as the tears fell steadily onto her oversized raincoat. "Ye... ye... yes!"

CHAPTER 14
ANGEL

ZOE STAGGERED FORWARD, stumbling and nearly falling onto the sidewalk as she kept her eyes pressed shut. Moist air greeted her, along with the smell of fresh rain. Other than knowing she was outside, she had no idea where she was or where her car was. But she immediately noticed something else. She didn't feel the rain. Shielding her eyes, she opened them just a little. No rain. Zoe took in the parking lot, the city beyond, and a sky that looked all wrong.

"What now?" Angel asked.

Spinning back to the double doors of the courthouse, Zoe remembered how Deandre had her use his belt to tie off the door. When she was a nurse in uniform, she always wore her gait belt, a long canvas belt used to support patients while they stood or walked.

Pulling the belt free of her waist, she wrapped it through the two handles and cinched it down, just as the first pursuer slammed into the door. The door opened a few inches before stretching the gait belt taut. The now familiar sounds of hungry moans and hisses permeated the doors as fingers appeared through the gap. They groped, grabbing at the belt and pulling.

"That should hold them for now. Do you have a car?" Zoe asked.

"No, my friend should be waiting on the other side of the courthouse," she said, staring up at the cloud-filled sky.

"Well, we can't stay out here. Those clouds look bad. Like it might start raining again. That's me over there," Zoe said, pointing at her car. "Can I give you a ride?"

A car horn sounded, followed immediately by the crash of a collision. Zoe spun just in time to see an explosion rise up in a mushroom cloud of fire and smoke from a road on the far side of the parking lot.

Behind them, more bodies slapped against the double doors as more hands appeared through the crack, pushing, clawing and pulling. Fear gripped Zoe. There were too many, and she worried her gait belt wouldn't hold them at bay for long.

"Come on!" Zoe said, running to her car.

The two women climbed into the SUV. Zoe fired up the engine and backed out of the space. A bloody palm slapped against her driver's-side window. A man with crazed red eyes stared at them through the window, his lips curled back in a hungry snarl.

Angel screamed, "Shit! Go!"

Zoe stomped on the gas pedal, accelerating too fast and nearly losing control. She rounded the courthouse in a slide, fishtailing on the wet pavement. The front door came into view, the pickup truck still wedged half in the building and smoking.

"My ride should be parked here. But... but I don't see him," Angel said, her eyes creased with worry. "Wait!

There! There's his car." She pointed at a black Cadillac backed into a space between a SUV and an old Corvette.

Zoe pulled up with her passenger side door to the front of the Cadillac. "I don't see anyone inside."

Angel opened the door and ran to the driver's side of the car, peering inside. "The keys are inside. Maybe he went in to get me?"

"If he went into the rain, then..." Zoe trailed off, not wanting to say it. "Angel, come with me. Until we figure out what is happening, come home with me."

A group of people appeared at the other end of the parking lot.

"I need to know if he's okay. If I leave and he's gone in to get me... he... well, he won't be happy."

Angel didn't need to say who the man was; Zoe understood he was her pimp. The group at the opposite end of the parking lot suddenly stopped and turned, appearing to sniff at the air. "Listen to me, Angel. We've got to go! Please come with me," she begged. She didn't know why, but she wanted so bad for Angel to come with her. She barely knew this woman, but they'd already been through so much. And she didn't like the idea of her being alone. "Please, Angel! Get in!"

The infected people at the other end of the lot broke into a run, charging straight at them.

"I... I can't. You go! The keys are in the car. I'll get in and wait. If he doesn't come back, I have a car. I'll be okay!" Angel said, her makeup-smeared face a visage of fear as she forced a smile and pulled open the driver's-side door.

The feeling of desperation consumed her. "Angel! Please," Zoe tried again.

"Thank you, Zoe! But please, go... Really, I'll be okay.

Thank you. Thank you for everything." She climbed in the Cadillac and slammed the door.

As the group of crazed sick people bore down on them, Zoe reached across the passenger seat and pulled the door shut. Preparing to throw the car in reverse, she glanced over at Angel once more, forcing a smile and giving a quick wave. She knew she would likely never see her again.

Angel waved back, a shared look of knowing in her eyes. Over the last couple hours, they had fought for their lives together and saved each other. In those harrowing moments, the only thoughts were of escape and survival. Exchanging phone numbers hadn't once crossed their minds, but now, Zoe wished she had some way to stay in touch with the stranger she'd shared a nightmare with. She didn't even know Angel's last name. Was Angel even her real name?

The two women gave each other a final nod, a goodbye nod.

Ahead, the group of sick people were coming her way. It was time to go. As she glanced over her shoulder to back up, Zoe's eyes found Angel once again. A hand appeared from the shadowed back seat, grabbing the woman by the face and yanking.

Zoe gasped.

Angel's eyes went wide as her head snapped back.

Zoe watched in horror as a man's face appeared from between the seats. His eyes were blood red, his mouth set in a hungry snarl.

"No!" Zoe screamed, but there was nothing she could do.

The man lunged in, biting down on Angel's throat. Blood sprayed the windshield as the woman's arms flailed wildly.

Zoe tore her eyes away as a wretched sob broke from her soul and tears spilled down her cheeks.

A rain-soaked man slapped wet palms down on her hood and shouted something, his lips drawn up in a feral visage.

Zoe stomped on the gas pedal as a Black woman with long braids wrapped in a bun reached her driver's-side door and began pounding on her window with her own face. As the SUV raced backward across the lot, the woman turned to give chase. Zoe realized with horror that the woman had no arms, just blood-soaked sockets where her arms used to be. The question of how a woman whose arms had been ripped from her body could still be alive and giving chase barely had time to cross her mind when she slammed into something behind her. Her head snapped back as the Xterra came to a sudden and jolting stop.

"No!" she shouted, slamming the gear shift into drive. She sped forward, colliding with several people as she whipped the SUV out of the parking lot and onto the main street. The tears running in trails down Zoe's cheeks made seeing the road almost impossible. "Oh, Angel! Why? Why didn't you just come with me?"

Around her, cars were abandoned – some wrecked, some burning. People were running through the streets, some chasing others. Houses along the street were burning too.

Zoe was in the center of Bloomridge. Ahead, the street was totally blocked with a pileup of wrecked vehicles. As she slowed, steering the SUV up onto the curb to make her way around via the sidewalk, she wondered how in the hell was she going to get out of the city and get home. If all this wasn't enough, the sky above was choked with deep red clouds unlike anything Zoe could have imagined. They roiled like an ocean in a storm. Thunder boomed, and once again a rust-colored rain began to fall.

Zoe wiped her eyes on the sleeve of her nurse's uniform. "Shit," she breathed, depressing a button on the dash to engage the four-wheel drive. If she were to get stuck or have car trouble, she'd be a prisoner in her car until the rain stopped – assuming she wasn't already infected from the moist air. She glanced up into the rearview mirror. Her heart skipped a beat as she realized her eyes were bloodshot. Jesus Christ! She was infected! She maneuvered onto the shoulder and slammed on the brakes, staring at her reflection in the mirror as fresh tears welled and spilled down her cheeks. Tears that were clear and free of blood. In fact, her eyes didn't look at all like Tom's or Deandre's had. Her eyes weren't bleeding either. They were red, but she'd been crying... and she looked like she'd been crying.

Zoe sucked in a shaky breath and pulled back out onto the road. *Calm down,* she told herself. *You've got to get home, and you can't do it if you're freaking out.*

Maneuvering around a few more abandoned vehicles, Zoe turned onto Route 9. She still had to cross over Interstate 55, but she could follow this route all the way to Mackinaw.

As she neared the last intersection before the overpass, a siren blared and lights flashed in her rearview mirror. A police car raced up behind her so fast she was sure it was going to rear-end her before she could get over. "What the hell!" she shouted, jerking her wheel to get out of the way.

The police cruiser nearly clipped the side of her car, ripping her mirror off as it passed.

Zoe screamed.

Ahead, a semi was crossing the intersection. "Oh, no," she breathed, seeing what was about to happen. The semi driver seemed to see it too and tried to accelerate. The cruiser didn't even brake as it collided with the cab of the semi.

Zoe watched, wide-eyed and mouth agape.

The explosion was fatal as both the semi cab and police cruiser exploded in flames.

At least two lives had just ended right before her eyes, and as awful as that was, Zoe's mind went straight to her more immediate problem. The burning vehicles were blocking her way onto the overpass.

CHAPTER 15
GIRL POWER

BEFORE PULLING ONTO BROADWAY ROAD, Oliver threw the brake. They were a few miles away from the church now. Far enough that he didn't need to worry about the runners catching up with them anytime soon.

"Let me see." He tried to keep his voice calm, but inside he was screaming. His heart was in his stomach, and he felt like he might puke. All this, the car crash, Sam, the zombies at the church. They had been so close to getting out of there in one piece, but in the end he'd failed epically. He'd let Jurnee get attacked, and worst of all, he'd let her get bit! Fuck!

Oliver looked down at the little girl. She sat in the middle of the bus's bench seat, hugging Princess and rocking back and forth, her eyes pressed shut. "I... I... I want my mom!" she sobbed.

Oliver felt his own eyes go blurry with emotion. *Don't you do it! Don't you dare let her see you cry,* he told himself. "Where did she bite you, Jurnee? Please, you have to show me."

The tiny girl with the Afro puffs kept her eyes shut tight as she rocked and shook.

Oliver searched for a wound, but she was all balled up, with her knees pulled to her chest and Princess held tight to her body. "I need you to be the brave girl I know you are and show me where it hurts. Is it your arm?"

Jurnee shook her head.

"Okay, what about your leg? Is it your leg?"

Again, the little girl shook her head.

Oliver searched her face, her neck, and her hands, but he saw no sign of a bite wound.

"She bit my back, Ol... Oliver! That mean monster girl bit my back!" She sobbed hard now, her breath hitching.

Oliver swallowed. "Turn around. Let me see."

Jurnee twisted in the seat to expose her back.

Oliver's heart sank. She was still wearing Sam's raincoat, but the back was ripped open now. Beneath the raincoat, a chunk of the little girl's North Face jacket was torn away. Dark blood crusted the purple material all around the tear. *Oh, no, please.* "I need to take your coat off, Jurnee. Here, let me help," he said, lifting her arm.

Jurnee slid her tiny arms out of the raincoat and jacket to reveal a pink T-shirt that read GIRL POWER across the front in glittery gold letters. Oliver turned her around to examine her back, not wanting to see what he feared he would.

The back of Jurnee's shirt had a small red stain the size of an open mouth. Oliver lifted the shirt to expose broken skin just below her right shoulder blade.

"It hurts, Oliver!"

"I know," he said, trying to swallow his own emotion. The girl's skin was bruised; where the top of the teeth had bit in, her skin was broken and bleeding. But the teeth had only barely broken the skin, and thankfully the wound didn't look deep, but it didn't matter. If there was something in the rain, and he knew there was, then it would likely be transmittable through a bite. After all, everyone knows when you get bit by a zombie, you turn into a zombie. What was he saying? That was stupid. Zombies didn't exist... until now. But that didn't mean it worked like it did in the movies, right?

Oliver's heart skipped a beat and then kicked into overdrive as a sudden realization dawned on him. Her shirt! There wasn't a hole in her shirt! Oliver lifted the purple North Face jacket to find that although it was missing a chunk of material, the inside layer wasn't bitten all the way through! And there was no hole in her shirt! Examining the jacket again, Oliver realized the blood on the outside of the lavender material must have come from the zombie's already bloody mouth. There was no way the zombie's blood or spit or whatever could have gotten into Jurnee's wound.

"Is it bad, Oliver?" the girl managed as tears rolled down her cheeks.

Oliver let out a breath. "No. No, it isn't bad at all! In fact, you're going to be just fine, kiddo."

"Can I pull my shirt down now?" Jurnee asked.

"Yes, of course you can!" He laughed with relief as a huge smile stretched across his face.

"Hey, it isn't funny. It feels bad!" she said, lifting her coat from the seat.

"I know, but when we get home, I am going to have my wife Zoe fix you up. She's practically a doctor. Then we'll have a big bowl of ice cream. How's that sound?"

"Ice cream?" she asked, looking up at him.

"Yep, but right now I need to take this jacket, okay?"

"But I need my jacket, Oliver," Jurnee protested.

"This one is messed up, and it's got that other girl's blood on it."

"The monster girl?" Jurnee whispered, her eyes starting to well once more.

Oliver nodded. "Now I need you to be a big girl and sit tight. Before you know it, you'll be eating ice cream. Hey, do you like dogs?"

The girl wiped her nose on her wrist. "If it's a nice dog. Why, do you have a nice dog?"

"I do. His name is Louie, and he's a very nice dog," Oliver said as he backed out into the aisle. His thoughts went to Zoe and the pressing need to get home now.

Returning to the driver's seat, Oliver punched in the air brake knob, and the bus let out a hiss. As he turned onto Broadway Street, the road ahead appeared clear. It was practically a straight shot now with only a dozen miles to go, and he'd be home. Above, the tortured sky let out a thunderous rumble and once again began to bleed a rust-colored rain.

CHAPTER 16
THE NEIGHBOR

ZOE COULDN'T GET around the flaming mess ahead of her on the overpass. This wasn't the only way home; however, it was the fastest. The burning wreckage left her no choice but to turn around. She would have to make her way to the road leading under Interstate 55. She cut through an adjoining neighborhood to the sound of constant gunfire. Occasionally, she would see people running through the street, and twice they ran directly at her car. An elderly woman in a bathrobe and slippers came particularly close. Luckily, Zoe didn't have to run the old woman over. But she would have if she'd had to, because she sure as hell wasn't going to stop. In fact, she never stopped, not even at stop signs or stoplights. If she stopped, she would expose herself to attack.

Three blocks into the neighborhood, she was gripping the wheel so tight her hands were beginning to ache. She just wanted to get the hell out of this town.

Finally, she made a right turn leading out of the neighborhood, the overpass coming into view just ahead. She noticed right away that the railing was broken and a car lay upside down on the road ahead of her, the passenger compartment completely crushed. She couldn't imagine falling from up there. As she looked up, she could see smoke rolling from atop Interstate 55. Something up there was on fire. *Damn*, she thought, nervous to even drive under the overpass. But what choice did she have? She wanted to get home. She needed to get home.

Quickly she maneuvered around the smashed vehicle and under the overpass. Once she had come out the other side, she let out a relieved sigh. No more neighborhoods from here, just country roads.

Twenty-five minutes later, she turned into the entrance to Summer Lake, the neighborhood she'd lived in for the last eight years. At first, aside from the strange rain collecting in burnt-orange puddles, everything seemed normal.

But normal wasn't to last. As soon as Zoe turned at the first stop sign, all hell broke loose. The first thing she saw was a firetruck sitting alongside the road with hoses stretched across the street. On the opposite side, a house, or what was left of a house, still smoldered. In the front yard, a man in a fireman's jacket lay on the ground with an ax handle sticking up from the back of his head.

As she eased past the firetruck, a crowd of eight or nine people stood gathered in a neighbor's yard. It wasn't until they turned toward her and began to run that she realized they were all infected. She stomped on the gas, speeding down the street before they could reach her. At the four-way stop, she turned right and began to make her way around the lake.

A woman emerged from behind a tall row of shrubs and staggered out in front of Zoe's car. Zoe gasped, reflexively slamming on the brakes. The thought of running the woman over flashed through her mind, but then the woman yelled.

"Help me!" the woman shouted, staggering and then practically falling into Zoe's driver's-side door. Frantically the woman yanked on the door handle. "Unlock it, please! Please, help!"

The woman's hair was soaking wet. It looked red; she supposed it could have been the rain or blood. Either way, Zoe didn't recognize the terrified woman and, even if she wasn't symptomatic now, it was only a matter of time.

"They're coming! Please!" she begged.

"I'm... I'm sorry," she said, pressing down on the accelerator. The Xterra tore away.

The woman gave chase, screaming for help as she ran barefoot down the rain-soaked street.

I'm going to burn in hell, Zoe thought, watching the woman in her rearview mirror. As the frightened woman gave chase, two figures appeared behind her. She gasped as they overtook the woman, pulling her down onto the pavement. As Zoe drove away, the red rain swallowed the horror of what she could only imagine was happening to the woman who had just wanted help.

She could have saved her... could have opened the door, but then what? Watch the woman become sick? Wait for her to attack like Deandre had? No. She couldn't have saved that woman; she would only have delayed the inevitable and put herself at risk doing it.

She rounded a curve and then turned onto her dead-end street, Brandywine Road. Heavily wooded, Brandywine Road was a naturally dark street made darker by an otherworldly sky of red. The street itself descended a steep hill towards the lake. Zoe didn't live on the lake, but her neighbor did. Hers was the second log cabin on the left.

Farther down the cul-de-sac, several other houses lined the roundabout near the water's edge. Each lot was large. A few homeowners, Zoe included, owned two lots. Most of the lots were heavily wooded. It was one of the features that had drawn her and Oliver to this area. Despite being in a subdivision, the location gave Zoe a feeling of seclusion, especially when seeing her neighbors required peering through the foliage of the trees. Well, until winter anyway. Then the leaves would fall, and you would get to see what your neighbors had been up to. Oh, look at that, the Donners put up a new woodshed. Well, they'll certainly be warm this winter.

Zoe glanced ahead towards the bottom of her dead-end street. From what she could observe, all seemed quiet. Turning into her own driveway, she felt a sense of relief fill her. Her home was intact, seeming just as she had left it. But her relief was short-lived. With the sky darkened, she'd expected to see light coming through the windows and for Oliver to have turned the porch lights on. Maybe he didn't want to draw attention to the house? *Or maybe he isn't here,* she thought. As she approached the garage, a sense of dread filled her stomach.

Zoe pushed the button on the garage door opener. *Please be here.*

The door rose slowly to reveal an empty garage. "Dammit!" Zoe shouted.

She pulled inside, jabbing a finger into the button to close the garage. The spring groaned; the door sank, and with it her heart. *Where are you, Oliver?*

She was careful getting out of the car, making sure none of the rust-red liquid touched her.

The garage connected to the house via the mudroom, so at least she didn't have the problem of getting from the garage into the house. Once inside, she locked the door behind her and went immediately to the bathroom to check her eyes. From what she could tell, they looked okay.

Louie gave a bark, voicing his displeasure that he hadn't been properly greeted. He also expected Zoe to let him out upon arrival, but it was raining. Could whatever was making people sick make her dog sick too? She couldn't risk it. "I'm sorry, Louie, but I need you to wait, at least until it stops raining."

The blue-nose pit bull let out a whine and cocked his head, as if trying to understand.

"Just for now, Louie. Just for a little while," she said, patting him on the head. She wanted to call Alexis and make sure she was okay, and she wanted to get ahold of Oliver. Why in the hell wasn't he home? She thought back to the text message. Sam had gone into the rain, but Oliver hadn't and seemed to know not to. But what was taking him so long? Sam in the rain meant she was infected. It meant she would likely attack Oliver. *Don't! Don't think like that!* It was only a thirty-minute drive from River City on a normal day. But this was anything but a normal day. Maybe he was stuck in traffic? She'd lost her phone to Tom, and they didn't have a house phone, so she had no way to call.

All she could do now was wait and pray. Looking down at her bloodstained uniform, she realized she could also get the hell out of these bloody clothes and shower. She placed the toe of one of her shoes against the heel of the other to kick them off when a hard knock came at the door.

Louie barked and bolted from the bathroom.

Zoe jumped, startling at the sudden commotion. *What the hell?* She crossed the living room. "Move, Louie, dammit!" she said, pushing him out of the way with her knee. The big pit shuffled to the side, his little nub of a tail wagging excitedly. Zoe stood on her tiptoes to peer out the square glass window at the top of the door.

Right away, she noticed two things: No one was there, and the rain had stopped again. She glanced towards the driveway, hoping to see Oliver's Jeep. But it would be odd for him to enter through the front and not the garage. As she peered out, a face appeared only an inch from the glass.

Zoe staggered back, nearly falling over the throw rug.

"Mrs. McCallister! It's Doug Henderson. I, um, I need to talk to you, please?"

Zoe's eyebrows bunched. Doug, the nice old guy from next door? Him showing up like this wouldn't be weird except that he never asked to talk to her. When he needed anything, it was always Oliver he'd asked for. Usually, he'd come over when he needed a hand with something, and then they'd talk about yard work and lawnmowers or... whatever guys talked about. Recently, Oliver had helped the old man move a log splitter to his backyard. Come to think of it, she didn't think she'd ever actually spoken more than a few words to him. A hello here and there. A wave in passing at the mailbox. "Oliver isn't home, Mr. Henderson, but I'll tell him you stopped by. Now, you should probably get home before it starts raining again."

"The rain, you say. Is that what's causing it?"

So, he knew something was going on. "Yes, I believe so. Best to stay out of the rain."

"The radio is right, then?"

"The radio? What did they say?" she asked, her curiosity piqued.

"They say to stay out of the rain. And, well, you see. That's why I came over. I, well, I need to talk to you, Mrs. McCallister."

Zoe stood up on her toes again and peered back out the

window. "Me? What can I help with?" she shouted through the door, trying to get a look at the man's eyes. But he'd moved to the edge of the porch, facing away from her as he assessed the sky.

"You're a nurse, right?" he shouted over his shoulder.

"Yes, why? Is something wrong?"

"Well, you see, my Betty isn't well. When all this started, she was out for her morning walk and got caught in the rain. Now she isn't herself. She's..." He trailed off.

Zoe dropped down off her toes, leaned her back against the door, and drew in a breath. She knew that what she had to tell him wouldn't be easy for the man to hear. "Mr. Henderson, listen to me. If Betty was caught in the rain, you need to isolate her. You need to lock yourself away from her. It's only a matter of time before she..." Zoe stopped. How was she supposed to finish that sentence? How was she supposed to tell the man his wife would try to kill him... to eat him?

"I understand. I... I came over here hoping for help."

"I'm sorry, Mr. Henderson, but I can't help your wife."

"Oh, I know that, dear. I'm afraid no one can help Betty now. I split her head so bad her brain fell out. I... well, I didn't even know it was possible to do that... to hit someone in the head so hard their brain fell out. I only used a five-pound sledgehammer. Can you believe that? One hard swing and it split like a pumpkin. Did you know it could do that?"

Zoe slapped her hand over her mouth to prevent the scream surging up the back of her throat like vomit as she slid down the door on legs turned to rubber.

"Did you know?" he asked again. "Mrs. McCallister?" The doorknob jiggled above her head. "Mrs. McCallister? Open the door, please."

Fear gripped Zoe, but despite her pounding heart she found her voice. "Go home, Mr. Henderson."

"Open the fucking door!" the old man shouted.

Boom! Something hit the door.

The vibration jolted Zoe's back.

She gasped, pressing herself into the door. She anchored her white shoes, already stained in blood from the courthouse, securely onto the wood floor as she struggled for purchase and to leverage her weight into the door.

Boom!

Jesus Christ, was the old man kicking the door? He was like seventy!

"You see! After she bit me, I had no choice! It hurts until you give in!"

Boom! The wood frame popped.

Zoe and Oliver each kept a gun by their bedside. If she ran for the bedroom to get the gun, the door wouldn't hold, but if she didn't, she might not be able to hold it anyway.

Boom!

"Mrs. McCallister, when Betty's brain fell out... I ate it. I ate every single drop. Every drop! Oh... ho! And once I tasted it, I knew, I knew, I knew!"

Tears ran down Zoe's cheeks. "Go away! Please, just go away! I have a gun, Mr. Henderson! I have a gun and Oliver is due home any minute!"

"As soon as I tasted it, I knew nothing would ever taste better! So do you see now?" His voice lowered to a soft, steady tone barely audible through the door. "You see, I can smell your brain. I can smell its sweetness. Like a honey pot. Now be a good neighbor... and open the fucking door!"

The window above Zoe shattered, showering her with broken glass. She screamed, scrambling away from the door.

She glanced back in time to see the head of the five-pound sledgehammer withdrawing from the broken window.

Louie lost it, growling and barking on a level Zoe had never heard before.

"I'm coming in!" the old man shouted.

Boom! The doorframe broke away, flinging the door inward and shoving the doorknob through the drywall.

Mr. Henderson crossed the threshold, the oversized hammer held above his head. Blood trickled down his cheeks as he sniffed at the air. "There it is!"

Zoe scrambled backwards on her ass, knowing she needed to get to her feet and run for the bedroom.

Louie charged forward, barking and with teeth bared to bite.

Mr. Henderson's lip curled as he took aim at Louie's head.

"No!" Zoe shouted.

Hands slapped down hard on Mr. Henderson's shoulders from behind and yanked him off his feet, jerking him out the door and onto the porch.

"Oliver!" Zoe cried, a mix of emotions washing over her like an ocean's wave. Oliver was alive! But now he was wrestling with a contagious man.

"Stay, Louie!" Oliver shouted as he snatched the hammer away from Mr. Henderson.

"I smell you too, Oliver! I smell you too!" the old man snarled.

"Oliver! Don't let him bite you!" she shouted.

"I know!" he said, his back to the door as he squared up with the old man.

Mr. Henderson clenched his fist and sneered. "I'm coming in!"

Oliver swung the hammer, striking the man in the side of the head.

Mr. Henderson's arms flailed as he fell backward off the porch and down the stairs, striking the back of his head on the sidewalk.

Zoe was up and at the door, mouth agape, as Mr. Henderson bled out from his fractured skull.

Oliver tossed the hammer. It bounced, clacking across the wooden deck. He turned to face her. "Are you okay?"

Zoe threw herself into his arms. "Oliver," she cried, unable to find words as she sobbed. The emotion was too much. Even though she hadn't allowed herself to really think it, the possibility of Oliver not coming home had been there in the back of her mind this whole time, and it was only now she realized just how frightened she'd been.

"It's okay, babe. I'm here now and thank god you're okay," he said.

She pushed herself back enough to look him in the eyes. "You stayed out of the rain?"

"Barely, but yeah, I did," he said, smiling.

"Oh, thank god." She began crying again.

"Oliver, can I come out now?" a little girl's voice called.

Zoe glanced over to the driveway to find a little girl standing in the doorway of... was that a church bus? Her pale pink shirt contrasted with her dark skin, and she was holding a small doll.

CHAPTER 17
WELL, WHAT WOULD YOU CALL THEM?

OLIVER CARRIED JURNEE onto the porch and set her down.

"You kidnapped a little girl?" Zoe said, eyeing Oliver in what appeared to be a combination of confusion and disbelief.

"No. I didn't kidnap her." Oliver frowned. Technically, wasn't that exactly what he and Sam had done? But it wasn't as though they'd had much of a choice. "Jurnee, this is Zoe. Zoe, meet Jurnee."

Jurnee stood shyly, one arm wrapped around Oliver's leg and the other around her doll. "You're the lady who's practically a doctor."

"And you're Jurnee?" Zoe said in disbelief. Oliver read her thoughts. The same thoughts he'd had when he learned the little girl had the same name they would have given their own baby had it been a girl. But the miscarriage had stolen that away from them.

Oliver met Zoe's eyes, pressed his lips into a tight line, and nodded. "Let's get inside and I'll explain everything."

Jurnee let out a short scream.

Oliver flinched, his fists rising. "What's wrong?"

"Oliver! That's a big dog!" Jurnee said.

Louie had made his way onto the porch, tail wagging and tongue licking.

Oliver blew out a relieved breath. "It's okay! He's like a big teddy bear. Alright, Louie, that's enough kisses."

Jurnee wiped her face. "That's enough kisses, Louie!" she giggled.

Inside, Oliver directed Jurnee to the bathroom. "Let's let Zoe look at that bite."

"Oliver! She was bitten? By what?" Zoe asked.

"It was a mean monster girl at the church. She bit my back!" Jurnee's eyes spilled fresh tears at the memory. "Oliver said you are practically a doctor, and you can make it better."

Zoe's eyes flashed to Oliver, a pained expression twisting her face.

Oliver held up his hand. "It's okay. It isn't what you think. She had a lot of layers on, and the bite didn't go through."

"But it still hurts bad, Oliver!" Jurnee scolded.

"I know it does. But Zoe is going to fix you up and then we'll get you that ice cream I promised."

"You're sure?" Zoe asked.

"I'm sure. See for yourself. But in the meantime, I need to secure the front door and then I'll have to deal with the rest of the house."

"Can I see where the mean girl bit you?" Zoe asked.

Jurnee nodded. "It hurts really bad. But maybe you're hurt too?" Jurnee said, looking at Zoe's legs.

For the first time since stepping onto the porch, Oliver looked at his wife, really looked at her. Her nurse's uniform was stained in dried blood so thick that pieces were flaking off, her top was torn, and her braids were disheveled. Even her tennis shoes were splattered with blood.

Oliver's eyes knitted together. "Hey, are you okay, Zo? I mean really?" he asked.

"Yeah, but I have a lot to tell you," Zoe said, smiling down at Jurnee, who seemed to also be assessing her bloody appearance for the first time. "It's okay, I'm not hurt. I was just helping people who were."

"And that's how you got blood on your pants?" Jurnee asked, pointing at Zoe's uniform pants.

Zoe's smile slipped as some memory pulled her back.

"Zo?" Oliver said quietly.

She shook away whatever memory haunted her and forced a smile. "Turn around for me and let's get you fixed up."

Oliver watched as his wife squatted down to get a good look at the girl's back. Since this whole crazy nightmare started, everything he'd done was to get back here to Zoe, all the while hoping like hell she'd be here when he did. Until right now, he hadn't considered what her journey must have been like. What had she been through? Clearly, whatever it was, it had been bad. He also hadn't allowed himself to imagine her not making it home. Now, as he looked at his wife, he dared to think what coming home to an empty house would have done to him. Christ, what had it been like for Zo to get here and find the house empty? She must have been going out of her mind. Then to finally make it to safety and their fucking neighbor tries to kill her! A new fear gripped him. They weren't safe at all. They were exposed.

Oliver placed a hand on Zoe's shoulder. "I need to run outside, but I'll be right back."

"Okay, please be careful and stay out of—"

"Out of the rain. I know, believe me, I know. That's why I want to do this now before the rain starts again."

Zoe dug through the cabinet and produced a small first aid kit. "Ollie, what are you going to do?"

"I'm going to get all those sheets of plywood I bought to finish the inside walls of my workshop and bring them into the house. I also have a bunch of two-by-sixes and two-by-fours. We need to board this place up. All the windows and doors. Once we get secure, we will figure out our next move."

Zoe pressed around the edges of Jurnee's wound to try and get it to bleed a little. This would help push out any debris.

"Ouch!" Jurnee shouted.

"Aww, I'm sorry. That part is over. Now I need to wipe it. That might sting a little, but I'll be gentle, okay?

"Okay," the little girl said, squeezing her eyes tight as she braced herself.

"You are so brave." Zoe smiled and wiped gauze damp with rubbing alcohol across the wound, ensuring she'd cleaned it thoroughly.

Jurnee winced. "Ow!"

"Oh, I know." Quickly she squeezed some Neosporin onto her finger and rubbed it onto the wound. "But the good news is we're all done with that part and now we get to put a nice big Band-Aid on it." She turned to Oliver. "Just please be careful. Even one drop of rain, Oliver, and..."

Oliver bent and kissed her cheek. "I know. Trust me, okay?"

Oliver retrieved the 9mil from his bedroom. He had a .45 upstairs on a bookshelf hidden in a hollow book, but he was a better shot with the .9.

Outside, thunder rolled in the distance and the cloud-choked sky threatened another bout of rain. Oliver grabbed a raincoat from the mudroom, lifted the hood into place, and ran for the woodshop. It was only a dozen or so yards from the house, but there was no way to get there without being exposed. He supposed if the rain started, he would do his best to keep his eyes shut and get back to the house.

Making multiple trips, Oliver began securing the materials he would need, along with his cordless drill and several boxes of wood screws. On his last trip, movement caught his eye across the wooded ravine behind his house. He froze, peering through the trees at one of his neighbors standing in the backyard.

It was Roger; he and his wife, Liz, had just moved into the neighborhood. They had two little ones, two and five. Oliver stopped short, a bundle of two-by-fours under one arm. What was he doing outside? Peering through the trees and across the ravine, Oliver couldn't tell if the man was infected, but he could see he was holding something in his hand. Oliver put a hand up to his mouth, preparing to give a shout across the ravine to see if the man responded, but then he hesitated. Roger hadn't seen him yet, and if the neighbor was infected, he would come running. Oliver knew he could make it inside before the man crossed the small patch of timber, but he really didn't want to risk having a crazed Roger on his porch or, worse, drawing the attention of more zombies.

"Why?" the man screamed, head tipped back as if speaking to the red clouds above.

Oliver ducked down, nearly dropping the bundle of

boards, watching as Roger began to sob, his wretched moans drifting across the ravine.

"You took them! Goddamn you! You took them!" Roger shouted, lifting his hand and the object it held to his head.

"Oh, dear god. Roger, don't—"

The report echoed through the neighborhood as an explosion of bloody mist sprayed the vinyl siding of Roger's house.

Oliver stood in motionless disbelief. His breaths came quick as his heart racked against his chest like a caged animal trying to escape.

Thunder boomed, bringing him back to the moment, and he realized he was still standing in his yard... still holding the two-by-fours, and still exposed to the sky above.

From around the side of Roger's house, several people appeared, sniffing at the air as they descended on Roger's corpse.

"Shit!" Oliver breathed, carefully hurrying onto the porch and back inside. He dropped the boards onto the floor of the mudroom, locked the deadbolt, and hurried into the kitchen to stare out the bay window. Jurnee had finished her ice cream and was now sitting in the bedroom playing Tetris on Zoe's iPad. It probably wouldn't have been her first choice, but the internet wasn't working and only a few games were already loaded. At least they still had power, but Oliver wondered how long it would last.

"What happened?" Zoe asked, following his gaze out the window. "I heard a gunshot."

"Look, over at Roger's place, you see there? Zombies. At least six."

"Zombies, Oliver? Don't be ridiculous. Those people are sick. Something in the rain is causing them to fall ill."

"'Don't be ridiculous?!' What the hell would you call

them, Zo? People are getting sick and losing their minds! When you kill them, they come back unless you destroy their brain. And when they *do* come back, all they want is to eat brains. Roger is under that pile of people being eaten as we speak!" Oliver sucked in a calming breath. "Listen, Jurnee is safe in the bedroom and the house is locked except for the front door, so let's start there. I'm going to need you to help me get the plywood in place and hold it while I secure it."

Zoe stared out the window at the mass of bodies ripping and tearing at what she now knew was their neighbor. "Jesus Christ, Oliver. What if the noise brings them over here?"

"We'll just have to deal with it because if we sit here doing nothing, we'll be exposed."

The two went to work boarding up the front door and covering the windows. As they secured the main floor of their home, each recounted all the events from the morning.

Oliver placed a screw into the magnetic drive guide of his cordless drill and ran a screw into the plywood. "So wait, after the guy... sorry, what was his name?"

"Deandre."

"Right. After Deandre went down in the bathroom you went back into the stall?"

"Yeah, but that's because Tom was coming after us."

"Tom? The little guy who used the scissors to kill the judge upstairs?"

Zoe shook her head. "No, it was a letter opener." She winced at the memory. "I can still smell the blood. There was so much of it coating the floor, and I was just covered in it. I've never smelled it so strong – not even at the hospital."

Oliver glanced down at the dried blood flaking off Zoe's uniform as he ran another screw into the opposite side. "You can let go," he said, motioning to the window. "So then it was just you and the prostitute inside the stall, and that's when she killed the clerk with her high heels?"

Zoe nodded. "Yeah, her name is... well, was... Angel. She was a sweet woman, Oliver. She saved my life. I just wish... I wish she had gotten in the car. She'd be here with us right now if she'd just gotten in! I should have made her."

Oliver couldn't believe what Zoe had been through. He thought the church had been insane, but all he'd done was fight zombies to get a key to the bus. Zoe had treated injured people in the midst of the chaos, nearly been shot in the face at point-blank range, and even had a man pick brains off her cheek and eat them right in front of her. Despite all this, she'd somehow kept her cool. She'd not only been brave, she'd also used her resourcefulness to survive. He felt strangely proud and scared shitless all at the same time. Jesus, to bond with those people and then lose them one by one. To be the only one to make it out of there.

Zoe grabbed the next piece of plywood. "Why couldn't she have just got in the fucking car?"

"Listen, Zo, it sounds like you begged her. You can't blame yourself for what happened."

Zoe slammed her eyes shut and shook her head. "You have no idea. It was so horrible!"

Oliver didn't say anything, but he didn't have to.

"Sam... Oh, Oliver, I'm so sorry! She was your best friend. I wasn't thinking. I shouldn't have—"

Oliver waved her off. "It's okay. I know you didn't mean to."

"Do you want to talk about it?"

He shook his head. Sam turning was the last thing he wanted to talk about. "You know it was Sam who heard Jurnee screaming from inside the car. If not for her, we wouldn't have gotten to her before the whole thing went up in flames. That doll she clings to, Sam went back for it, and when she did, the rain let loose. I told her to just forget the doll, but she went anyway."

"I'm so sorry. Hey, don't you think it is odd that her name is Jurnee? Do you know how she spells it?"

Oliver nodded. "Yeah, and you won't believe it."

"J U R N E E?" Zoe guessed.

Oliver nodded.

"Hell of a coincidence."

"Yeah," he agreed, but he could see Zoe's wheels spinning. Part of him wanted to ask if she thought it all meant something – like if it were some cosmic sign – but he didn't want to reopen old wounds. Instead, he told the story of the church.

"You went back in for a freaking key and left her on the bus?"

Oliver pulled a face. "Hey, I knew what I was doing, Zo. I made sure they all followed me."

"Given what you used to do for a living, I figured you could just hot-wire anything."

Oliver laughed. "No, that's not how it works. Clients would give me keys. I didn't have to hot-wire."

"Yeah, well I'm glad you were able to get away. I hate to think how all this would have played out if you'd been gotten stranded at the church. Also, hot-wiring or not, I'm glad you don't do that kind of work anymore."

Oliver swallowed and nodded. "Yeah. Hey, I'm just glad you're okay, and I'm proud of how you handled yourself." He set his drill down on an end table, turned to Zoe, and hugged her, pulling her to his chest. At that moment, he never wanted to let go. "Not exactly what I had in mind for date night."

"No. Me either," Zoe said solemnly, pulling away. "Listen, before Mr. Henderson got into the house, he mentioned the radio was warning people to stay out of the rain."

"I think we already know that."

"I know, but do you remember when you were going through that prepper phase? Do you still have that emergency radio?"

"I do. It's on one of the shelves downstairs with the canned food. And it wasn't a phase. I just got busy and didn't keep at it," he countered defensively.

"I didn't mean to imply... look, it's a good thing. The internet is out, the local stations are offline, and both our phones are gone. But maybe if we can tune in and get updates, we can find out how bad it is and maybe how widespread. Oh, and that canned food... we may need that."

Oliver sighed and reached for her again, taking her hand in his and giving it a reassuring squeeze. "You're right. Let's finish this and get the glass sliding door covered, then I'll go dig it out."

Zoe looked up at him, nodded, and smiled.

How did she do that? How did she smile despite it all? Forced as it was, it was there, a smile so simple and perfect. It wasn't lost on him, the strength it must have taken to twist the terror of all she'd witnessed into a smile of any kind, let alone a perfect one. Against incredible odds, they had both survived the horror of the day and made it home. Whatever tomorrow and the days beyond held, in this moment, here with Zoe, he felt like the luckiest man in the world.

Oliver smiled back at her.

CHAPTER 18
WORST-CASE SCENARIO

OUTSIDE, rain pattered against the skylights as the red sky bled into darkness. Zoe had changed her bloody clothes, washed up, and retrieved her .357 from the bedside table. She now wore the gun awkwardly on her hip as if she were a gunslinger from the Wild West. Next, she'd warmed up some chicken and rice leftover from the day before. Now she sat across from little Jurnee, wondering how a six-year-old could eat so much.

"You like that?" Zoe asked.

Jurnee nodded – "Mm-hmm" – and shoved another spoonful in her mouth. Through a mouthful she asked, "Am I spending the night?"

"I think so. We don't have a house phone, and the radio says we need to stay inside." Oliver had found the radio among the supplies in the basement, but the emergency alert system wasn't telling them anything new, only playing the same message on repeat. After several minutes of scrolling through radio stations only to find more of the same, Oliver had shut it off, telling her he'd come back to it later, after securing the upstairs windows.

Upstairs, the drill buzzed away as Oliver covered the last of the windows. Despite everything that was going on, she needed to talk to him. To really talk to him. A question burned inside of her. One she had hoped Sam could answer. But with Sam gone, and her text to the woman going unanswered, she'd no choice but to ask Oliver himself... she had to know.

"Because of the monsters?" Jurnee asked.

"Uh? Oh, no. There are no monsters, but people are sick, and the rain isn't safe," she said, pulling her attention back to the girl as she spooned in another mouthful of chicken and rice. "Jurnee, do you know where you live? Do you know your address?"

Jurnee nodded. "I live at 2121 South Pine Street, Indianapolis, Indiana."

"Indiana?"

Jurnee lifted her glass of water and took a big drink. "Yep, but I think it's far away from here."

"Jurnee, who were you traveling with?"

"My mommy. We were visiting my grandma in River City. But I don't know where she went? There was a big crash and screaming and then Oliver came."

Zoe's heart sank. From what Oliver had said, the driver was dead. "Do you know your grandma's address?"

She shook her head.

"Okay, how about phone numbers? Do you know your grandma's phone number?"

Again, Jurnee shook her head.

"What about your dad's phone number?"

"Weeeellll, I don't really know. He always calls me because mommy says we can't call him." Jurnee looked down at her plate.

"Does he not live at home with you?"

"Nuh-uh, he's an army man. Mommy said he's on the other side of the ocean and that's really far because the ocean is really big," she said, fidgeting uncomfortably.

Zoe realized that was probably enough questions for now. "Well, we'll keep you right here with us until we figure this out, okay?"

"Uh-huh," she said, chewing another mouthful of chicken and rice.

Oliver bounded down the stairs from the upper loft and announced, "That should do it. We're all buttoned up. I drilled a few peepholes in the plywood covering the bay window, sliding glass door, and front door so we can see out." He motioned between the kitchen and living room toward the sliding glass doors where plain tan plywood obstructed her once beautiful view of the side yard. "We won't be able to go out the sliding glass door because I screwed the plywood to the doorframe. Same with the front since the door and frame were busted. For the back and garage door, I just covered the doors themselves since they both have deadbolts."

"Can I watch TV?" Jurnee asked.

"Well, the internet is offline, but we have DVDs. Let's go to the living room and see what we can find."

"Do you have Disney movies?" the girl asked hopefully.

"We sure do. Let's go pick one out and I'll watch it with you," Zoe said.

Jurnee lit up, grabbing Princess off the table as she climbed down off the chair.

Twenty minutes later, Jurnee lay quietly sleeping under a blanket, nestled on the couch. Carefully, Zoe got up and joined Oliver in the kitchen. "Hey, babe, she's asleep. Anything new?"

Oliver dragged both hands down his face and yawned.

"No, nothing. Just the same message on repeat. Stay in your homes. Stay out of the rain. If someone is infected, separate yourself from them. Local law enforcement and the National Guard are on their way and will transport all healthy people to a safe zone."

"But what about the safe zone?" she asked. "Maybe it isn't as widespread as I feared."

"Or maybe they're full of shit," Oliver said, standing and crossing the kitchen. "I'm going to make some coffee. You want some?"

"No. Not this late."

"Well, I can't sleep. I'm way too wound up and that last round of gunfire sounded like it was coming from right across the street."

"So you don't believe anyone is coming?" she asked.

Oliver pulled the coffee container from the cabinet and dumped a couple of scoops into the filter. "Zoe, this same message has been on repeat for the last hour that we know of. Shouldn't there be some kind of update by now? I can only find three stations still on the air, and it's the same repeating message on all three." Oliver reached over and turned on the faucet, filling the pot. "I just don't have a good feeling about this."

"Me either," she admitted. "Not after what I saw today. Not after what I saw sick people doing to each other." She closed her eyes as the memories, still too fresh to fully process, flooded her mind.

"Zombies. They're zombies," Oliver said evenly.

"Oliver, there's a logical medical explanation for this. There is no such thing as zombies."

"I watched a little teenage girl with a butcher knife buried in her chest right where her heart should be attacking a windshield because she wanted to eat my brain.

I broke a woman's neck and it didn't even faze her. She still came at me, her head sideways, teeth snapping. I watched my best friend tell me she wanted to eat that little girl's brain!" Oliver said, pointing toward the living room couch. "What the hell would you call them?"

"Hey, keep your voice down. Look, I know. It's just... there is something in the rain..." She shook her head in frustration. "Something... something not from Earth."

"So, you're telling me that your theory is aliens, and that's somehow less ridiculous than zombies?"

"No. I didn't say it was ridiculous. But yeah, I guess the whole thing is ridiculous, but here we are," Zoe said, throwing her hands up. Now that she thought of it, the idea of zombies wasn't really all that far-fetched if what they were dealing with was a parasite. "If I could just study it somehow," she said.

Oliver frowned. "Study it? You mean one of the zombies?"

"Yeah, well, their blood anyway."

"Well, our dead neighbor is lying on the lawn."

Zoe nodded. "That might work."

"I was joking."

"Oliver, I have a theory."

Oliver hit the button on the coffeemaker and turned back to her, his face genuinely curious. "Okay, what are you thinking?"

"I think we're dealing with a parasite."

"A parasite?"

"Sure, there are plenty of examples right here on Earth of parasites that utilize mind control to manipulate the host. Last semester, we studied all sorts of parasites. Mostly we studied the helminths, like tapeworms, flatworms, and roundworms. But we also studied protozoa. These are microscopic ones that can't be seen with the naked eye. Of course, the most infamous parasite is the emerald wasp. We didn't really spend much time on it because it can't infect a human, but it basically turns cockroaches into zombies to provide food for the wasp's larvae. If this is an alien parasite, then that could explain what's happening."

Oliver nodded along. "Right, zombie wasps. Those I've heard of. Don't they attach themselves to the backs of cockroaches? Well, I don't think these are attaching themselves. And I don't think they're microscopic either. I could see the perforations in Sam's eyes. So if I could see tiny holes, I should be able to see what made them, right?"

"Maybe. At least they'd be larger than any we've seen so far. Maybe they're attaching themselves directly to the brain in order to control the host. Or maybe they're some type of alien helminths, or perhaps something completely new. They could be microscopic in the rain and then grow once they enter the host."

"Wait, you're saying they can mutate?"

"No. Not exactly. Parasites can change as they advance through their life cycle."

Oliver sighed heavily. "Okay, so what does that mean for us?"

"Well, that depends. Often parasites need perfect conditions to complete their life cycle. We know that whatever this is transfers through the rain upon contact with the host. What we don't know is how long the parasite, if that's what this is, can live if it doesn't land directly on a host. If the parasite can only transfer upon contact from the rain directly onto a human host, then that is our best-case scenario."

The coffeemaker hissed and percolated, signaling it was finishing up.

Oliver crossed the kitchen, retrieving a coffee mug from the cabinet. "That's the best case?" Oliver asked.

"Yes, because we know for certain that it will cause an infection with contact to a human. So we know how to avoid it. Hey, on second thought, pour me a cup too?"

Oliver nodded, pulling a second coffee mug from the cabinet. It was Zoe's favorite mug, white with a periodic table on the side that read I USE THIS MUG... PERIODICALLY. Oliver had gotten it for her when she started going to school to get her LPN. She watched as Oliver filled both mugs. He started to say something and then stopped.

She knew he wanted to ask the burning question. "What?" she asked.

Crossing the kitchen with two steaming mugs, Oliver seemed to find his courage. "Okay, so what's the worst case?" he asked.

She pulled in a deep breath. "The parasite infects all other mammals, or worse still, the parasite goes on living when it hits the ground, infecting our water supply. If it does, it's only a matter of time before we're all dead."

CHAPTER 19
TINY MONSTERS

OLIVER HANDED ZOE her cup of coffee and collapsed into the kitchen chair, his mind reeling at the knowledge his wife just dropped on him. He held her gaze, wondering how in the hell he'd ended up with a woman so much smarter than he was. Searching for a glass-half-full response, he said, "So if this is the worst case, we become vegans and boil our water."

"It might work for a while, but we won't survive for long that way. We'll slip up or we'll eat a vegetable that's carrying spores or god only knows, but it will get us eventually." Zoe closed her eyes, drawing in a deep breath. "Anyway, we're getting way ahead of ourselves. It's just a theory and I could be completely wrong."

"I don't think you're wrong, Zo. You're the smartest person I know," Oliver said, smiling at his wife.

Zoe returned the smile, but it quickly fell away. "Hmm. Well, glad you think so, but we need proof and we need a phone. We have to figure out this situation with Jurnee, and I need to check on Alexis and my parents. I need to know they're okay."

Oliver knew the odds were they were not okay, but he simply nodded. "I can search Mr. Henderson. Maybe he had a cell phone on him. If not, I think searching his house is a good next step."

"You would go out there? Oliver, I don't think—"

"I know," he interrupted. "But we may not have a choice. Look, the rain seems to come and go. Right now, I don't hear it. I think it stopped again. Let me just go out and check his body first. Then, if we have no luck, we'll decide if the trip is worth it."

Zoe gave a reluctant nod. "Wear your rain jacket and keep your hood up – oh, and wear those goggles you have in the garage. The ones you use to weed whack. And I have a whole box of rubber gloves. You have to wear those if you're going to touch his body. I mean it, Oliver. You have to be so careful."

Oliver could see the creases of worry on Zoe's forehead. "Of course I will."

The sky was a black veil. Oliver had no way to know how long the rain would hold off, but he knew from the hopelessly dark sky that the clouds were still up there, threatening to send death his way at any moment. Never had he feared the weather like he feared it now.

He couldn't go out the front or sliding glass door; he'd made them immobile. So instead he went out through the garage, opened the garage door, and quickly ran around to the front porch. It was only a few steps down the sidewalk. The porch light illuminated Mr. Henderson's body well enough for Oliver to see. Quickly he patted the man down with gloved hands as he cautiously avoided stepping in the pool of blood around the man's head. Despite the rain having watered it down, there was still plenty present on the sidewalk, and he wanted to stay clear of it. Checking the man's jeans and beneath his flannel shirt, he found no phone. *Damn*, he thought. Turning to the door, he shook his head, knowing Zoe would likely be watching him through the peephole he'd drilled in the plywood. From somewhere beyond his yard, a woman screamed. *Time to go.* Turning on his heel, he ran back into the garage.

Zoe was there at the interior garage door. Oliver hit the garage door button as he climbed the stairs into the house and slammed the door.

"No luck. Listen, I have my 9mil. I think if I'm going to go to the Hendersons', now is the time."

"I don't know, Oliver. Did you hear that scream? And what about the rain?"

He followed her back into the kitchen. "I know but..." He trailed off, the objects on the kitchen table catching his eye. "What's this?"

"Remember my theory? Well, this is how we're going to find out if I'm right."

"The microscope I got you for your microbiology class?" he asked, eyeing the Amazon purchase.

She nodded. "Yep."

Oliver had gotten it for her for Christmas. At the time, she hadn't the heart to tell him microscopes weren't required for microbiology because they were provided in the labs. Hell, he hadn't known that. Pretending to be over the moon for her gift, Zoe had spent Christmas Day looking at samples that had come with the kit. Months later, she'd told him the truth and how the gift had turned out to be useful as hell. She'd ended up using the heck out of the thing, often bringing home samples from school to help her study her quizzes.

Zoe pursed her lips in thought. "Now I need a few samples. A sample of Mr. Henderson's blood, a sample of the rain from a puddle or even a sample of water from the koi pond, and then a fresh sample before it hits the ground."

He loved that Zoe was naturally intuitive and curious, and he wanted to understand what this was too, but another part of him just wanted to focus on their basic survival needs. Oliver was sure the power would go out soon, and they'd probably lose their fresh water supply after that. Plus, their food supply was only good enough for a few days.

He pulled off one of the rubber gloves. "Zoe, is this really what we should be focusing on right now? I mean, we need to get a phone, and we need to understand how long this is going to go on. Our food won't last long."

Zoe attached a needle to a syringe and then set it down next to two others she'd already prepared. "Of course, all those things are important, Ollie, but wouldn't it be a whole lot easier if we knew what this was and how potentially dangerous even walking across a wet lawn might be?"

Damn, he really wanted to get to a phone, but she was right and he knew it. And besides, she'd called him Ollie, her pet name for him. She knew damn well she always got what she wanted when she called him that. "Okay, but we need to hurry. It could start raining any minute, and then who knows how long it will be before I can get over to old man Henderson's place."

Zoe smiled. "Okay, we'll hurry."

Collecting the sample of blood from Mr. Henderson was easy enough despite how much Oliver hated doing it. Zoe had offered, but he wasn't keen on letting her stand under a questionable sky. Once he'd handed off the sample to Zoe, Oliver went out back to collect a syringe full of water from their koi pond. Across the ravine, darkness hid whatever might still be in Roger's backyard. Standing upright, his syringe full, Oliver paused to listen. Darkness might hide what he couldn't see, but it couldn't hide the hungry growls and grunts of the zombies as they fed. He didn't hear anything except the noise of locusts and other night bugs. Normal sounds. Still, he wondered if they were there, standing in Roger's backyard. He felt like a kid alone in the dark. Like at any moment something would crash through the foliage, catching him before he could get back to the house. Christ, he wished he could hear them feeding. The silence was almost worse. If he could hear them, he could tell where they were.

Quickly he turned back to the house and hurried inside like a child running from the night.

"Got it," he announced triumphantly.

Zoe looked up from the microscope, her eyes wide.

"What is it?" he asked.

"I think I was right. It looks like a worm, but..."

"But?" Oliver asked.

"But not like any worm I've ever seen. It's got legs and... teeth."

"So they don't normally have teeth?" Oliver asked, looking over her shoulder.

"No. Not like this. Here, see for yourself," she said, turning the microscope.

Oliver pressed his eyes to the eyepiece as a monster came into focus. "Whoa."

"What do you see?" Zoe asked.

Maggots, Oliver thought but didn't say it, because this was no maggot. Maggots didn't have legs. He squinted, realizing the only similarity this thing had to a maggot was that it was wormlike. "I see a sort of flat worm with legs sticking out the sides. But I don't see any teeth. Oh wait, the one next to it! It's all teeth. I mean it's flipped on its back, isn't it? I think the whole length of it is... is teeth!" Maggots didn't have teeth either. At least not that he knew of and certainly not like this. Absently, he wondered if these smelled like maggots? No, probably not. Maggots were huge compared to these. Plus, these things were whiter, flatter, and way scarier.

"Right, but what do you not see?" Zoe asked.

"Not see? I don't understand," he said, keeping his brows pressed tight against the eyepiece as he peered through the two small windows into another world.

"They aren't moving, Oliver. Except, they were when I first placed the sample on the slide. Just for a handful of seconds."

"What does that mean?" he asked, finally pulling away from the microscope and meeting her eyes.

"It means that when the sample was inside Mr. Henderson, the parasites were still alive. And inside this syringe, they are alive. But when I exposed them to the air, they died," Zoe said, excitement filling her voice as she carefully prepared a new slide using the pond water sample.

"Well, that's something," Oliver said hopefully.

"It is hopeful, but I wouldn't bet my life on it. Not yet," Zoe said, turning the microscope and leaning in.

"What do you see?" Oliver asked, knowing this was the more important of the two samples. If they were alive in the water, then humanity might be screwed.

"I see them. They're in the water too! But they're much smaller than the ones in the blood sample. Which means they grow once inside the host."

"Are they moving?" Oliver asked anxiously.

"No. These appear to be dead too."

Oliver blew out a breath like a man who'd been read the verdict of not guilty. "Okay, so what now?"

Zoe lifted her head from the eyepiece. "Look, this isn't my field of expertise, but I worry they could just be going dormant. I need a sample of the rain before it hits the ground. I want to see how in the world these things are surviving a fall through our oxygenated atmosphere. Maybe then I can make sense of it."

Nodding, Oliver said, "Well, right now it isn't raining and we need a phone. I want to go for Mr. Henderson's now, while the rain is holding off and it's dark out."

Zoe nodded, but her face was a visage of fear and worry. "Are you sure?"

Oliver drew the gun from his shoulder holster and placed it on the kitchen table. "I think I have to. You need to check on your parents and Alexis, and I need to check on Sarah." Oliver's parents had passed away, and his sister, Sarah, was his only living relative. She was all the way over in California. He hoped whatever this insanity was, it wasn't widespread – or at least hadn't spread all the way to Cali.

"Please be careful, Oliver. Remember the rain. Straight there and straight back," Zoe warned.

"Roger that, Mom. No talking to strangers and back before the streetlights come on." He smiled, zipping up the raincoat.

"Oh, you got jokes. I'm serious, Oliver. Promise me."

He dropped the smile and nodded, securing his goggles and lifting his hood into place. "Of course. I promise, babe. I'll hurry." And with that, he kissed his wife on the lips, lifted the pistol from the table, and ran out the back door.

CHAPTER 20
NAILED IT

ZOE WATCHED as Oliver's silhouette vanished into the darkness. "God, Oliver, please be careful." She turned back towards the kitchen, deciding to occupy the minutes by reviewing another sample of the blood from Mr. Henderson, but as she began to prepare the slide, the house shook with a thunderous boom.

What could only have been the front-facing windows exploded in a pop of shattering glass. Zoe's ears popped too and her chest rumbled. Thankfully, the plywood covering the windows and doors held, shielding the interior of her home from what surely would have been a shower of glass fragments.

From the living room, Jurnee screamed.

Zoe ran across the kitchen and into the front room as something slammed into the front of the house and then the roof. What followed sounded like a thunderstorm of softball-sized hail pelting the roof. One of the skylights popped and cracked, but somehow it didn't shatter.

"It's okay, Jurnee! Go to the kitchen! Hurry!" Zoe shouted.

Jurnee ran past her, screaming.

Zoe reached the front door and peered out the small hole Oliver had drilled into the plywood covering. She gasped. Until that moment she hadn't understood what was happening, but instantly it became clear. Across the street where the Miller family lived, fire burned out of control, turning what used to be a two-story A-frame into burning debris.

The whole house had exploded. Now she realized that the large hail pelting their house wasn't hail at all; it was raining down bits of the neighbors' house.

On her porch, a chunk of the Millers' roof burned wildly. Zoe strained to see, quickly realizing their log cabin was going to catch fire if she didn't do something.

She ran back to the kitchen and removed a small fire extinguisher from under the sink. Both the front door and the sliding glass door were boarded up tight. She would have to go out through the garage.

Jurnee cried out, "What's happening?"

"It'll be okay! Stay in the kitchen, Jurnee! I'll be right back." She ran through the house, across the mudroom, and into the garage. She hit the button on the opener. Still no rain. Scanning the yard and the street beyond, both now lit by the light of the neighbors' burning debris field, Zoe stepped out onto the driveway. Wasting no time, she ran down the sidewalk, stepping over Mr. Henderson's corpse, and onto the porch steps. The fire had already caught the wraparound porch on fire and the flames were climbing the support post, threatening to ignite the roof.

From somewhere behind her, a man yelled. "Too fast! You bitch! I was too fucking fast! Blow me up! You wish! You bitch!"

Zoe whipped around, her eyes widening with fear as

she searched for the source of the sudden outburst. Across the street, in the yard of burning rubble, a man stood in tattered clothes, with his back to the street, laughing. "You-ou haha, yummy bitch! All that delicious candy, wasted! You'd rather blow yourself up than let me have a taste! You bitch!"

"Shit!" Zoe breathed, wanting nothing more than to get the hell back to the safety of the house. Turning back to the burning porch, she took aim at the base of the fire and squeezed the handle, sweeping the extinguisher back and forth. Within a few seconds, she had squelched the flames.

Above her, the sky rumbled threateningly.

Stealing a glance back over her shoulder, she saw the neighbor man crossing the street towards her yard. *Shit, he must have heard the extinguisher.*

"Will you give me a taste?" he shouted.

"Oh god!" Zoe threw the extinguisher onto the ground and ran back towards the safety of the garage. As she crossed the threshold, the sky barked out another roar and let loose a downpour. *Oh, no! Please be inside, Oliver.*

The man was running up her drive now.

She slapped the button on the garage wall and drew the .357 from her hip holster. The garage door squeaked to life, its cranking spring muffling the sounds of the man as he shouted profanities at Zoe. "Please. Please!" she begged, hoping like hell the door closed before the crazed man got in.

The door was halfway closed, but Zoe could see his face clearly, illuminated by the garage door light. Flesh was burnt and missing from his face, and his eyes spilled blood down his cheeks.

Zoe assumed her shooter's stance and thumbed back the hammer.

The man ran harder now. He wasn't going to stop! He was going to dive under!

Zoe took aim near the bottom of the door.

"I got you! You bitch!" the man shouted, and dove.

The door met the floor and went silent.

The man slammed into the garage door.

Hands shaking, Zoe held her breath, the gun trained on the door.

"You bitch!" came the man's muffled voice. But there was no way he was getting through that door. Zoe holstered her gun, climbed the three steps back into the mudroom, shut the door, and locked the deadbolt. "Oliver!" she shouted. "Jurnee, is Oliver back?"

Jurnee stood in the kitchen, eyes wet, with Princess hugged tight to her chest. She shook her head.

A fist pounded on the back door.

Zoe jumped, her hand grabbing for the gun on her hip. "Oliver!" she shouted hopefully, hurrying to the door. She flung open the door to find Oliver coated in rust-colored rain.

"Oh, Oliver! No!"

Oliver kept his goggle-covered eyes downcast and pointed a gloved hand towards the laundry piled up on the laundry table, ready to be folded.

Zoe spun, grabbing a towel and shoving it into Oliver's hands.

Oliver covered his face and then said through the towel. "I don't think I got any rain in my mouth, but maybe on... on my skin. Can you help me get... get out of this rain gear?"

"Don't move!" Zoe said, retrieving a pair of gloves off the kitchen table. She noticed too that Oliver was grunting, sounding as if he were in pain. She stepped out onto the back porch, pulling the latex glove on with a snap.

Carefully, Zoe pulled back his hood, cautious not to turn it inside out so none of the rain water dripped onto his neck. "Okay, take the towel from your face so I can get you out of this jacket."

"Are you okay, Oliver?" Jurnee called, peeking out from the doorway.

"I... I will be. But you stay inside, okay?" Oliver grunted.

"Are you hurt?" Zoe asked, tossing the rain jacket aside. She searched him for any sign of injury, but the back porch light was dim.

Carefully, he removed his goggles and nodded.

"What? Where?" she asked, her eyes frantically searching his.

"Look down," he managed.

Oliver was standing on a piece of charred two-by-four. At first it didn't register, but then she saw the nail sticking through the top of his foot. "How did... Shit! Did rain get inside that?"

"I don't see how. I was only in... in the rain for a second. I hadn't even made it inside when the Millers' house exploded. The damn blast knocked me right off my feet." Oliver grunted and shifted his stance. "The whole place must have been filled with gas to explode like that. Anyway, I... I came running back to check on you, and I didn't see the board lying in the grass. "

"Oliver, we have to get you out of these pants and into the shower right now. And that means the nail has to come out."

Oliver nodded.

"Don't move!" Zoe said, running back inside. She grabbed a bottle of rubbing alcohol from the bathroom cabinet and returned to the porch, squatting down next to

Oliver's foot. She unscrewed the lid and dumped a quarter of the bottle's contents over the nail. Standing back up, Zoe stepped on the board. "Lift your foot. Do it as fast as you can."

"This sucks." Oliver exhaled, then took a deep breath and jerked his foot into the air. "Son of a bitch!" he shouted.

"Good. Now don't think about the pain. Get those shoes and pants off. Let's go!"

"Easy for you... you to say," Oliver said through gritted teeth. But he obeyed, cursing under his breath the whole time as he discarded everything down to his boxers, including his blood-soaked sock. When he finally looked up, his eyes met hers once more. "It's going to be okay, babe. I love you."

She wanted to scream. Didn't he understand what he'd done? "Okay, let's just get you in the shower," Zoe said, her heart racing as concern of a worst-case scenario threatened to paralyze her with fear. Please, god... please don't let him get infected... not him! She realized at that moment she still loved him... more than ever. More than she ever thought she could. Despite her suspicion of his infidelity still lingering in the back of her mind, she couldn't bear seeing Oliver become a victim to this horrible parasite. Not her Oliver.

Limping and bleeding badly, Oliver stepped across the threshold back into the laundry room. Zoe was right on his heels. To her left, Jurnee stood in the doorway to the kitchen, her eyes suddenly as wide as saucers. Zoe started to say, 'It's going to be okay,' when the little girl let out a high-pitched scream just as hands grabbed Zoe around the throat and yanked her backwards out the door and onto the porch.

She landed hard on her back. Immediately she began kicking and grabbing for purchase.

Groping hands released her throat, instead finding her

shirt collar as they pulled, dragging her backwards. "My treats! Mine!" the voice of her attacker exclaimed.

Screaming, Zoe's fingernails scraped along the porch planks, bending and snapping as she was dragged towards the edge of the porch... towards the rain.

CHAPTER 21
REFLECTIONS IN THE DARK

IT HAPPENED SO FAST. One second, Zoe was right behind him, the next, she was halfway across the porch and about to be pulled into the rain by some crazed maniac! Adrenaline surged through Oliver, the pain of his foot instantly forgotten as he stepped forward and dove, landing hard on his stomach. He grabbed Zoe by the ankle, halting her movement toward the rain.

"No! This one is mine! Get your own! Get your own!" the man from across the street shouted. Oliver remembered the guy's name was Jim, but he didn't really know this neighbor. The man was fairly new to the neighborhood. Not that it mattered now.

Jim planted his feet against the porch step and leaned back, leveraging all his weight and strength.

"Oliver!" Zoe screamed, prying at the man's hands, still trying with all she had to free herself, but it was no use.

Oliver felt himself slipping forward across the wet porch as Jim used his leverage to pull them both. In pain and not paying attention, he hadn't seen where Zoe had placed his gun. Though he probably couldn't get to it now even if he knew where it was. "No... You... Don't!" Oliver shouted, hooking his injured foot onto the doorframe in a last-ditch effort to stop himself and Zoe from being pulled further. Pain shot up his leg as the puncture wound atop his foot pressed into the doorframe, but he ignored it.

Little hands wrapped around his other ankle. "No you don't!" Jurnee repeated in a shout.

Oliver glanced back to see the brave little girl leaning back with all she had.

Despite Jurnee's efforts and his foothold on the doorframe, Oliver knew he couldn't maintain this. He was going to fail. If he didn't find a solution quickly, Zoe would be pulled off the porch and into the rain. If he let that happen, it wouldn't matter if he could free her from Jim's clutches. Dammit, if only he had his gun.

"Please, Oliver! Don't let me go!" Zoe begged.

Thunder boomed from above as a flash of red lightning lit the sky and the yard beyond. The red glow illuminated Jim's strained face and flashed in his wild, bleeding eyes. But it was the reflection from the stainless steel of Zoe's .357 holstered on her hip that caught Oliver's attention.

"I'll eat my candy right here! Right here! Right here!" Jim chanted, raising his fist.

"Zoe! Gun!"

Zoe's eyes lit with recognition as she groped for the gun at her hip.

Jim, still gripping a fistful of Zoe's shirt in one hand, slammed his raised fist down atop her head.

"Ah!" Zoe shouted, drawing the gun.

"Jurnee, close your eyes!" Oliver ordered.

"Open up!" Jim shouted, smashing his fist down again.

Zoe flipped the gun towards her feet, towards Oliver,

and then covered her head to defend against the next blow sure to come.

A surge of rage-fueled hope flooded Oliver as he let go of Zoe's ankles, grabbed the gun, and raised up onto his elbows.

Jim, no longer pulling on Zoe and instead intent on cracking her head open to get to her brains, ignored Oliver as he raised his fist high in the air. His tongue poked out in concentration, his bloody eyes focused fully on Zoe as he licked his lips in anticipation. "Mine!" he snarled.

As Jim's fist dropped for a third time, Oliver fired, shooting the crazed neighbor in the face.

Jim fell backward off the step and into the rust-colored rain.

Zoe sat up and threw herself into Oliver's arms. He hugged her, never wanting to let go. "Are you okay?"

Zoe pulled back, her eyes meeting his. "I... I think so?" she said, touching the top of her head. "Oliver?"

"Yeah?"

"I... I love you."

"I know, and I love you too, babe," he said, his own voice choked with emotion.

"Are you crying?" she asked.

"No. I'm just... my ears are ringing a bit and the pain in my foot... and I'm not sure if I'm..." He trailed off, not wanting to say what he was thinking. What he feared was likely.

Zoe pressed her lips into his, kissing him hard on the mouth and not letting go. He didn't want her to let go, but part of him wanted to pull away, to not let her put herself at risk of catching what he likely had. But he didn't pull away. He sat there in his underwear, exposed to the night air and bleeding on the back porch as a deadly storm rained down only a few feet away.

As Oliver kissed his wife, a sudden and urgent need to tell her a truth he'd been keeping from her overwhelmed him. He'd watched what happened to Sam and he knew if he didn't act now, he might lose his mind in the moments to come, and if that happened, he might never have another chance to come clean.

Oliver pulled his lips from hers and looked her in the eyes. "Zoe, I... I have to tell you something."

Behind him, a tiny voice asked, "Oliver, can I open my eyes now?"

CHAPTER 22
COMING CLEAN

ZOE SQUINTED, trying to hear Oliver's words above the ringing in her ears and the throbbing in her head.

Behind them, Jurnee stood in the doorway, looking terrified.

Oliver turned and said something.

Jurnee opened her eyes.

"Come on. It isn't safe out here, and we need to get you inside and washed off," Zoe said, pushing herself up.

Oliver nodded and stood. Together they made their way back in the house.

"Get in the shower. I'm right behind you." Zoe knelt down in front of Jurnee. "I'm going to help Oliver wash up."

"And get a Band-Aid on his foot?" she asked.

Zoe forced a smile. "Yep, and get a Band-Aid on his foot. But we're going to be right through that door in the bathroom. I'll even leave the door open. You want to finish your movie?"

"Okay. You locked the other door, right?"

"Mmm-hmm. Everything is locked up tight," she said, feeling like she might vomit. The thought of Oliver turning into... into whatever in the hell those things were was too much. She heard the shower turn on as she hurried into the living room and reset the movie for Jurnee.

In the bathroom, she undressed and climbed into the shower with Oliver. She took the Dr. Bronner's soap and filled her palm. "Turn around."

Oliver turned and she lathered his back, running her hand over the circular scar beneath his shoulder.

"Did you soap up really good?" she asked.

Oliver nodded.

"I know I didn't get any in my eyes or mouth, but I rinsed with mouthwash anyway," he said, his voice shaking.

Zoe put her arms around him. "You're okay. You're going to be okay. Do you hear me? You have to be."

"And what if I'm not?"

"Don't even say that, Oliver McCallister. How does your foot feel?" she asked.

"Like I ran a nail through it," Oliver said, turning around to face her. "I need you to lock me in the basement tonight. I'll sleep down there. It's the only—"

"What? No!" Zoe protested.

"Zoe. Listen to me. You know I'm right. You have to isolate me until we know for sure."

She hated it, but she knew it was true. "Okay, but first I need to treat that foot. Aside from pain, how does it feel? Can you wiggle your toes?"

Oliver winced and nodded.

"Any numbness?"

"No. It just hurts like hell, but honestly, it's not my biggest worry right now."

Zoe wouldn't say it out loud, but maybe it should have been. If any rainwater had gotten into that wound... No. No, she wouldn't think like that.

"How's your head?" Oliver asked.

"I'll be fine. Just a headache. He didn't break the skin."

Oliver brushed her wet braids over her shoulder and rubbed his thumb across her cheek. "Babe, are you okay?"

She shook her head, pushing back tears she didn't want him to see. "No. No, I'm far from okay." Wanting desperately to change the subject, she said, "Hey, outside you said something to me. It sounded like you wanted to tell me something, but after that gunshot I thought my ears were bleeding. And you know the really fucked-up thing? That isn't even the first time today a gun has been fired within a couple feet of my head. Can you tell me what you were trying to say?" she asked, searching his eyes.

Oliver held her stare.

"Oliver? What is it?"

"I... I know you texted Sam."

Zoe's breath caught, but she didn't say anything. She didn't need to say anything. Sam must have told him before she... before she turned.

"There's something I need to tell you, Zoe, and I know you're going to be upset, but—"

"Stop," she said, putting a hand on his chest.

Oliver frowned. "But, Zoe, I need to get this off my chest before—"

"Stop." Just an hour ago, she would have given anything to know who Oliver had been cheating with. She would have given anything for him to just be fucking honest and tell the truth. To explain how he could have betrayed her with god knows who. And wasn't it just convenient for him to want to unload this crap on her now on the worst freaking day of her entire life. "No, Oliver. Not now, I can't take this now! Now that the world is ending and you think you might die, you want to come clean? What about me? Do you ever think about me? You couldn't have told me all this before?" Water ran hot over her back as steam rose between them. Zoe felt herself becoming more and more angry. "You know what? Fine! Let's do this on your terms, you selfish asshole! Who is she? Who were you fucking, Oliver?"

CHAPTER 23
BROKEN PROMISES

THIS WASN'T how Oliver had planned to tell Zoe the secret he'd been keeping for all these months. Now, as he stood in the hot water holding his naked wife in his arms, he stared at her dumbly. Hindsight being twenty-twenty, he realized Zoe was right. It wasn't fair to do this now. But what if he didn't have tomorrow? He didn't want to die with this secret between them.

"Well! Who is she? How long has this been going on?" Zoe asked, pushing him back and crossing her arms over her breasts.

He'd been so stupid. All this time, him being so secret, pushing her away. He had nearly driven them to a divorce. Looking into Zoe's eyes, he understood just how bad it really was. Left with no answers, she'd been forced to draw her own conclusions. A huge smile spread across his face.

"Are you fucking smiling?" Zoe asked in disbelief.

Oliver nodded.

Zoe stared at him like she might actually punch him in the face.

Oliver held up his hands in surrender. "I'm smiling because as pissed at me as I feared you would be when you found out why I was really coming home late all this time, it never even occurred to me you would think I was having an affair. You're right, Zo, I'm an asshole. But you're wrong too. I never cheated on you. I would *never* cheat on you!"

"What? Then... I don't understand." Frantically, Zoe's eyes searched his. "If not cheating, then what have you been keeping from me?" she asked, her tone skeptical.

Oliver nodded. "I know. Listen to me. When we lost the baby and I saw how bad you were hurting, I would have done anything... anything to take away your pain. I knew how bad you wanted a baby and I did too, but with your school and my income, paying for in vitro was impossible."

"Oliver, what did you do?" Zoe asked.

"I took on a sort of second job, and that's what I've been keeping from you."

"A second job? A second job you couldn't tell me about? What job would you keep from me and why?" But before Oliver could answer, her eyes lit with realization. "Repo? Have you been working for Georgie?"

Oliver pressed his lips into a tight line and nodded.

"Goddammit! Getting gunned down once wasn't enough for you? You remember when you asked me to marry you from that hospital bed? I had one condition! One thing you had to swear to never do!"

"I know, but—"

"No 'but,' Oliver! You promised you would never work high-asset repo again – or any repo, for that matter! So that's it? You've been moonlighting for Georgie?"

"It's the only way I could get us the money we needed for in vitro."

"I never asked for it! I never would have wanted you to risk your life for this, so don't you stand here and tell me you did this for me! Admit the truth. You did this for yourself!"

That wasn't completely true, but she wasn't wrong either. He did take the job to raise the money that would give them another chance at having a baby. But there was another part of him that longed for the work. He wasn't just good at repoing high assets – he was the best. It didn't matter if the assets were planes, yachts, high-end luxury cars – if you wanted it repossessed, Oliver would locate it and secure it. There had been only one exception to his perfect track record. One nearly fatal mistake that had almost cost him his life. The memory of burning lead ripping through his body still haunted him. But she was right. He missed the adrenaline rush.

Oliver reached past her and shut off the water. "I'm sorry, Zoe, but isn't this better than finding out I cheated on you?"

Zoe stepped out onto the floor mat and lifted two towels from their respective hangers, throwing one at Oliver before wrapping the other around herself. Eyes wet with tears, she said, "You may not have cheated, but you broke a promise, and worse, you lied to me."

"I know, and I'm sorry. But I wanted to surprise you with the money to get the in vitro. You know how expensive this is?"

"Oliver, I don't want to talk about this anymore."

"Are you really going to leave it like this?"

"You left me wondering what I'd done wrong. Questioning my worth as your wife! As your lover! You let me think the worst! And now you think because you didn't fuck someone else, I should just be okay?"

"But—"

"I need time to process this – time to think, and honestly, we have bigger things to worry about," she said, looking down at his foot. "C'mon, we need to get you bandaged up. We can't let it get infected."

Zoe was right. It wasn't like he could go to the doctor, not now and from what he could tell, not for the foreseeable future. "Okay," he said, reaching for her. "Just know that I love you and I never meant to hurt you."

"What you did – lying to me like this, thinking that you would just do what you want and ask for forgiveness later – it isn't okay, Oliver. What if... what if you had gotten killed?" She pulled her T-shirt over her head. "Did you ever think how I would feel getting a call you had been shot or killed god only knows how? No, of course you didn't. Because you only think about yourself. Listen, I said I don't want to do this right now."

He didn't want to let the moment end this way. "Zo. You remember the night we met? We were at that karaoke place on Fifth Street. You were with friends from work."

"And you were there for a bachelor party. Of course I remember. You were singing."

"I came down off the stage and sang to you. Do you remember the song?"

"Oliver, where is this going?"

"Please?"

Zoe crossed her arms again. "It was INXS, 'Never Tear Us Apart.'"

Oliver smiled. "That's right. I saw you in the crowd and I knew instantly I was meant to sing you that song, meant to be with you forever. I walked right up to you, took your hand, and sang to you. Look, I fucked up, okay? I admit it, but we're not going let this tear us apart, right?"

He reached for her hand just like he had that night over eight years ago, but she pulled away, snatching a clean pair of sweats off the toilet and tossing them to him.

"I do remember, Oliver. I remember you sang that if you hurt me, you'd make wine from my tears... Well, all you've done is make me cry." Her voice cracked as her eyes welled up.

Oliver's heart clenched. "Oh, Zo. I never meant to..."

"No. You never do." Zoe straightened and wiped her eyes. "Now come on, get dressed and come to the kitchen where you can sit down and I can work on your foot."

Oliver sighed. *Damn,* he thought. He knew his wife well enough to know pushing her any further would only end badly. She needed space, and he needed to let her have it. Plus, she was right. He glanced down at his swollen foot and the reddish-black puncture wound. "Okay, babe," he said in surrender, pulling on the sweats, careful not to let the cuff drag across the wound. The damn thing hurt like hell, but it was nothing compared to being shot through the shoulder.

Zoe was stoic now, all emotion buried back inside. "When was the last time you had a tetanus shot?"

"Seriously? Tetanus is the last thing I'm worried about."

"You'll be pretty worried when your jaw locks up and you get muscle spasms and a fever. Untreated, tetanus can kill you." Zoe's tone was matter-of-fact.

"Less than two years ago, when I cut my arm open on that broken mayonnaise jar at work."

Zoe nodded in recollection. "That's right. Turn this way and let me see your eyes."

Oliver did as his wife asked. She was now treating him more like a patient than a worried lover. "Clear? Because I feel... normal."

"Clear. Now check mine," she said.

Oliver frowned. He hadn't even thought of the possibility that Zoe could be infected, but she had been close to the edge of the porch and that asshole from across the street had beaten her over the head with his bare fist. Oliver squinted, staring into Zoe's brown eyes. They were red, but more like you would expect of someone who'd just been crying. He remembered how bad Sam's eyes had looked, and over such a short period of thirty minutes. Zoe's looked nothing like Sam's had.

"Well?" she asked.

"Oh, sorry. No, your eyes look fine."

"Are you sure? Why in the hell did it take you so long to answer?" she asked looking into the mirror.

"I was thinking about Sam, and what her eyes had looked like before..." Oliver started but couldn't find the words to finish. "Anyway, yours look fine."

Zoe seemed to soften. "I'm sorry about Sam, Oliver."

"Me too," he said.

She hugged him. "Go to the kitchen. I'll grab supplies and be right there."

Trying not to put weight on his foot, Oliver limped into the kitchen. In the front room, he heard *Fantasia* playing on the television and Jurnee giggling. "You sure drink a lot, Louie. Good thing they have you to clean up this mess!"

Oliver frowned, hurrying around the corner. "Oh, come on!" he shouted.

"What's wrong?" Zoe asked, appearing next to him with bandages and the bottle of rubbing alcohol. Zoe gasped, the bottle slipping from her hand. "Louie, no!" she shouted.

Oliver's eyes followed the steady stream of dripping water to the cracked skylight above, and immediately he understood what his wife must have already known. They were too late. Louie stood in the center of the room, lapping at a puddle of rust-colored water pooling beneath the skylight.

CHAPTER 24
UNDEAD OR ZOMBIES

"JURNEE, please tell me you didn't touch that water, did you?" Zoe asked, her heart pounding as she pulled Louie away from the growing puddle.

"Nuh-uh. No way! I'm not drinking water from the floor!"

Oliver shuffled into the living room with a towel and a large stockpot.

"Oliver, careful not to touch the water! And for god's sake, keep that foot back," she said, taking the towel and the pot from him. "Here, just get Louie back," she said, trying not to let the tears fall as her own emotions threatened to overwhelm her and take control.

She dropped the towel over the puddle and then ran to the laundry room.

"What are you doing?" Oliver called after her.

"Getting bleach!" she shouted back. She grabbed the gallon jug from the shelf above the washer, then a roll of paper towels and a pair of gloves off the kitchen table. She set the bleach down, donned the gloves, and poured several cups' worth into the pot. She bagged the towel and splashed bleach over the wet area, sopping it up with the paper before sliding the pot with bleach into place.

Turning back to Oliver, she met his eyes with a knowing look. Louie sat next to Oliver, obediently watching as his tail wagged happily.

"We have to put him in his kennel until we know for sure," Oliver said.

Louie had been a gift from Oliver shortly after they lost the baby. At first, she had been pissed Oliver had got her a dog. She felt like he was saying, 'Hey, I know we just lost the one thing in the world you wanted more than anything but here's a puppy to make up for it.' But over time, she had become attached to Louie, and in a sense he was like a child. Now she couldn't imagine the blue-nose pit not being part of the family. Her stomach ached at the thought that she might not only lose Oliver to this madness, but she was also most certainly going to lose Louie.

The tears Zoe had managed to hold back would no longer be stifled. She had been through too much, and this was the last straw. A sob broke from her and she bolted for the bedroom, slamming the door behind her. She ran and threw herself onto the bed like a child, burying her face in her pillow and sobbing.

She lay there on her stomach, crying her heart out. It wasn't just Louie. It was the courthouse. It was Deandre. It was Angel. It was not knowing if Oliver was infected. Then there was Jurnee. How in the hell was she supposed to get this girl home? What if there was no one in her family left alive? What if Oliver got sick? How was she supposed to do this without him? Part of her was so pissed at Oliver right now. Running over there and putting himself at risk all for a freaking phone that probably wouldn't have worked anyway! And then there was what he'd dropped on her in the shower. She should have been happy her husband wasn't cheating on her after all, but that didn't change the fact he'd lied. He'd still betrayed her, but in a different way. She took a deep breath and tried to calm herself. Right now, she couldn't think about that crap because the other part of her, the biggest part, just prayed he would be okay. And on top of all of it, her dog was probably infected!

Oliver appeared in the doorway. "Babe? Are you okay?"

She sat up and wiped her eyes. "Where's Louie?"

"In his kennel."

"And Jurnee?"

"Enthralled with Mickey Mouse."

She sighed. "I'm sorry I ran out of there, it's just..."

"You don't have to explain. This whole thing is insane," Oliver said, shifting his weight.

Zoe pushed herself off the bed. "Oh, Oliver. Your foot! I totally forgot."

"It's okay. It isn't even bleeding anymore," he said, forcing an unconvincing smile.

It wasn't okay at all. What the hell was she doing in here crying when there was so much to do? There was no time for this. *Suck it up and get to work,* she told herself, pushing herself off the bed. "C'mon. Go to the kitchen and sit down."

Oliver smiled again, and this time it seemed more genuine. "Thanks, babe."

"You won't be thanking me when I pour rubbing alcohol over that puncture wound," she said, following him out of the bedroom.

"You seem a little too happy about this." He gave her a backwards glance.

"Me?" She forced a laugh as she pulled on a fresh pair of gloves.

Oliver eased himself down in the kitchen chair as Zoe stared into his eyes. She pressed her thumb against his eyelid and lifted one, then the other.

"Well?"

"They still look clear, so far," she said, unscrewing the cap from the bottle of rubbing alcohol. She wanted to lay into him again about how reckless and stupid venturing over to the neighbors' was, but as she stared into his eyes, she saw something. Even though his eyes showed no sign of bleeding or irritation, they were full of something else. Oliver could try and play it off like he was fine, but his eyes were windows to a truth he couldn't hide. He was frightened. More than frightened. He was scared shitless. Going off on him now wouldn't do anything that he wasn't already doing to himself.

"It's been over an hour. It happened a lot faster for Sam," Oliver said, his voice full of ten emotions at once.

Zoe nodded as the horrible memories of earlier in the day flashed through her mind. "Yeah, I watched several in the courthouse turn, and I don't think it took any longer than thirty minutes for them to start acting strange. Here," she said, handing him a clean washcloth. "You might want to bite down on this." She lifted his foot. "Damn, Ollie, it's really swollen."

"Just do it."

She poured the alcohol over his foot.

Oliver grimaced, squeezing his eyes tight. "Ugh!"

"I told you it was going to hurt. Now, I need to wipe it, and that's going to hurt too. Then we'll add some Neosporin and get it covered."

"You said you watched them turn... turn into zombies or lose their minds?"

"Still with the zombies, Oliver? Really?" she asked, her

face skeptical as she carefully placed a Band-Aid over the puncture on the top of his foot, then the one on the bottom, and began to wrap his foot with gauze.

"Look, I know zombies don't fit into your medical definitions, but you did notice, right?"

She stopped and looked up at him. "What exactly are you asking me?"

"Okay," he started. "For now, forget the word zombie. Just think about it from a medical perspective. When I was with Sam and she started to act differently, she could still think and talk, yet she wanted to..." Oliver paused, glancing toward the front room where Jurnee lay on the couch watching TV. Lowering his voice, he continued, "To eat Jurnee's brains. It started slowly, with a smell, and she complained about being hungry, starving. For Sam, talking about food and hunger was completely out of character for her. Then even when she went full-on psycho, she was still talking... still thinking. But then when I kicked her backward out of the truck, she landed on her head. I'm sure that fall should have killed her, and now, reflecting back on it, I'm sure it did. But she came back. Her head was bleeding badly and her neck was twisted horribly, like it was broken. Sam never spoke after that. She only moaned, Zo." Oliver closed his eyes and shook his head as if with this simple gesture he could shake away the horrible memory. "My god, when she moaned... It was... it was awful. It was an undead moan. "

"Oliver, you can't be ser—"

"Hold on. Just stay with me here. At the church, they were all dead when I got there. Don't you see?"

Zoe's eyebrows bunched. "See what?"

"The undead ones don't talk. Once they're really dead, they change from thinking and speaking crazy people to...

well, to undead. And they have only one mission – eat the living. You're looking at me like I'm crazy, but I know I'm right. At the church, a man with half a face and one eye missing smashed through an office window with his face... his face. Then there was this woman." Oliver closed his eyes at the memory. "I broke her neck, Zo. Like... bad. Way worse than Sam's. The church lady couldn't even lift her head off her shoulder, but still she came on, mouth snapping open and closed. How? How is that medically possible?"

Zoe finished the gauze wrap, her frown deepening as she replayed what she'd seen in the courthouse. Deandre had called them zombies too, and that man, Chuck, Deandre had shot him in the chest. He was dead – for sure dead. Then he vanished. At the time, she hadn't wanted to believe he could have left the atrium of his own accord. Then there was Tom, and then Deandre himself. Once they had seemingly died, they stopped talking – instead, they... they moaned. Oliver was right. Once they had died and then became... well, undead, they seemed focused on one thing... consuming brains. It was like their cognitive skills were limited to this singular activity.

"I see the wheels spinning. What are you thinking?"

"I think the parasite can keep the human host functioning unless the brain is destroyed. I don't know how it does it, nor do I know why the parasite needs brains, but clearly there's something in brain tissue the parasite requires, and it will make the host do anything and everything to get it what it needs."

"So it infects and controls the mind first, and then when the person dies, it controls their whole body?" Oliver frowned.

Nodding, Zoe finished the wrap and tore a piece of medical tape free from the roll. "Yes, I mean I have no idea how the parasite is doing it, but yes. That has to be it!" She started to stand and then paused, sitting back on her heels.

"What is it?"

"Knowing how they become..."

"Zombies," Oliver finished.

Zoe's eyebrows bunched. "I was going to say undead."

Oliver shrugged. "In zombie movies, that's literally the definition of a zombie."

Zoe shook her head, hating the word zombie. She didn't know why, but it still sounded so ridiculous to her. "Whatever you want to call them. What I was going to say is that knowing this isn't really that helpful. I need to look at the rain under the microscope, and now I can," she said, pushing herself up. "We have rain dripping from the skylight."

"Right! Good call," Oliver agreed.

On the kitchen table sat the microscope, the kit that came with it, the samples from earlier, and Zoe's first aid kit. Rifling through her supplies, she retrieved a sterile test tube. This would work fine for capturing a sample, she thought, as movement from the corner of her eye caught her attention. She looked down at the old samples. Two syringes sat side-by-side, one filled with water, one filled with blood drawn from Mr. Henderson.

Zoe froze, staring at the blood-filled syringe. She could have sworn...

The blood swirled and the syringe moved.

CHAPTER 25
ANSWERS

ZOE BACKPEDALED, gasping and falling into Oliver's lap.

Instinctively, Oliver's hand went to her waist, steadying her. "What happened?"

"You didn't see that?"

"See what?" he asked, glancing over her shoulder and scanning the table. He didn't see anything.

Zoe pointed. "The syringe with the blood in it. It moved!"

Zoe stood and Oliver pushed himself up. He reached forward, lifting the blood-filled syringe from the table.

"Be careful," she whispered as if she were afraid to startle whatever was inside.

Oliver examined the tiny syringe. He didn't see anything at first, but then the blood seemed to ripple. "What the hell?" He watched as something tiny and silver slipped along the glass and then vanished again.

"They grew," she said.

"Yeah, and there's more than one in there. Look. See that?" He held the syringe up to the light above the table.

"The others are smaller though. I wonder what that means?" His thoughts drifted back to the pungent maggots he'd frequently encountered at his job. Maggots don't stay maggots. They change into flies. Were these things only growing... or were they changing?

"Survival of the fittest?" She shrugged. "Maybe the larger ones are feeding on the smaller ones? Maybe they will consume each other until there is only one left. Ollie, this is huge. They've been in that syringe for – what? – a little over an hour, and they've gone from microscopic to visible with the naked eye! Clearly they're thriving in human blood and growing at an exponential rate."

Oliver marveled at his wife's ability to be excited about the growth rates of an alien parasite. The thought of it scared the shit out of him. Hadn't she seen the movie *Alien*? Carefully, he set the syringe back on the table. "Now what?"

"Rain sample."

"Right."

Oliver stood, careful not to put pressure on his right foot. Following her into the living room, he stifled a yawn as Zoe held a test tube beneath the dripping ceiling.

"You look exhausted," Zoe said, appearing to fight back a yawn of her own.

Following her back to the kitchen, Oliver topped off his coffee. "I am exhausted and so are you, but I know there's no stopping you until you've figured this out. You want some more coffee?"

"Thanks, I'm good. But, hey, are you sure you don't want to try and get some sleep?"

Oliver shook his head. "Not a chance. Tired as I am, there's no way I could go to sleep, not until I'm one hundred percent sure I'm okay. Besides, I want to mess with the radio some more, see if I can find a station broadcasting something other than that damn recording."

While Zoe went to work looking at samples, Oliver sat next to her at the kitchen table and messed with the radio. It was no use. There were even fewer stations playing the emergency alert than before, and there were no new communications. His and Sam's favorite rock station had gone completely off the air. The local country music station was still repeating the same message between what could only have been prerecorded commercials, two of which seemed to play with the most frequency. One was an ad for huge cost savings for Illinois residents if they converted their home to solar, and the other was for an upcoming concert featuring Bubba Phats at the River City Civic Center on October twenty-eighth for "one hell of a good night of boot-stomping country hits." *Yeah, well, I think your show's canceled, Bubba.*

He also found three stations on the AM side playing the broadcast, including the National Public Radio station. Not a good sign. If NPR was broadcasting the same message, then this had to be countrywide. That meant his sister, Sarah, and Zoe's friend Alexis along with her parents were all likely... Well, he didn't want to think about it. Nothing he could do for them right now.

None of the AM stations were playing commercials either, so he flipped it back to the country station. The solar commercial was playing again. Idly, Oliver wondered why this station had commercials running and the others didn't? Was the country station more automated? Did it really matter? No. Not one bit. But an idea was forming. One he hadn't fully worked out and wasn't ready to share with Zoe... not yet. He needed to think it through.

Pulling a long sip of coffee from his mug, he pushed the radio aside. "Learn anything new?"

"Yeah, actually I did. They are alive in the rain sample but die quickly after I place them on the slide. Could be a number of reasons they're dying."

"Like?"

"Well, like a change in temp," she offered.

"But wouldn't the fall through the atmosphere have killed them then? I mean the temps change drastically between our atmosphere and the ground level."

"True," she said, pursing her lips in thought. "I'm still leaning toward exposure."

"Exposure in what way?" Oliver asked, switching off the radio.

Zoe pulled a slide and replaced it with another. "I presume it's the makeup of our atmosphere. If I'm right, they have a limited time to find a host."

"That's a good thing! But if that's the case, how do they survive the fall through the atmosphere?"

"Strangely, it's the rain itself. It isn't rain at all. I mean it is, but it isn't only rain. There's water but there's also another substance in the rain I can't identify. Some sort of liquid coating."

"Liquid coating?" Oliver asked.

"Like an amniotic fluid protecting the parasites."

"I have no idea what that means," Oliver admitted.

"Well, I'm not even sure that's what this is, but it reminds me of the fluid that protects a fetus. Now that I've taken a close look and worked with the liquid, it does have this sort of viscous motion to it," she said.

Oliver smiled.

"What's funny?" she asked.

"You're just so damn smart is all."

Zoe narrowed her eyes. "Are you trying to kiss ass because you know how pissed I am?"

"What? No. I was just... Look, it was just a compliment," Oliver said, already regretting he'd said anything at all.

Zoe smiled, but her smile was ornery.

"Oh, you're messing with me, aren't you?" he asked, with a smirk.

"No. I'm still really pissed," she said, pressing her eyes back onto the eyepiece.

Oliver swallowed, unsure what to say next. Say the wrong thing and a fight could ensue, and he was too damn tired and stressed. Instead, he peered down into his coffee, swirling the mug in a tiny circular motion. "So now what?"

Zoe sighed. "I think I've learned all I can from the rain sample. Now I think we test my theory."

"Test your theory? How do we do that?"

Zoe picked up the syringe with Mr. Henderson's blood. "We expose this to the atmosphere and see if they die."

Oliver's eyes went wide. "You want to let those things loose?"

Zoe shook her head. "Not let them loose. I'm talking about a controlled environment."

Oliver dragged both hands down his face. The adrenaline had long worn off and exhaustion had set in. He was tired and irritable, and his foot was throbbing. He wanted nothing more than to say, 'Babe, can we do this in the morning? I am so tired and Jurnee will probably wake up early,' but he could see she was in the zone. "Okay. So what's the plan?"

"Right. I'm going to remove the needle because the parasites are too big to pass through now. Then I'll put one-third in a test tube with nothing, one-third in a test tube with water, and we can leave the remaining one-third in the syringe."

"Why leave any?"

"Because we know they're alive in the blood, at least for now, and I want to see if they change any further over the next few hours."

Oliver yawned again. The coffee apparently wasn't doing shit to keep him awake.

"Go lie down, Oliver. I'll wake you up if I find anything. I promise," she said, placing the cap back over the needle and then unscrewing the needle hub from the lock.

Tired as he was, and despite the fact Zoe knew what she was doing, Oliver was reluctant to leave her alone with those things. Instead, he watched as she prepared to add some of the blood from the syringe into the pond water. As she pressed down on the plunger, blood squirted into the test tube, diluting as it swirled in the water.

Oliver leaned in, now able to see the silver parasites as they swam through the bloodstained water. "Wow, there must be a dozen of them! They look about, what, two millimeters long?"

"Yeah. I'd say that's about right, but there were probably thousands when they were microscopic," Zoe whispered in fascination. "Look! They've stopped swimming. They're... writhing."

Oliver squinted. "They're dying is what they're doing!"

"Okay, let's try a sample with no water," she said, squirting another two-thirds into an empty test tube, then corking it. "There. That's three-quarters air and one-quarter blood."

Oliver watched curiously as she tipped the tube back and forth carefully, letting the blood coat the inside and mix with the air.

Holding the corked test tube horizontally, she said, "See there. They're moving along the glass."

Zoe was right. The bastards were crawling along the blood-slicked glass like little toothy centipedes. Then, like the ones in the water, they stopped crawling and began squirming.

"Same as the water! They're dying," Oliver announced.

"I can't say this with certainty, but from this experiment I think we can say with some confidence that these things can't live long without a host. They essentially need to land on a host. If they don't, the elements will kill them quickly."

"That means we have a chance! A chance that once this rain finally stops for good, the spread will slow!"

Zoe nodded. "Maybe, but we have another test we need to perform. And if this test fails, I don't think humanity has a chance."

"What test?"

"I would like to look at the blood of an exposed animal. And now that we know the sample from the leaking skylight had live parasites in it..."

"Louie?" Oliver asked.

"Have you checked on him since you put him in the crate?"

"No, and I haven't heard a peep." Oliver pushed himself up from the kitchen chair to go check, but then he paused. "Hold on a second. You're not going to try and draw blood from Louie... are you?"

Zoe lifted her mug of coffee toward her lips and then stopped. "Well, yeah. That's what I was thinking."

"Zoe, have you ever drawn blood from a dog?"

"No, but I've seen it done. They usually pull from a vein in the lower leg."

"Let me check on him first, and if he seems normal,

maybe you don't need to look at his blood. If he's bleeding from the eyes, then I think we know all we need to know."

Zoe pressed her eyes together and Oliver realized she was fighting back tears.

"I'm sorry, Zo. Look, stay here and let me go see what we're dealing with," he said, flipping on the light in the mudroom. Once inside, he knelt next to Louie's crate. "Hey boy, how are you feeling, huh?"

Louie stood up inside his crate, his tail wagging and tongue hanging out.

Oliver stared at the dog's eyes. Eyes that were clear and normal. "You okay, pal?"

Louie whined and licked at the cage. He looked normal enough. Oliver smiled. "Zo, he looks fine."

"You sure?" she asked.

Oliver could hear her chair sliding out from the table and the wood floor creaking as she approached the door.

"I'm sure. But let's keep him in his crate tonight and by morning we should be positive, right?"

"No, not positive. We don't know how this might manifest inside a dog. It could take longer. But if he still seems himself in the morning, let's draw some blood and be sure," she said, her face a visage of worry.

"Fair enough," Oliver said, taking his wife's hand. He forced a smile, not because he felt like smiling but because he felt like she needed to see it. "Zo, it's going to be okay."

"How, Oliver? How is any of this going to be okay?" she asked, tears spilling down her cheeks.

Oliver squeezed her hand. "Because we have each other, and as long as we have each other, we will get through this. Hey, it's been almost two hours since I was exposed. I think by now..." Brightening, he said, "You think I'm okay?"

"I think you must be. No one I've seen has taken this long to change." Zoe smiled through her tears.

"So, you think I can sleep with you tonight?" he asked shyly, as if he were asking for the first time. If she didn't feel safe, he wouldn't argue, but he hoped so much that he wouldn't have to sleep alone. After everything that had happened, he didn't want to be by himself.

Zoe met his eyes, her head slowly bobbing up and down. "I'd like that, Oliver. I'd like that a lot."

CHAPTER 26
SHAKESPEAREAN NIGHTMARES

ZOE FLAILED as a greasy face appeared from the darkness. Parts of the cheeks were missing, revealing teeth that gnashed and ground, caked in bits of flesh. The man's mouth, void of lips, did nothing to prevent bits of grey matter from spilling and rolling down his chin. In her horror, Zoe recognized the too-familiar face as it glowed white as dead coral from the blackness... white as a ghost. The undead face was Tom's. The slight, balding clerk from the courthouse. Closer he came, teeth gnashing and grinding, brains squishing and spewing. More and more spilled like vomit from Tom's mouth. An impossible amount. Chunky brains, wet and dripping like oatmeal.

Undead Tom leaned in close.

Zoe pushed back into something... a wall? Everything else was black except Tom. He was leaning over her now. There was nowhere to go. No escape.

Bits of brain were falling onto her lap... filling her lap!

Tom bent closer and closer still, his brain breath washing over her like something spoiled. He tried to talk, but no words came, only a full-mouthed moan. "MMMM... SSSSSS... TAAAA!"

Tom reached with bloody fingers, his lipless smile longing for her. Longing for her brains.

From somewhere in the darkness, a woman's scream. "Help me, Zoe! Don't let them eat me! Don't let them eat my brains!"

"Angel! Angel, please! I'm sorry!" she cried out.

Zoe looked down to find her lap filled with brains. But now they weren't brains at all! Something was wrong! The chunky oatmeal was moving, squirming in her lap! Toothy worms wriggled like maggots. She screamed. "No! Get them off of me! Oh please! Please god!"

Tom choked out a laugh as more and more parasites spilled from the balding man's mouth.

"Get it off!" she shouted again.

Tom grabbed her, shaking her shoulders. Laughing and shouting, "Wake up, Zoe! Wake up!" But it was no longer Tom's voice, and it was no longer Tom's undead face puking into her lap!

"No! Oliver, please! Not you! Not you!"

Undead Oliver coughed and retched, and his eyes popped out and dangled from their retinas like two dice hanging from a car's rearview mirror. From the now hollowed sockets came more and more gooey parasites, falling in chunks like sausage from a meat grinder. "No! Please! No!" she cried.

Undead Oliver's face sloughed off to reveal a laughing skull. Undead Oliver lifted his skull from his shoulders and held it out to face himself.

The voice changed then. Still Oliver's but with an English accent. "Alas, poor Yorick! I knew him, Horatio, a fellow of infinite jest, of most excellent fancy. He hath borne me on his back a thousand times, and now, how abhorred in my imagination it is! My gorge rises at it. Here hung those lips that I have kissed I know not how oft."

Hamlet? The undead Oliver was reciting *Hamlet*?

The skull spun in his palm to face Zoe now, shouting at her through an overflowing mouthful of writhing worms, spilling and spitting from the skull's mouth. "Zoe, it's okay! You're okay!"

Zoe's eyes sprang open. She gasped and flailed, swiping her hands across her hips. "Get them off!" she shouted, launching herself upright.

"You're okay, babe. Just breathe," Oliver said.

"What happened? Did you have a bad dream?" Jurnee's tiny voice asked from somewhere near her.

Zoe felt around, realizing she wasn't covered in parasites. She wasn't in her bed, either. She was on a couch. Exhaling with some relief, she drew in a steady breath, trying to bring her breathing under control. "I'm sorry. I... I mean yes, it was just a dream, hon. Go back to sleep."

Near her, she heard Jurnee moving closer. The little girl cuddled up next to her. "Do you want to hold Princess?" Jurnee asked.

"Thank you, but I think I'm okay now," she said, feeling her racing heart slow.

"Okay," the little girl said, pulling her doll to her chest and rolling onto her side.

After they'd finished in the kitchen, they had made the decision to sleep in the basement. Random gunfire, screams, and even a series of explosions had reminded Zoe of the neighborhood on the Fourth of July. Except it wasn't the Fourth of July, and when a random bullet hit the house, the decision to sleep downstairs seemed the safest choice.

She had also foregone the idea of locking Oliver away

from them. She figured the hours that had gone by with no symptoms meant he was not infected, and so they took a chance and decided to sleep together. They did leave Louie in his crate. After all, he had clearly drunk the water from the leaking ceiling, and Zoe knew for a fact the water had contained live parasites.

The basement couch wasn't the ideal arrangement, but at least it was a sectional, so despite it not being the most comfortable to sleep on, it had plenty of room to spread out. Initially, she and Oliver had tried to convince Jurnee to sleep on the small twin in the spare bedroom, but the little girl wasn't having it. Zoe couldn't blame her for not wanting to sleep alone. She didn't want to be alone either, and so they all ended up together on the couch.

Waking up to Oliver's calming voice was the best gift this morning could have offered. "Oliver?" she whispered.

"Yeah?"

"Are you feeling okay?"

"Sure, just freaking hungry."

Zoe's heart skipped a beat and she felt her throat constrict. "Hungry?"

"Yeah, I mean with everything going on, I hardly ate anything yesterday, and now I feel like I'm starving. What I wouldn't give for a stack of pancakes right about now."

Zoe let out a breath and hugged Oliver tight as she ever had.

"Wow, what was that for?" he asked.

"I'm just glad you're okay. Hey, what time is it?"

Oliver shifted next to her, turning and reaching. A moment later, his iPad lit up. "Five thirty."

Next to her, Jurnee's breathing became steady, a sure sign she had fallen back asleep.

"I don't think we have any pancake mix, but you want some eggs and bacon?" Zoe whispered.

"You serious? Aren't you tired? We were up past midnight."

"I don't want to go back to sleep. Really, I'm wide awake now," she said, carefully slipping out from under the blanket.

"Well, let me help." He rolled onto his side and sat up. "I want to check on Louie anyway."

The fact that Louie's health might determine the fate of humanity wasn't lost on Zoe. If this parasite affected animals like it did humans, humanity might be doomed.

Upstairs, they peered into his crate as he whimpered and wagged his tail excitedly.

"Look, he's okay. I can let him out," Oliver said.

"Wait! Not until I look at his blood."

"But he seems fine," Oliver argued. "And he needs to go out."

"Oliver, he could be a carrier. I need to know his blood is clean before I'm comfortable."

"Well, we better do that before breakfast or he's going to freak out."

Louie's blood turned out to be clear, but that didn't mean the parasites weren't living in his stomach. Zoe couldn't test for that, but she was able to check his saliva and collect a stool sample when Ollie finally took him out. Both were negative for the parasite. It seemed humanity might have a chance after all, as long as they could survive each other.

The sky, too, was clear. Clear and blue, all signs of the red rain clouds gone.

"Thank god for blue skies," Oliver said.

But the blue skies weren't to last. Over the next two days, red rain showers blew in and out sporadically, often with little warning. Zoe worried that Jurnee would continue to ask about going home, but she didn't. Perhaps she intuitively understood they had no way to take her home and phones weren't an option. She wondered if the little girl knew on some level that something bad had happened to her mom. Zoe didn't ask, and Jurnee never mentioned it.

Jurnee's favorite pastime was watching Disney movies. By the end of the first full day they had completed a Disney marathon. She already knew all the character names and was intent on memorizing the lines. The rest of the time, Jurnee seemed to enjoy playing thinking games, like Chutes and Ladders and Go Fish. Oliver was even teaching her how to play chess when he wasn't peering out the holes he'd drilled in the plywood-covered windows, inventorying supplies, or messing with the radio.

At least a dozen times a day, he would scroll the AM and FM stations, but as of this morning only one country station continued broadcasting. Nothing but a couple commercials and the same old recording. *Stay inside. Help is coming...* yada yada. Zoe was beginning to feel like this whole thing was much worse than they could ever have imagined. On the bright side, at least the power somehow remained working and the water continued to run from the faucet. Oliver had even taken a barrel and filled it from the tap, anticipating that eventually their luck would run out.

Unfortunately, the internet remained out. If only she could just google what the hell was happening out there. It was like they'd jumped back in time a hundred years overnight. No internet, no television, no radio, no phones.

As for her, when not helping Oliver or watching movies or playing games with Jurnee, she was lost in thought. It was weird, all this time to think. It was also weird not having her face stuffed in a book studying for hours on end or racing through a nursing shift at the hospital. With all this time to think, she considered the parasite and what it was doing to the world. Her thoughts drifted to Alexis; was she alive, dead, or undead? Images of her friend turned zombie invaded her thoughts. Her friend was out there either hiding from the madness, or worse... becoming part of it.

She also thought about Oliver, his secret, and all the lies he'd told her to keep it. She wondered: If this hadn't happened and she found out, what would be different? Would she have left him? Would she have stormed out of the house right back to Bloomridge and into a Holiday Inn? She knew a few girls from school she could have stayed with. Maybe she would have just booted Oliver out. He was the liar. He could go sleep in the hotel! She honestly didn't know what she would have done. But here she was, forced to stay whether she liked it or not. The more she thought about it, the angrier she got. He'd betrayed her. She still didn't know what to do or how to feel. Could she even love him after all this? It was all just too much to think about. She wished she could call Alexis to talk. She'd always had Alexis, and now that was gone.

Around noon on the second day, Oliver tore himself away from the front room window and said, "Zoe, we need to talk about food."

Zoe pulled herself away from her thoughts. "Okay, what are you thinking?" she asked, knowing that with water still functioning and some in storage, their biggest concern was food. They didn't have much to begin with, and they were now feeding three.

"Well, I think the rains have slowed enough for me to venture to the neighbors'. This time, I can go in the daylight. Even if a storm blows in, I'll see it coming in time to get back."

"I don't know, Ollie. It seems like a huge risk. We don't know what's happening out there, but we know there're still a lot of people in the neighborhood." The gunshots and screams hadn't slowed over the past two days, and all day yesterday the house smelled like a fireplace as smoke blew across their yard from somewhere up the road.

"We might have enough food for two more days. But look, whether we wait two days or I go now, we can't stay in this house forever."

She knew he was right. They could make it a few more days, but the food selection would start getting pretty rough. They'd finished off the eggs yesterday, and all that was left were some freeze-dried rations and canned beans. With her being in school, she and Oliver hadn't been doing their best at grocery shopping. It was a kind of a fly-by-the-seat-of-your-pants approach with very little planning or forethought from day to day.

Zoe didn't like the idea of Oliver going back out there. But she knew he was right. It was different now. It was day, the sky was clear, and besides, if they didn't find a way to get food, they wouldn't make it.

Reluctantly, Zoe nodded.

Oliver forced a smile. "Okay then. It's midday now. No better time than the present. I'll get ready." He turned to leave the room. "Trust me, Zo, it's going to be alri—"

A sudden pounding came from the front door.

CHAPTER 27
NO SOLICITING

"HEY, NEIGHBOR! ANYONE HOME IN THERE?" a voice called through the front door.

Jurnee, who had been watching DVDs, leapt off the couch and ran for the kitchen, throwing her arms around Oliver's leg.

Oliver looked at Zoe and held his finger up to his lips. He knelt down and whispered, "I need you to be as quiet as you can and go down to the basement like we practiced. Hide in the spot I showed you until I come and get you. Okay?"

Jurnee nodded and ran for the basement stairs, taking Princess with her.

"Look, we heard someone in there. Now open up and let's have a conversation!"

Louie's deep growl filled the living room as he cautiously placed himself between Oliver and the front door.

Oliver motioned to Zoe and then to the kitchen table where her .357 sat holstered.

Quietly she eased over to the table and drew the gun.

Oliver nodded, vanishing into the bedroom and returning with his 12-gauge pump and two pairs of shooting earmuffs. He tossed Zoe hers and donned his own. He didn't own as many guns as some people he knew, but he had a 9mil, his .45, a lever-action .30-30 that had belonged to his father, a little .22 pistol boot gun, and a few hunting shotguns that were family heirlooms. The Savage 12-gauge pump was an assault shotgun he'd purchased a few years back specifically for home defense. It had a shortened barrel and a five-round magazine.

"We know you're in there. We can smell you and we're coming in one way or another," the man said matter-of-factly.

Zoe's eyes went wide. "Oliver, they're infected," she said, talking so quietly she was almost mouthing the words.

He nodded his understanding. These were infected but not undead. Though the craving drove them, they were the ones who could still communicate, still strategized.

The cabin had an open-concept layout, allowing them to see across the front room to the front door from the kitchen. Oliver motioned her to take cover behind the kitchen counter. The counter was a peninsula and offered the only structure between the kitchen and the front door. "Listen here, asshole. You'd be best to leave. We are heavily armed. You try and come in, you die!"

The man on the other side of the boarded-up door laughed.

Footsteps pounded around the side of the house. People were running across the wraparound porch. How many, he couldn't say for sure. With the glass sliders covered with plywood and the kitchen window too, they would find no entrance into the home from either point.

"You got more than enough in there. All that creamy

sweetness and you think you ain't gonna share it? I smell... I smell... three! Three treats! Now open the fucking door!"

The plywood covering the front door flexed as the man attempted to kick it in. "Let! Me! In!"

On the side of the house, glass shattered as the would-be intruders busted the glass sliding doors and kitchen window.

The man at the front door kicked again, smashing the doorknob through the plywood covering the door from the inside.

"Oliver!" Zoe screamed.

Oliver ran forward, pumping a shell into the shotgun as he lifted it.

Louie, still standing in front of the door, held his ground and barked like mad.

"Get back, Louie!"

Reluctantly the pit bull obeyed, stepping back and ducking low, ready to pounce. His barks of warning stopped as he settled into a low growl. If the man made it inside, there'd be nothing Oliver could do to stop the loyal dog from protecting his territory. Hell yes to that. But what he didn't want was to accidentally shoot the dog.

"Louie, hold!"

The man kicked again, breaking the plywood loose from the doorframe on one side.

Stopping a yard from the door, Oliver fired.

Buckshot blew through the door in a narrow spread.

The man grunted.

Oliver pumped the gun and fired again.

Everything went quiet.

Oliver pulled down his earmuffs and stole a glance back toward the kitchen.

Zoe poked her head up from behind the kitchen counter, her eyes darting around.

Oliver stepped forward, peering through the fist-sized hole in the front door.

Outside, the fallen man began to move, pushing himself up from the deck. Instinctually, Oliver understood the man was no longer a breathing, thinking human. He was an undead – a zombie that would stop at nothing to eat their brains.

The zombie threw all its body weight at the door, again and again. The plywood splintered as the doorframe cracked and snapped.

Oliver raised the gun and aimed where the man's head should be. He fired, pumped the gun, and fired again.

In the kitchen, the plywood covering the window above the sink cracked and then busted. A piece of firewood came through the window, landing in the sink.

"I'm coming in!" a bearded man shouted, pulling himself up onto the windowsill. He slid forward, busting the tall faucet as his palms slammed down onto a stack of dishes, shattering them under his weight. "I'm coming in to get what's mine!"

Behind the man, another silhouette appeared, pushing the man farther inside. "Hurry up – there's plenty for all of us!"

"Shit!" Oliver shouted, limping for the kitchen. "Shoot, Zo!"

Louie, barking like a maniac, ran right in front of Oliver, tripping him. He went down hard, the shotgun sliding across the floor.

Oliver scrambled forward. "Dammit, Louie! Move!"

"Better than sugar! Better than creamy caramel!" the

bearded man said, standing in the farm sink as water sprayed wildly from the busted faucet.

"Zo! Shoot, dammit!" Oliver said, reaching for the shotgun.

The man leapt from the sink.

Clack! Clack! Clack! Clack! Clack! Clack!... Click.

The man in the sink fell face first, his head bouncing hollowly off the hardwood floor.

Oliver blinked up at Zoe. She stood poised in a shooter stance, still pulling the trigger. *Click. Click. Click.*

A monster of a man leaned in the window. "Well, that's just more for me!" He gripped the windowsill and launched himself headfirst over the sink.

Zoe, eyes wild and hands trembling, continued to pull the trigger. *Click. Click. Click. Click.*

The giant man sprang to his feet, lunging forward.

Oliver was on his feet with the shotgun in hand, but in that split second there was no time to pump the gun. Oliver threw himself into the larger man, and they both crashed into the refrigerator. The fridge tipped back, slamming into the wall.

The man punched Oliver in the face, grabbing the shotgun and trying to rip it from his hands.

Louie lunged in, bit down on the man's calf, and began shaking it like a chew toy.

Wrestling the man for the gun, Oliver knew he had to keep his hands on it or they were all dead for sure.

The man twisted, slamming Oliver into the stove. A sharp pain shot through his lower back. The man took one hand off the gun and punched Oliver in the face with his big meat-mitten of a fist.

Oliver's head slammed back into the microwave and he felt the door smash inward. Despite the flash of light and pain through his head he stayed conscious, seizing the opportunity to twist the shotgun and smash the stock into the man's face. His nose exploded in a gush of blood.

Louie continued to pull at his leg, and the big guy went down onto one knee.

Behind him, Zoe stood with the .357 cocked back over her shoulder as if she were going to throw it like a baseball. But she didn't throw it; instead, she pistol-whipped the man across the back of his head.

"You bitch!" the man shouted, twisting to look over his shoulder at the cause of this new pain.

Oliver pumped a round into the chamber. "Move, Zo!" he shouted, placing his foot against the man's side and kicking.

The man fell onto his opposite side, his head smashing through one of the lower cabinet doors.

Zoe backpedaled out of the kitchen.

Keeping hold of the man's leg, Louie continued to growl and pull. Blood gushed from the infected man's leg as the pit bull shook the appendage like a rag doll.

"Raaaahhh!" the man roared, punching Louie in the head.

"Back, Louie!" Oliver ordered.

Louie released the leg but stood his ground, emitting another deep growl, all his teeth bloody and bared to bite again.

The man tried to stand.

"Stay down or die, asshole!" Oliver shouted.

"Mine! Your goodies are mine!" the man said, ignoring Louie, the gun, and the fact he no longer stood a chance. He reached up, grabbing the counter to pull himself up.

Oliver fired the gun.

Discharging the shotgun at practically point-blank

range was instant and fatal. The man's now mostly headless body sagged to the floor.

At the sound of the report, Louie ran from the room.

Oliver wasted no time pumping another round into the shotgun and moving over the dead bodies to the window. Snatching a dish towel, he covered the busted faucet and peered out the window, looking left and then right. The porch was empty save a rack of firewood that now lay toppled and scattered across the porch.

Oliver pulled down his earmuffs. "I think there were only three," he said, turning to Zoe. "Are you okay?"

"I'm not hurt, but you... are you okay?" she asked, assessing his bruised face.

The guy had punched him hard enough to knock a tooth loose, but his jaw was still working, so he was pretty sure it wasn't broken. Oliver worked his jaw around and then said, "I'm okay. But I wasn't asking if you were hurt, Zo. I'm asking, are you okay?"

"I... I mean, we didn't have a choice, right?" she said, her hands still shaking.

"No. No, we didn't. We did exactly what we had to do... we survived," he said, kneeling down in front of the sink. He reached underneath, shutting off the hot and cold water. "I have a few more two-by-sixes in the garage. I'll have to secure the window and door. Can you go check on Jurnee? I'm sure she's scared shitless right about now."

"Oliver, *I'm* scared shitless."

He reached for her, wrapping her in a tight hug. "I know, babe. Me too, but you were awesome. You didn't freeze up and we're both alive because of what you did."

Her body trembled in his arms. "And what about all this?" she asked, motioning around the kitchen.

Two bodies lay sprawled in their kitchen, blood and bits

everywhere, busted appliances and cabinets, and he was sure he still heard water running from somewhere. He glanced over at the fridge as a puddle grew from beneath it, stretching out across the wood floor. The water line for the ice maker must have broken during the struggle.

Pulling his attention back to Zoe, he rubbed his hand over her back comfortingly and forced a smile. He had a feeling she wasn't going to like what he was about to say. "Yeah, listen, Zo. I've been thinking about this for a while now, and after all this" – he waved a hand at the kitchen – "I'm sure."

Her eyebrows knitted together. "Sure of what, Oliver?"

"Remember what I said about going to the neighbors' to find food?"

She nodded, a look of dread coming over her face.

"Well, forget all that. We need to leave this place."

CHAPTER 28
THE WHITE WORM

ZOE FELT like she was about to have a panic attack. She had just killed a man in their kitchen, and now Oliver wanted to leave the only safe place they had left in this world.

"But where will we go? It's absolutely insane out there. The internet isn't working. The radio isn't broadcasting anything but that same damn emergency message telling everyone to stay inside. And what about the rains? Wouldn't we be better to clean this up and stay put? I mean, you said you have more wood. We can fix the window and —"

Oliver placed his hands on her shoulders. "Zo, do you trust me?"

Well, that was a strange question. She frowned up at him. No. She didn't trust him. A few days ago, he'd admitted to lying to her for the past several months. He'd gone back to a job that had nearly gotten him killed! A job he'd promised never to go back to again.

"I know what you're thinking," Oliver said.

"Do you?" she asked.

"That was different. What I mean is, do you trust me to keep us safe?" he asked.

Without further hesitation, she nodded. She knew that no matter what, Oliver would do everything he could to protect her. But that didn't mean leaving the safety of their home was a good idea. She needed more. "Do you have a plan? I'm not getting in a car and just driving away with no destination... no plan. That sounds like suicide!"

"Of course I have a plan. Like I said, I've been thinking about this for a while, even before these assholes broke in. Our survival isn't just about getting somewhere safe. I mean, sure we need security, but we also need food. We can't just board ourselves in and hope this all ends before we starve. And sure, I can search the neighbors' houses, but it will be a recipe for violence every single time. Now, don't get me wrong, it may still come to that, but I think I have a better plan."

Zoe tossed her earmuffs on the table. "Okay, but our kitchen, and probably our basement are flooding. Let's get this place secure and check on Jurnee, then let's hear your plan."

Oliver smiled and nodded, letting out a relieved sigh. "Right," he said as he bent and retrieved the piece of busted plywood that had been covering the window.

Zoe forced a smile. "I said I'd listen, Ollie. I didn't say I'd agree."

Oliver stood up and headed for the basement door. "Fair enough. I'll check on the kid and then I'll grab some boards for the window."

"I can check on her," she said.

"No. Just sit tight and catch your breath – you don't look so good."

"Asshole."

Oliver smiled. "You know that's not what I meant. Seriously, take a minute and I'll be right back," he said, vanishing down the basement stairs.

Zoe closed her eyes and let out a long sigh. She wished that when she opened them, this would have been a dream... a nightmare. Like many times over the last few days, she thought of Alexis and wished so badly she could talk to her childhood friend. Was she okay, or was she one of them? And what of her parents? What about Oliver's sister, Sarah? Was she safe? Had this damn disease reached that far? Maybe Oliver was wrong and this wasn't happening everywhere. No. She was kidding herself if she believed that. Opening her eyes, she looked down at the kitchen table strewn with medical supplies, boxes of ammo, and bloody syringes. Had this become their life now?

On the table a puddle of blood pooled, sticky and dark. Wait a sec, that wasn't right. The syringe holding the nearly four-day-old sample from Mr. Henderson's blood sat broken. Zoe leaned in, observing a trail of blood leading away from the puddle to a tipped-over cereal box that was leaning on the fruit bowl in the center of the table. Cautiously she reached for the box, pinching the flap between her thumb and index finger.

Zoe drew in a breath and held it, standing the cereal box back upright, then yanking her hand as she jumped back.

Under the box lay a worm thing with claw-like legs. It was the same image she had seen under the microscope, only this version was every bit of three inches long. No wonder the syringe had broken. The white worm was lying on its back, squirming. From top to bottom, what she assumed was a long mouth held razor-sharp sharklike teeth that scissored into each other as the strange mouth flexed open and closed, like a fish out of water struggling for air.

Zoe's eyes stretched wide as the thing wiggled and then went still as she watched.

Picking up a pen, she leaned forward to poke the worm when she heard a moan behind her. She spun only in time to see the bite coming for her face.

Zoe screamed as the man she'd already shot half a dozen times threw himself at her. She jerked her head to the side as teeth clacked by her ear.

How was this happening? She'd shot him five times practically point-blank in the chest and once in the head. At least that's what she thought she had done, but the red gash across the man's brow told her she had only grazed his skull and not penetrated it.

Twisting to get away, Zoe shoved, but the undead man groped for her, snatching a fistful of her braids, jerking her off her feet.

Zoe landed hard on the hardwood floor, expelling all her air. She tried to gasp but couldn't get a breath.

The man hissed and moaned, throwing himself atop her, mouth snapping shut hard enough to break teeth as he bit at the air like a dog trying to bite a fly.

In the mudroom, glass shattered and wood splintered.

From the basement stairs, Oliver shouted her name. "Zoe!"

"Oliver," she tried but no sound came as she pushed against the man's bullet-riddled chest with all she had. She felt his broken chest bones shifting under her palms.

She couldn't hold him up and she couldn't breathe!

Blood dripped from the man's eyes onto her shirt as panic surged. Either her hands were going to push into the man's broken chest cavity, or her arms were going to buckle. A terrifying thought consumed her.

She couldn't hold the red-eyed man. He was going to collapse atop her and eat her face.

As her arms gave out, hands grabbed the man's shoulders, dragging him off her.

She kicked him away as Oliver tossed him to the side and drew his pistol from its holster. He leveled the gun at the man's face.

Zoe, still unable to get a breath of air, slammed her eyes shut and slapped her palms over her ears.

Clack! Clack! The bullets ripped through the man's head.

From the mudroom came a chorus of hisses and moans.

CHAPTER 29
THE HORDE

HIS WIFE'S attacker tipped over onto the hardwood floor with two exit wounds out the side of his head.

"Get up, Zoe!" Oliver urged as he pulled on her hand.

Zoe stood wheezing for breath she couldn't seem to pull in. She must have gotten the wind knocked out of her.

In the mudroom, moving shadows accompanied the sound of undead moans. Oliver let go of Zoe's hand and ran forward, slamming the door between the kitchen and the mudroom. Holstering his pistol, he grabbed a kitchen chair and wedged it under the doorknob.

Bodies slammed into the mudroom door and it cracked with a pop.

"C'mon, Zo! This isn't going to hold them long!" He pulled her hand, leading her towards the basement stairs. "Go!" he ordered, turning back to the kitchen.

"What... what about you?" she wheezed.

"Right behind you."

More moans and hisses as a bloody hand broke through the wood door.

Oliver scrambled for the shotgun, knocking a box of shells off the table. "Fuck!" he shouted, kneeling down as he raked his hand across the floor. He glanced up as several more hands reached through the hole in the door. They grabbed and pulled, snapping the wood panel of the door. Hands became arms. Blindly, they reached and groped for the chair.

Louie appeared at his side, barking like a maniac.

"Oliver, get down here," Zoe begged, but he knew there were too many. He had to do what damage he could before they breached the door.

Releasing the empty shotgun magazine, he tossed it down the basement stairs. Quick as he could, he shoved shell after shell into the loading port until it wouldn't take anymore, then pumped the gun and jammed in another. Raking his hand across the floor again, he picked up a handful of shells and stuffed them in his pocket.

"Get back, boy," Oliver ordered as he leveled the gun at the door.

Louie, still barking, backed up a few steps.

One of the groping zombie hands found the back of the chair and yanked it free, knocking it onto the floor. Another hand clutched the doorknob, twisting it.

Oliver braced the shotgun against his shoulder and rushed forward. As the door started to open, Oliver kicked it with his sore foot. "Fuck!" he shouted again. The broken door slammed shut.

Wasting no time, he fired buckshot through the hole in the door, tearing open flesh.

Pumping the shotgun, he fired again and then again. The buckshot ripped through arms and dropped fingers onto his side of the door as the relentless undead continued to shove and press. Missing fingers or even hands didn't seem to matter to these things. Once they became zombies, they felt no pain.

Catching movement in his peripheral vision, he turned to find Zoe at the top of the stairs with her hands over her ears. "Come on, Louie!" she begged, trying to reach for the dog. "Get down here!"

Oliver pulled the trigger again. *Boom!* Buckshot separated an arm at the elbow. Again he pumped the gun and pulled the trigger, but this time there was no deafening report, only a soft click.

"Take this!" he shouted, tossing Zoe the shotgun. He picked up the .45 from off the table. He wasn't the best shot with the .45, but at this distance he didn't need to be. He pointed the gun at what he figured was head level and fired over and over, blasting holes in his own kitchen door until the gun reported the same soft click as the shotgun.

On the other side of the mangled door, the moans continued.

How many of these bastards were out there? The door flexed in, snapping the hinges. "Down! Down! Down!" he shouted, making for the basement stairs.

Behind him, the door crashed inward, followed by a flood of undead.

With the .45 empty, Oliver drew his 9mil. from its shoulder holster and fired at the heads of the first three zombies as they pushed into the kitchen. One was a teen already missing part of his face and badly burned. As he reached forward, Oliver realized the teen's right hand was completely gone. The other two were adults, both women. Despite the close range, he was sure he missed two of the three, but there was no time to shoot again.

He ducked into the stairwell, slamming and locking the door. As he turned to descend, his feet became tangled.

Oliver knew he was going down and there was nothing he could do about it.

Hands outstretched, Oliver landed hard, feeling his wrist strain as his elbow folded. His shoulder made a crunching sound as it impacted the stair.

Luckily the basement stairs were carpeted, offering some small level of cushion as he tumbled downward, smacking the back of his head off the bottom step before finally spilling out onto the basement floor.

Upstairs, it sounded like a herd of elephants stomping across the hardwood floor. Bodies crashed into the door. Even through the pounding in his head, Oliver heard the hisses and moans of the dead.

"Are you okay?" Zoe asked.

Oliver pushed himself up, rotating his shoulder slowly. Nothing felt broken and it still worked. "I think so."

Jurnee sat on the couch, looking terrified as she squeezed her doll.

"It's not going to hold. We have to leave now. Where's Louie?"

Zoe's eyes threatened to spill tears. "He didn't come down the stairs!"

CHAPTER 30
THE PLAN

ZOE RAN to the gun safe as Oliver reloaded shells into the shotgun. Behind her, Oliver shouted, "Grab a box of 9mil., a box of .45, and a box of shotgun shells."

It had been quite the argument when Oliver had purchased the safe last year. He'd wanted the giant ugly metal box to reside next to their bed, and she wasn't having it. She'd never been so glad to have won an argument as she was right now, pulling boxes of ammo out of the safe.

"Oliver! What's the plan?" she shouted, running back into the room.

"I can't tell how many are up there, but it must be a lot. I think they were drawn to the house by the initial gunshots. The good news is that the door is solid, not like the one in the mudroom. It will hold for a while, but they're going to get down here," he said, crossing the room to the egress window. It was the only other way out of the basement and the only window in the whole house she and Oliver hadn't covered with plywood. The window exited out beneath the wraparound porch and couldn't be easily seen with the lattice covering the opening beneath the porch. Because they were sleeping in the basement and the window was well hidden from the outside, they had decided to leave the window uncovered.

Oliver leaned the shotgun against the wall and drew up the blind, peering out through the window. "No rain."

"We're going out that way?" Zoe asked. She'd never imagined they would actually have to use the window.

"Well, we aren't going back up there." Oliver drew and released the magazine in his 9mil. She handed him a box of rounds, and one by one he loaded the magazine.

"Jurnee, we have to leave," Oliver said.

Upstairs, the undead beat relentlessly on the door.

The little girl jumped up and ran to the window.

"I can't believe we're doing this. What if there are more of them outside?"

"I think the noise will have drawn them all in, and if there are one or two, I'll just have to deal with them on the way to the bus."

"We're taking the bus? Where? And what about clothes... Jesus, Oliver, Jurnee doesn't even have shoes on and what about Louie? We can't leave him up there!"

"Babe. Do you have a better idea? Your car is in the garage, which is locked. Our clothes are up there, which is a problem. I can get us to the bus, which is not locked. Also, I left the keys in the ignition."

Zoe's mind raced. They had some food down here, and a bathroom. It wouldn't be great, but they could last a few days down here if they had to. "I... I don't know. Maybe if we stay quiet we can wait them out... Maybe... maybe they'll leave. And what about Louie? I'm not leaving him."

Above them, something hit the hardwood floor so hard it sounded like the whole ceiling was going to come down. What followed was the sound of smashing glass.

"Sounded like they flipped the kitchen table," Zoe said, looking at the ceiling.

Oliver shoved the reloaded spare magazines into his pocket and the shotgun magazine into the shotgun port. "Look, I know you don't want to hear this, but that door isn't going to hold long enough to wait them out. They know we're down here, and they won't stop until they get through. I've watched enough apocalypse movies and read enough zombie books to know that society is in the process of a collapse that we may not recover from. Not in our lifetime anyway."

"What are you saying?" she asked.

"Zo, I don't think anyone is coming. And I don't think this is going to just blow over."

He was right. She didn't want to hear this, not because she thought Oliver was crazy with all this talk about zombies but because she knew it was all true. Medically speaking and based upon what she had seen on the kitchen table, this parasite was potentially a humanity killer. She wondered how many people had already fallen.

Zoe took a deep breath and swallowed. "So what's your plan, Oliver?"

"Right." He shoved his arm through the shoulder strap of the shotgun and hurried across the basement to a linen closet. He jerked the door open and retrieved a gym bag. "Now that the guns are reloaded, we need to fill this bag with the rest of the ammo. You remember I told you about the church, the one on that country road about a mile off Broadway? It's the right turn just past that piece of property we always dreamt about buying someday." He handed her the bag.

"The church full of undead that nearly killed you? The one you barely escaped from? The one where Jurnee got bit in the back?" She locked eyes with him. "Yes. I know the church. Please tell me you're not suggesting we go there."

The look on his face told her that was exactly what he was suggesting. He turned, hurrying back to the furnace room where they kept the gun safe. Zoe stayed on his heels. "You can't be serious."

"Not to live... not even to stay. But yes, I am suggesting we stop by there on our way."

Above them, wood scraped across the floor. It sounded as though the zombies were rearranging their furniture.

They stopped in front of the safe and Zoe held open the bag as Oliver emptied the shelves of ammo. Then he retrieved the small .22 deuce-deuce, knelt, and strapped the ankle holster to his leg.

Oliver glanced up. "I see the look and I know what you're thinking, but the pantry in that church held enough food to keep us alive for months."

"We don't even know if that food will still be there! And what about the zomb... the sick?"

Oliver pulled his pant leg over the holstered gun and stood. "It's okay. These are by definition zombies and you might as well embrace it."

"I'm being serious. This is insanely risky," she said, shuffling the contents of the bag around to make more room. Next to the gun safe were shelves where Oliver had stored some provisions. That was back when he'd had it in his head that they were going to become preppers. She grabbed some freeze-dried packets of soups and scrambled eggs from the shelves, dropping them into the bag.

Oliver pushed the door to the safe closed. "Zo, it's no riskier than staying down here and waiting for those things to break through. And even if we somehow kill them all or wait them out, our house is fucked."

"Oliver!" Jurnee scolded.

They both turned to the door, only now realizing Jurnee had followed them into the room.

"I thought you were waiting by the window," Oliver said, his face flushed. Zoe realized the look was one of embarrassment. Something inside her found his embarrassment endearing.

"Well, I'm only six, Oliver! And there are monsters up there, and I don't want to be alone! Everyone knows you don't leave a six-year-old alone with monsters!"

Zoe dropped the bag and knelt, pulling the little girl into her arms. "I'm sorry, Jurnee. We should have never left you alone. And Oliver is sorry too, aren't you, Oliver?" she asked, giving him the side-eye.

"Of course," Oliver said, picking up the bag.

Upstairs, the pounding changed, becoming harder and louder, like a fist had been replaced by a foot or maybe a shoulder. That or someone much stronger was punching the door.

"We have to go, Zo. At least with the church we could pull a huge load of food and not have to worry about finding more for a while. Maybe by then something will change. Maybe the rains will stop for good, and maybe the military will show up."

Zoe held little Jurnee's hand in hers as Oliver took Zoe's other hand, quickly leading them back through the basement over to the window.

"But after the church, then what? Let's suppose we get the food. Where will we go?" Zoe asked.

Oliver dropped the bag at the base of the window. "Right. That's the next part of my plan. Just past the church on the same road is this mansion. It's like a farmhouse but modern. It has an attached four-car garage and like four chimneys. The place is huge. But the best part is the bridge across the creek that runs through the front of the property along the road. At the end of the short bridge is an iron gate. Behind the house is an open field. There's nothing planted in it right now, so it will be easy to see anyone coming. Plus, the property itself is fenced in with a decent-sized stone wall. You remember that commercial playing on the radio advertising solar power?"

How could she not. The commercial must have played a hundred times over the last couple days. "Of course."

"Well, the best part is the garage is covered in solar panels. Now I know that doesn't seem important while we still have power here, but trust me when I say this isn't going to last. I'm actually surprised it hasn't already gone down. So yeah, I'm suggesting we load as much food as possible into the bus and take that house for ourselves."

Zoe's mind raced at all the possible flaws in this plan. "You said there were like a dozen of those things in the church and you want to go back there? Even if we somehow don't get ourselves killed at the church, you think the owners of this house you saw are going to just welcome us into their home to live with them?"

"When I drove by the house, a car was wrecked in their front yard. Something had already happened there. Look, I know this all sounds risky, but last time I was at the church, I was alone and my concealed carry pistol is in my Jeep, which is at base. All I had was a pipe. But now it's different – I have you and plenty of firepower. If those things are still inside the church, we can handle it. As for the house, I don't know what we'll face, but if it's occupied, we'll have plenty of food to trade and weapons to help protect everyone inside, which at this point I think is way more valuable than money." He took both her hands in his and squeezed. "We can do this, Zo. We have to, because the alternative isn't good."

Jurnee pointed up at the window. "Are we going through there?"

Oliver held Zoe's gaze, urging her with his eyes.

She knew he was right. They couldn't stay here indefinitely. Even before their kitchen was destroyed and contaminated with blood and guts, the inevitable fact was they were going to run out of food and would likely lose power soon.

"Okay, but what if the food at the church is gone? What if someone is in that house and they don't want to share? What then?"

"Then we move on down the road until we find a safe place."

Above them, the ceiling shook. Zoe glanced up to find some of the white tiles darkening with blood and other bodily fluids. The rancid smell of death had found its way into their basement, reminding her of the bloody courthouse bathroom, and she suddenly felt like she might be sick.

She took a deep breath, feeling her heart race at what she was about to say. "Okay, Ollie. Let's do it. Let's get the hell out of here."

CHAPTER 31
COME AND GET SOME

OLIVER KNELT and zipped the bag, then heaved it over his shoulder opposite the shotgun. "Your .357, is it loaded?"

Zoe nodded. Her face was creased with worry.

"We can do this, Zo. I promise we can do this." He motioned to the window. "We climb out and stay under the porch until we get to the front. I kick the lattice loose and we run for the bus. Easy peasy."

Again, Oliver peered out the window through the lattice into the yard. Still clear. No zombies and no rain. Thank god for small miracles. When he flipped the latch and lifted the window, a gush of cool air rushed in.

Upstairs, the door cracked with a pop. What followed was a smashing of wood, hungry cries, and bodies falling down the stairs.

"Go! Go! Go!" Oliver said, lifting Jurnee through the window.

At the base of the stairs, bodies piled onto the floor. People who used to be his neighbors writhed in a tangle of dirty, bloody undead. They hissed and growled as they scrambled to get to their feet. Wasting no time, the undead crawled and stumbled, finding their feet in mere seconds.

Oliver pushed Zoe through the window. "Go!" he shouted again as he slammed the window shut, spinning to face the rushing mob. He thought he'd have more time, more warning that the door was going to fail, but the damn things came through so fast!

"Oliver!" Zoe screamed.

"Go, Zoe!"

The first zombie was a woman, probably in her thirties. A gnarled gouge in the thigh of her pink yoga pants flayed open to show bone. She wore a bloodstained tube top and was missing an eye and her left arm below the elbow. Oliver let the shotgun fall from his shoulder, lifted it, and fired, removing most of her head from her shoulders. As a bonus, the buckshot peppered a portly man who'd been unlucky enough to be rushing forward right behind her. At least one of the pellets must have hit the man in the head because he dropped like a sack of potatoes.

There was no way he could turn his back on this mob in time to climb through the window. A frightening movie scene flashed through his mind. Dozens of zombie hands snatching him off the windowsill as he tried to escape. They tugged him back into the crowd, forcing him down onto the floor as they fed on him. No fucking way was he going out like that! "Get to the bus!" Oliver shouted, firing again and again as he moved away from the window towards the bathroom. More piled down from the stairwell. Too many to count. The bathroom was his only chance.

As the rush of undead surged forward, Oliver stepped into the bathroom and slammed the door, locking it. Experience told him he had about five minutes tops before the door was destroyed.

The first body that hit the door cracked the panel.

Okay, maybe one minute, he thought, spinning toward the other door.

Even before Oliver had stepped into the bathroom, a very simple plan had started to take shape. The basement was set up so that each room was connected to form a sort of circle. The entertainment area connected to this bathroom, which had a second door connecting to the spare bedroom. The spare bedroom connected to a hallway that led back to the entertainment area. Off that hallway was a large walk-in storage closet and the furnace room. In theory, if he could make it across the bedroom and down the hall, he could essentially circle back behind the horde of undead and escape back up the stairs. *In theory*. "Okay, Oliver, piece of cake."

A fist busted through the door and groped for the handle.

"That's right, you son of a bitch! I'm in here! Come and get some!" he shouted, exiting into the bedroom and shutting the door behind him. There was no lock on the bedroom side of the door. Quickly, Oliver threw the bag of ammo and shotgun onto the bed, grabbed the dresser, and slid it in front of the door. Since the door was at the corner of the wall, he did his best to angle the dresser between the door and the wall so that it was wedged. It would take twenty men to push that door open now and they'd have to shove the dresser through the wall to do it.

Oliver hoisted the bag over his shoulder and picked up the shotgun. The key now was stealth.

Quietly, he moved across the carpeted room that he now realized was soaked from the broken water lines in the kitchen. Cold water gushed into his shoes with each step.

His hands were shaking so bad that the gun was rattling louder than he liked.

Taking a deep breath, he tried to steady himself. Slowly he peeked around the corner into the hall, half expecting a zombie to be there, waiting.

The hallway was dark but clear, with only the sounds of the undead filling the hall. At the other end, just around the corner, were the stairs and his only chance of escape. He hoped like hell the entire mob was focused on the bathroom and that the stairs were clear.

He eased forward into the hall. What would he do if they rushed him? Run back for the safety of the bedroom. Then what? Wait them out like Zoe suggested?

He took another step, the smell of feces and death assaulting his senses.

If he had to retreat back to the bedroom, would the door even hold them at bay? At least he could lock that one from the inside, but he'd need to reinforce it. Maybe he could use the bed frame to somehow brace the door. Then, with the bag of ammo, he could pick them off one by one through the door. In the back of his mind, he knew he wouldn't win that battle.

He neared the end of the hall and stopped. Around the corner he could hear their desperate groans and pained cries. It was almost like whatever was driving them to feed on human flesh and brains was using hunger pains to motivate them. Maybe the parasites had the ability to multiply the pain by a hundred or a thousand? Carefully he peeked out around the corner.

There must have been thirty zombies crowding around his bathroom, pushing and shoving like they were in a mosh pit at a heavy metal concert. The door to the bathroom was completely destroyed now, and the small space was full of even more undead as they attacked the second door. Each zombie's tormented moan and angry hiss oozed desperation for a bite of Oliver's flesh – a taste of his brains.

Staring at the back of the zombies' heads, he noticed something for the first time. Until now, he'd only fought them face-to-face, but seeing them from this view revealed something very strange.

All the undead seemed to have an oval-shaped bulge at the base of their skulls. Even creepier, as Oliver stared at a bald, shirtless man near the back of the crowd, he could see the knot was moving. The oval bulge seemed to convulse beneath the skin.

What the hell? He'd have to tell Zoe about this if he lived long enough to get the hell out of here. He withdrew back behind the wall and took a deep breath. *Stay calm, Oliver – you got this.* All he had to do was round the corner and dart up the stairs.

In a strange way, this reminded him of repoing. Many times, he'd had to sneak into a private marina, airport hangar, or someone's garage and take an asset without getting caught. However, the penalty for getting caught might be a physical confrontation or, worst case, getting shot, but at least he'd never had to worry about being eaten alive.

Oliver swallowed dryly and leaned out from behind the wall again, this time stretching farther and glancing up the stairs. Remnants of the broken door lay strewn downstairs, stained in thick patches of viscous blood.

Three bodies lay twisted on the stairs, the remains of earlier headshots.

Oliver ducked back behind the wall and readied himself. Now or never.

As Oliver slowly eased around the corner, preparing to

make a run for it, his heart stalled and he froze. At the top of the stairs, a silhouette appeared in the doorway.

No. No. No! he screamed in his mind. *Stay, Louie. For the love of god, stay and do not—*

Louie barked and started down the stairs.

The mob of undead turned.

With only a dozen feet between the zombies and himself, Oliver ran, racing up the stairs, stumbling over the bodies and slipping in blood. "Go, Louie! Dammit, move!"

Louie turned around, racing back up the stairs.

Oliver didn't dare look back, but he didn't need to. He could feel them surging up the stairs after him, their desperate cries turning into moans of excited anticipation.

At the top of the stairs, Oliver caught a glimpse of the overturned stove and refrigerator. He didn't give them a second thought as he pressed on around the corner, nearly falling over the out-of-place kitchen table, which lay upside down.

Reflexively, he jumped the table, feeling pain shoot through his wounded foot.

Zombies fell over each other as they crested the stairs. They scrambled behind him, some crawling, some managing to stay on their feet.

Ignoring the stabbing pain in his foot, Oliver made for the back door.

As he crossed from the kitchen into the mudroom, he couldn't help but notice the smell. Not the smell of shit or blood or death, but something else. Gas. He smelled gas.

The stove, he thought.

"Louie! Outside!" he shouted.

Louie bolted out the back door just ahead of him. Was he really about to do this?

Oliver cleared the porch and spun, raising the shotgun.

Zombies filed out the door.

Oliver fired – but not at the zombies. Instead, he fired at the bay window, still covered in plywood. Buckshot peppered the wood, but nothing happened. "C'mon, dammit!" Oliver fired again and then again.

The first zombie, the shirtless bald man from the basement, was on him now and he realized he'd made a horrible mistake. He should have kept right on running. Jerking the .45 from its holster, he shot the zombie point-blank. The next one didn't make it off the porch after the shot blew through her right eye and out the back of her head in a starburst of blood. But there were just too many. "Please. Please. Please," Oliver begged, pointing the handgun at the bay window. *Clack! Clack! Clack!*

Whoomp!

Inside, the house ignited, lifting the roof and blasting a ball of flame out the bay window and back door.

Oliver felt a wave of heat slam into his body as the force of the explosion picked him up off his feet. As he flew backward, darkness closed in. The last thing Oliver saw before unconsciousness claimed him was a horde of burning zombies flooding out of the back door and running straight for him.

CHAPTER 32
THE BUS STOP

ZOE PULLED open the broken bifold door of the bus to reveal a bottom step covered in red liquid and glass shards – the result of a broken glass door and the small foot-sized hole in the passenger-side corner of the windshield. She picked up Jurnee, placing her on the next step up, which appeared to be dry. Jurnee climbed up into the aisle, Zoe skipping the same step to join her. A quick glance around told her everything else seemed dry. She knew from her research if the red rain didn't land directly on you or maybe even in your eyes, mouth, or some other open wound, the parasites would die quickly. It seemed the parasite could only last seconds without a host. Still, she wasn't about to put that to the test by splashing through that shit. "Jurnee. Listen to me. I need you to wait here, okay?" Zoe said, staring out through the fractured windshield of the bus.

Jurnee, clutching Princess, looked horror stricken and began to cry. "You can't leave me here!"

Zoe knelt down in the aisle. "Listen to me. Oliver is stuck in there and he needs my help. Can you be brave for just a minute and wait right here... for Oliver?"

Jurnee wiped her nose on sleeve and nodded. "You promise you'll hurry?"

"I promise," she said, standing up to survey the front yard. She didn't know what to do, but she knew she had to do something. Maybe she could draw them out and give Oliver time to escape. If he was even still alive. *God, don't think like that.*

With no sign of the sick, she made her way back down the steps. She decided she would circle around the garage side of the house to the back door and start shouting. Maybe she could draw them up from the basement and give Ollie a chance to—

Boom! Boom! Boom! Instinctively, Zoe dropped down into a squat. That was a shotgun! And it was coming from the backyard! Zoe stood and ran across the driveway and around the garage.

Clack! Clack! Clack! Whoomp!

The ground shook and the window in the garage blew out. Reflexively, Zoe threw her hands up, not understanding. Something had exploded, but it wasn't until she rounded the corner that she realized the full extent of what had happened.

Zoe stopped, taking in the scene. Their home was burning. Flames rose from the roof and the windows. But her attention quickly went to the man lying in the grass. "Oliver!"

She ran toward him as the sick, all of them set aflame, appeared from the back door like a swarm of burning monsters.

Louie stood behind Oliver, gripping his flannel shirt collar in his jaws as the loyal dog tugged, frantically trying to drag Oliver away from the burning undead.

But they rushed ever forward from the flaming porch,

falling down the steps. They clawed their way forward, crawling as if the flames did nothing to deter them from their prize. They acted like they couldn't feel that they were on fire! That they were being burned alive! Or maybe, more aptly, that they were being burned unalive.

Zoe pulled the .357 from her hip and shot the first one as it grabbed Oliver's ankle. The shot missed the head but hit the thing in the shoulder.

She ran forward again, getting even closer. Holding the gun in both hands, she assumed a shooter's stance and this time at three yards she blew the burning man's head apart.

Zoe turned and faced the crowd. Three of the sick collapsed short of reaching them, the flames or maybe the explosion having caused enough damage to halt them, but seven more still scrambled forward. She fired over and over, killing only two more before she ran out of rounds. "Wake up! Wake up, Oliver!" she begged, lifting his shotgun. She pumped the gun and pulled the trigger, but nothing happened. "No! No! C'mon, Oliver! Wake up!" she shouted, slapping him in the face.

Three of the remaining sick were on them, pulling at Ollie's feet. One – a woman maybe, though it was hard to tell due to the bald head and blistered skin – bit down on Oliver's foot.

Oliver's eyes fluttered open. "My gun," he moaned, lifting his hand and the pistol it held.

She snatched the .45, pointed and fired, shooting the woman through the top of the head.

The burnt woman collapsed onto Oliver's feet.

Zoe shot four more in rapid succession. Despite the nearly point-blank range of the shots, half missed the heads of the sick. Still, by the time she had spent every round in the .45, all the sick that the flames hadn't completely consumed were dead.

"Oliver?" Zoe breathed, collapsing back onto her ass. "Are you okay?"

"I think so," he moaned, pushing himself into a sitting position. Together they watched as the roof of their home collapsed upon itself.

"That's everything we had," she said, knowing somehow that none of it mattered. All that mattered was that they were alive.

Across the yard, motion caught Zoe's eye. "Get up, Oliver."

"Yeah, just give me a sec to clear my head," he said, holding a hand against the side of his face.

"No time. Get up now!" she said, standing and heaving the duffle bag of ammo onto her shoulder. "Now! Move!"

"Zo, what the shit..." He trailed off, seeing what she saw.

From the south side of their yard, dozens of people were appearing from the thin sliver of woods separating their house from the next street over.

A pained scream sounded from a morbidly obese woman in a flower-patterned nightgown. Her war cry seemed all the permission the sick needed as they surged forward from the woods in a flat-out run.

Zoe pulled Oliver up as he swayed on his feet. "We have to run!" she shouted.

"Everything is spinning!"

Zoe held on to his hand, leading a hobbling Oliver around the garage with the sick right on their heels.

"Get up there, Louie!" she shouted.

Louie barked and ran up the stairs and onto the bus.

"Louie!" Jurnee cheered.

Scrambling onto the bus, Zoe dropped the bag, shut the door, and jumped in the driver's seat.

"Can you drive this thing?" Oliver asked, falling into the seat next to Jurnee.

"We're about to find out!" she answered as the mob of sick people slammed into the front of the bus and began to climb.

Zoe turned the key and the bus groaned to life with a rumble. "Just like a big SUV, right?" she asked.

Oliver didn't answer.

"Oliver?" she called over her shoulder as she backed out of the drive.

"Uh-oh, I think he must be tired," Jurnee said.

Zoe stomped on the brakes, throwing a man in a blood-soaked plaid shirt from the hood into the already fractured windshield.

The man came through in a shower of broken glass, landing upside down on the stairs. Hissing like an angry snake, the man righted himself, jumped to his feet, and raced up the stairs.

"Hold on, Jurnee!" she shouted, stomping on the gas just as the man stepped onto the landing.

The bus lurched forward, sending the man tumbling down the aisle towards the back of the bus.

Zoe kept the gas pedal to the floor and her eyes to the rearview mirror as she raced up the hill. Branches raked along the driver's side as she practically steered the bus into the ditch. She couldn't stop. Not yet. There were too many giving chase, but despite her desperate attempt to get the bus as far away as possible before stopping, she couldn't let the man on the bus get to Jurnee. She tried to see Oliver, to understand what had happened to him, but between the sick man making his way back up the aisle and trying not to wreck the bus, she couldn't see him.

Jurnee screamed.

Louie jumped from the seat, colliding with the man before he reached Jurnee. Louie locked his jaws around the man's throat and they both went down into the aisle.

Zoe smashed a green plastic mailbox as she made the turn off Brandywine Road and onto Lake Drive. She stopped the bus, hoping she had created enough distance between herself and the mob of undead. She pulled herself from the seat and drew her .357. "Jurnee, cover your ears now!" she said, raising the gun. "Louie! Come!"

Louie let go of the man's throat; he ran back to Jurnee, turned, and growled.

The man stood, his torn throat exposing his esophagus. Still he rushed forward as if oblivious to his mortal injury.

Zoe fired two rounds. The first missed completely, but as the man's head snapped back, she knew her second shot had hit home. The man fell onto his back.

Outside movement caught her eye. "Shit!" she announced, jumping back into the driver's seat. The sick were coming up the hill in a flood. It reminded Zoe of the River City 5K zombie race on Halloween.

Stepping on the accelerator, she raced down the road. The neighborhood looked like a war zone. Many of the houses lining the street on both sides had been burned. Others were ransacked. Cars were parked haphazardly in the road, in yards, and in one case, smashed through the front of a house.

Zoe navigated through the neighborhood. There were multiple times she had to traverse the shoulder to maneuver around abandoned cars, but it was when she was about to turn onto the road leading them away from the neighborhood that she saw a scene that stole her breath.

A small passenger plane had crashed, coming to rest in a farmer's field. But along the way it had completely leveled three houses, flipped several cars, and left three other homes with severe damage. Only four days had passed since this nightmare began, and this was what had become of the world... at least her world.

It wasn't until she was outside of their neighborhood on the country road and surrounded by empty cornfields that she felt safe enough to stop.

Zoe pulled the brake and rushed to Oliver and Jurnee.

Tears spilled down Jurnee's cheeks. "I think Oliver got hurt."

Oliver sat leaning against the window.

"Oliver! Oliver, wake up!" she shouted, her eyes frantically searching for any sign of injury. Confused, she glanced at Jurnee, her eyes pleading for the answer.

Jurnee pointed at Oliver's waist.

Beneath him, a red stain pooled.

"Oh, god no!" She grabbed Oliver and leaned him forward. His back was wet with blood that was leaking into his jeans. Her eyes followed the wet stain up his shirt to a hole in the area of his scapula. "Oh, Oliver," she whispered. Pulling the shirt away from his skin, she stuck her fingers through the hole and yanked, ripping it open. An inch-wide shard of glass protruded out of his back.

Zoe glanced back toward the front of the bus, where two plastic boxes were mounted near the ceiling above the dashboard. One read BODY FLUIDS CLEANUP KIT in white letters while the other read FIRST AID in bold red letters. Zoe ran for the kit.

Returning, Zoe said, "Jurnee, I don't want you to watch

this okay?" She moved Oliver's head so it rested against the seat in front of them.

"Is Oliver going to be okay?" Jurnee asked, sniffling.

Zoe fought back the overwhelming panic threatening to consume her. The truth was, she had no idea. He was bleeding badly and without a stethoscope she couldn't tell if his lung was punctured.

"I... I don't know," she said, refusing to lie to the little girl. "Now look away, okay?"

Jurnee gripped Princess tight in her arms, slammed her eyes shut, and turned away. "Please be okay, Oliver! Please!"

That was the moment Zoe knew – one hundred percent, she knew. She not only loved her husband, she was in love with him. She hated what he'd done to her, but like stars needed a night sky to shine bright for all to see, she needed Oliver. Without him, there was no light inside of her – no shine.

Zoe blinked back her tears and took a deep breath. *I'm a trained professional. I can fix this,* she told herself. This fact should have been reassuring, but in reality, all her training was telling her just how bad this injury could be. Her mind raced with possibilities. Nerve damage, severe muscle damage, a punctured lung. In any normal circumstance, they would be on their way to the emergency room.

She gripped the shard of glass with the tweezers and pulled.

One inch, then two, then three. "Damn you, Oliver McCallister," she breathed. Fresh blood poured from the wound. She dropped the shard into the plastic kit and slapped a gauze pad over the wound, applying pressure. Despite her rising panic, her medical mind went to work. He hadn't punctured his lung. Zoe knew this now because the blood wasn't frothy, which it would be if it had been coming from his lung. Also, the shard itself had been angled oddly, so maybe it hadn't gone straight in and thus not as deep. Another bit of good news: She was ninety percent sure she'd gotten all of it out. The fact the shard still held a point meant that it was likely fully intact. *Okay, stop the bleeding,* she thought, pressing hard against Oliver's back.

"Can I look?" Jurnee asked.

"Okay, but there's a lot of blood. Are you sure you want to?"

Jurnee nodded, opened one eye, and peeked over. She opened the other and leaned over, trying to see. "Is he okay now?"

"I don't know. He lost a lot of blood," Zoe said, trying to keep her voice even. "Now I need to get this bleeding to stop."

"Can I help?" Jurnee asked.

Zoe's eyebrows lifted. "Actually, you can. Can you hold this over his wound and press as hard as you can?"

Jurnee nodded.

"Okay, it is very important you don't let go and that you push really hard because that pressure is what's going to help stop the bleeding." She motioned for the girl to climb over her. The thought that she was having a six-year-old help treat a major wound wasn't lost on her. She hoped she wasn't doing something that would give the poor kid nightmares, but after what Jurnee had already seen, if she was going to have nightmares, this probably wouldn't be what haunted her in her sleep. Besides, as long as she didn't lift the gauze, she wouldn't have to see the cut. Plus, Zoe needed the extra hands for what came next.

Jurnee stood on the seat, placed her palms over the

gauze as if preparing to give CPR, and pushed down. She made a face as if straining with all she had.

"Good. Now just hold that for a moment while I get some tape ready." In the kit she located a variety of bandages, from Band-Aids to compression wraps, but because the wound was in his back, she didn't think a pressure dressing would work well. To her surprise, she noticed the Steri-Strips. Most kits didn't come with them, but for whatever reason this one did, or perhaps someone had added them. Either way, short of a needle and thread, they were exactly what she needed. Steri-Strips were a cross between a Band-Aid and a suture. They didn't require the use of a needle and thread but had incredibly strong adhesion to hold cuts together.

She prepared the strips and opened a new package of sterile gauze. "Okay, you can let go, but when you do, I need to take that gauze off, so close your eyes."

"I want to see how you fix it," Jurnee said firmly.

"Are you sure?" Zoe asked.

Eyes still wet, Jurnee straightened, her face poised. "I'm sure."

"Take the gauze off."

Jurnee lifted the blood-soaked gauze to reveal the one-inch-long wound. The bleeding had slowed to a near stop.

Looking up at the girl, Zoe said, "Are you okay?"

Jurnee nodded, not looking away from the gash. "That's a bad owie," she whispered.

"It is, but we're going to tape it back together." She forced a smile, but internally she wanted to scream. *Oliver, damn you. Don't you do this to me. Not now, not here!* She hadn't even had a chance to tell him she'd forgiven him for lying to her. She had. She would! If only... *Just please wake up!*

"Then will Oliver wake up?" Jurnee asked.

Zoe's smile slipped. "I... I think he needs to rest for a while." The truth was she didn't know. He'd lost so much damn blood. But her worst fear was that he wouldn't wake up at all... that he'd slip into a... She couldn't finish that thought. She wouldn't let herself go there.

Pushing the horrible thought out of her mind, she wiped the wound with iodine from the kit, dried it as best she could, and squeezed the wound back together, taping it closed with the three Steri-Strips. To her surprise, Jurnee watched attentively, never taking her eyes off Oliver.

"Now what?" Jurnee asked.

Zoe looked out the window of the bus across the barren fields. The sun was high in a sky of scattered clouds. On the horizon, darkness crept closer. It looked like rain was coming. Zoe looked back to the broken windshield. "We have to go," she said, leaning Oliver back in the seat. Still unsure of the damage to Oliver's insides, she left him sitting up and leaning against the side of the bus. "Can you stay here and keep an eye on Oliver?"

Jurnee nodded.

Zoe grabbed the girl and pulled her to her chest, hugging her tight. "Thank you, Jurnee," she said, forcing a smile. She didn't feel like smiling, but the thank-you was sincere. This little girl was brave as hell. Despite the horrors of what they'd both been through to get to this point, she was glad Jurnee was here – glad they were together.

Louie jumped up in the seat next to Jurnee and lay down.

What now?

Now she would follow Oliver's plan.

She would drive the bus to the church. If Oliver hadn't woken by then, she would go inside herself and get all the food she could. Then she would get to the mansion Oliver had described.

All she had to do was get there before it rained, not get eaten by the sick, and hope like hell Oliver's farmhouse mansion was abandoned.

With her determination solidified, she climbed back in the driver's seat. Okay, so what could go wrong?

In the distance, thunder rumbled, drawing her attention to the horizon. Eerie red rays of sunlight punched holes through a sky slowly crowding with heavy, bloodstained clouds, like puffy cotton balls filled to the brim and ready to spill.

Zoe pressed in the brake knob and pulled the bus back onto the road. *Oliver, please be right about this.*

ACKNOWLEDGMENTS

As always, I want to thank my dear wife. Once again you allowed me the time I need to create my crazy stories, and for this I thank you and appreciate you.

Mom – even today, many years after your untimely departure from this world – you still inspire me in my life and my work. I miss you.

I want to thank my editing team, specifically Kristen Tate at the Blue Garret. Here we go again, book 1 in a brand-new series! I am so grateful to get to work with you again.

A special thanks to the readers who took the time to not only read my work but also review it. Reviews are incredibly important to authors, and I appreciate each and every one.

Finally, I want to thank my fellow writers and readers in the BookTok community who, over the last couple years, have welcomed me in, lifted me up, and made me part of this very special community. Thank you for getting excited with me.

Otto Schafer
October 31, 2023

ABOUT THE AUTHOR

Zoe, Oliver, and Jurnee are still a long way away from safe, and while their destiny is still uncertain, yours doesn't have to be. To stay abreast of how the next story is progressing, go to www.ottoschafer.com to sign up for my newsletter. In the meantime, I have a complete modern-day fantasy adventure to keep you busy while you wait. Click here to check it out: God Stones (5 book series) Kindle Edition (amazon.com)

If you enjoyed *Rust-Colored Rain*, I'd love to hear from you and hope that you could take some time to post a review on Amazon. Your feedback and support will help this author continue to create future works for your enjoyment. I want you, the reader, to know that your review is very important. If you'd like to leave a review, just go to my author page on Amazon. I wish you all the best and thanks again.

Check out my website and blog: www.ottoschafer.com
Connect with me on social:
Instagram – www.instagram.com/ottoschaferwriter
Facebook – www.facebook.com/ottoschaferauthor
TikTok – www.tiktok.com/@ottoschaferauthor

ALSO BY OTTO SCHAFER

A history hidden from the world. A truth long sought, but better left unfound. Will two teenagers survive the magical secrets they unearth?

Oak Island, Nova Scotia. Breanne Moore blames herself for her mother's tragic death. So when her archaeologist father is invited on an exciting new dig, she's determined to tag along and keep him safe. But as the mystery leads them closer to the island's secret, Breanne's dreams are filled with visions of a strange boy she's never met... and a world of flaming carnage.

Petersburg, Illinois. Sixteen-year-old Garrett Turek is the unofficial leader of his fellow outcasts. Grappling with a volatile relationship with his stepfather, he avoids his home life by helping an eccentric accountant restore a historic Victorian house. But when he and his crew stumble upon a crusty journal in the basement, Garrett uncovers a dead president's key to a secret world-saving society.

As Breanne and her dad seek clues to a treasure hidden deep

beneath the surface, they trigger a dangerous magic that should have stayed dormant forever. And when Garrett closes in on the truth, he'll question everything he thought he knew and find trust in a girl from far away as they prepare to battle a dangerous foe.

Can the two would-be heroes fulfill a powerful prophecy and save the planet from destruction?

The Secret Journal is the first book in the sensational God Stones YA contemporary fantasy series. If you like unusual pairings, well-researched historical backgrounds, and heated suspense, then you'll love Otto Schafer's coming-of-age adventure.

Destiny awaits those brave enough to turn the page!

Click here to check it out: God Stones (5 book series) Kindle Edition (amazon.com)

www.ingramcontent.com/pod-product-compliance
Lightning Source LLC
LaVergne TN
LVHW100522110826
845146LV00002B/741

* 9 7 9 8 9 8 6 0 7 6 0 6 5 *